John Paxton Sheriff was born in Liverpool and spent much of his childhood in Wales. He served in the army for fifteen years, married his childhood sweetheart and had three children before moving to Australia. Returning to live in Wales, he realized his dream of becoming a full-time author, and has also written extensively for local newspapers.

AN EVIL REFLECTION

A tragic road accident on a bleak moorland road lures PI Jack Scott to the Isle of Mull, and into a web of intrigue stretching back thirty years. On the island he's soon convinced that the crash that killed Bridie Button was no accident. He and his colleagues investigate possible connections with crimes in Mull, Oban and Liverpool as the death toll mounts. Then in another road accident that almost mirrors Bridie Button's tragic end, Scott's close friend Sian Laidlaw is injured. The violence is too close for comfort. A solution must be found . . . a murderer is on the loose.

Books by John Paxton Sheriff
Published by The House of Ulverscroft:

A CONFUSION OF MURDERS
THE CLUTCHES OF DEATH
DEATHLY SUSPENSE
DYING TO KNOW YOU

JOHN PAXTON SHERIFF

———————◆———————

AN EVIL REFLECTION

Complete and Unabridged

ULVERSCROFT
Leicester

First published in Great Britain in 2008 by
Robert Hale Limited
London

First Large Print Edition
published 2009
by arrangement with
Robert Hale Limited
London

British Library CIP Data

Sheriff, John Paxton, *1936* –
    An evil reflection
    1. Private investigators- -Fiction. 2. Murder- -Investigation- -
    Fiction. 3. Traffic accident investigation- -Scotland- -
    Mull, Island of- -Fiction. 4. Detective and mystery
    stories. 5. Large type books.
    I. Title
    823.9′2–dc22

    ISBN 978–1–84782–710–4

Published by
F. A. Thorpe (Publishing)
Anstey, Leicestershire

Set by Words & Graphics Ltd.
Anstey, Leicestershire
Printed and bound in Great Britain by
T. J. International Ltd., Padstow, Cornwall

This book is printed on acid-free paper

For my wife, Patricia Ann

Author's Note

Total police strength on the Isle of Mull is 1 sergeant and 4 constables. These personnel are split between the police stations at Tobermory, Bunessan, Salen and Craignure. In writing this novel I have tinkered with the ranks, and brought in a Detective Inspector and a Detective Sergeant. They, like all the characters in the novel, are figments of my imagination.

I have also made subtle adjustments to the island's geography. While the place names will be recognized, the terrain has been moulded to suit the story.

Acknowledgement

For some of the above, and for all the other information on Mull that has been used or remained in the background, I am indebted to John Wilson, of Lochdon, Isle of Mull. His assistance has been invaluable. Thanks, John.

PROLOGUE

November, five o'clock in the afternoon, and at a latitude of 57° a bitter wind was whistling down from the heights of Ben Nevis. It moaned its way along the length of Loch Linnhe, picked up salt spray as it reached the coast of mainland Scotland and crossed the Sound of Mull, then hissed angrily in across the rocky shore of the Isle of Mull to lash with sheets of rain the rusty truck bouncing and rattling up the hill out of Craignure. The vicious cross wind buffeted the vehicle, adding to the driver's problems. Ice already frosted the uneven road and rimed the wind-screen, condensation inside the cab was forcing the driver to scrub the glass with the back of a gloved hand, and visibility would deteriorate further as dusk turned into night.

The sparse lights of Craignure slowly fell away behind the roaring, smoking vehicle. Before too long they were entirely obscured by distance, driving rain and the low clouds streaming across hills and moorland. The driver was alone in the rapidly fading light, cocooned in a draughty, rattling cab where the temperature was just a degree or so above

1

freezing. Diesel fumes were strong enough to burn the nostrils. Worn tyres were sliding on the slick, icy road. Headlights, their cracked glass coated with mud and blurred with condensation, delivered the weak light of a waning moon and were a sick joke.

The road ahead ran through Lochdonhead, brushed the northern end of Loch Spelve then began a short climb towards higher ground. By the time the truck roared over the rise and began a long, snaking descent, the driver's eyes, arms and nerves were already aching with the strain. Each bend in the road sent the vehicle sliding on black ice; each slide had to be corrected by a fierce grip on the steering wheel, a turn into the skid; each correction threw the vehicle into the next bend with the front wheels at the wrong angle so that each slide became more difficult to correct.

After almost four miles of desperation in which the driver was always on the verge of losing control, the bends eased, became fewer and less severe. But the worried driver knew that in another quarter of a mile, as the road began its tortuous twisting and turning through Glen More, there was a section where it dropped steeply. At the bottom of that stretch, the camber was all wrong. Maybe it had been correct when they built the road, but over the years the Scottish climate had played havoc with the surface and its underlying hardcore and, at a point where the pitted tarmac sloped fiercely away to the right, drivers had to negotiate a tight left-hand turn leading into a short, steep climb.

On the outside of the bend, on the wrong side of that tricky reversed camber, the ground fell away for about sixty yards across a lumpy, boulder-strewn field of coarse grass and heather that finished up in a dense clump of pines.

It was a single lane road, with no crash barrier, no solid dry-stone walls, just a fence with rotting posts and rusting wire — and no room for vehicles to pass.

The driver took a deep breath, with one hand dashed away a film of perspiration, then gripped the greasy steering wheel. Tyres hissed along the icy road. The yards rolled away. The road curved, dipped again, then began a short climb. The truck slowed. Its labouring engine was knocking, steel hammers beating on anvils, the din ringing in the night. Smoke billowed from the loose exhaust. Like a beast in pain it crawled up to the crest, seemed to hover there for an instant.

Driving sleet lashed the windscreen. The

driver took another deep breath, made sure a foot was poised over the brake pedal's worn rubber tread. Then the truck's bonnet dipped. It picked up speed, yawed on the road's slick surface and careered down the hill towards the treacherous bend.

Suddenly, as the truck was about to enter that sharp bend, the foot hovering over the brake pedal stabbed down. Fiercely. Both front wheels locked. The truck slid across the reverse camber. Instinctively, foot seemingly anchored to the brake, the driver turned into the skid — but that pointed the sliding vehicle towards the right hand verge, and the road was swinging left.

With a crackle of breaking timber, the truck demolished the fence. Posts were sheared like rotten teeth. Wire snapped like old guitar strings. As if propelled from a ramp the truck flew from the verge, dropped with a crash on to the frosty grass and spun through 180°. Moving backwards, it careered down the slope. It crashed into a huge boulder, slewed sideways and toppled on to its canopy with the crunch and squeal of tortured metal as the tubular metal framework buckled. Sliding like a toboggan it bore down on the stand of dark pines. Another boulder spun it again. It rolled, leaped, slammed down on to its wheels. Then, still moving fast, it crashed into the trees and ploughed through. Branches snapped like gunshots. A front tyre burst. The truck lurched drunkenly to the right. Steam gushing from the holed radiator, it hit the trunk of an enormous, immovable pine tree and rocked to rest with a tinkle of broken glass.

Silence.

The driver's door, jarred out of true by the crash, creaked open and swung wide. A body lay slumped over the buckled steering wheel. An arm dropped, hung limp, gloved fingers slack. In the sudden quiet that marked an eerie lull in the wind and rain, all that could be heard was the wet patter of blood on the floor of the shattered cab.

PART ONE

1

Friday

It was DI Mike Haggard who had bestowed on me the name Ill Wind during the Gerry Gault case, but on that bleak November morning at Bryn Aur I was smugly reflecting on the curious fact that such winds inevitably blow somebody some good. Equivalent to pleasing some of the people all of the time, and all of the people . . . but I'm sure you know how that one goes . . .

It was the tail end of a storm that had swept down from Scotland. Rain was lashing the office windows as fierce squalls tore along the twisting, rocky course of the Afon Ogwen. Wind moaned across the yard, hissing like the cold breath of a thousand angry snakes through the naked branches of the oak tree, then dying to a fading moan as it buffeted the slate roof of my toy soldier workshop and swept onward and upward to flatten the brown heather blanketing the high slopes of the Glyders.

What was I doing? I was sitting at my desk with a silly grin on my face — swivelling lazily and without care. And why? Because the violent cacophony of the storm made it impossible to concentrate inside the office (which ruled out wading through boring accounts); my Scottish colleague Calum Wick was already slaving away over a hot melting-pot casting toy soldiers for stock which removed any need for me to risk stumbling in a force nine gale across slick slate and wet gravel to the workshop; and if I couldn't concentrate inside, stand up straight outside, and non-vital work was already being done — well, a wind by any other name and so on and so forth . . .

So I was grinning and swivelling, dreaming up more clever aphorisms and mentally debating the relative merits of Colombian and Kenyan coffee and wondering which to brew and how Calum was going to make it back across the yard to drink it — when the phone rang.

'Jack Scott,' I said above the roar of the wind.

It was Sian. I melted into the swivel chair as all around me the tumult faded into insignificance.

'Soldier Blue,' I said softly.

'How's it going, sleuth?'

'Nervously. Me pacing the floor believing this moment would never come.'

'I'd expect nothing less.'

'Indeed. When one case ends another begins almost at once with a mysterious phone call, yet nothing was happening — '

'Everything comes,' she said, 'to those who wait.'

'But the phone call coming from you is certainly a first.'

She chuckled. 'Mm, I've missed you, too.'

'Yes, but how are *you* coping? It's a mere seven days since I sat drying your tears as we cuddled halfway up Declan Creeney's stairs with police sirens howling and the man himself twisting slowly at the end of a rope.'

'Goodness, what's this, old-fashioned shock therapy?'

'No, this is the 'cruel to be kind' theory that sees jockeys clawing their way back into the saddle when their shattered ankle's still encased in plaster.'

'Pretty close to what happened, actually.'

'What does that mean? You're back into crime — and without my permission?'

'Sort of. The real reason I rang is because I've been hearing rumours. About a man's death that could be murder.'

'How did he die?'

'The truck he was driving went off the road. He ended up with its full weight on his chest, and was crushed to death.'

11

'From those bare facts, I'd call it an accident.'

'They think not.'

'Where was this?'

'Glen More, on the Isle of Mull.'

'Mull. Mm. And here's me thinking you were supervising an outward bound course for jaded executives at Cape Wrath.'

Another chuckle came over the phone, warming a morning cold and wet enough for the sure-footed sheep nibbling on the heights of Glyder Fawr to tread with caution.

'Executive on an outward bound course means wannabe macho but handle with kid gloves: the weather turned too nasty for the tender office types, so we headed south. That was a week ago. I've been too busy to phone.'

'Mull in November,' I said, 'is not exactly Lanzarote.'

'We'll manage. But you're right, and it explains the truck wreck. The driver went off the road at an accident black spot, in atrocious conditions: wind, driving rain, black ice. No other vehicles involved — as far as I know.'

'Nasty, but not unusual given those circumstances.' I paused, considering. 'If he was crushed beneath the vehicle, he must have been thrown out of the cab. So if it was a filthy night, with no other vehicles involved, why are the police looking at murder?'

'I'm not sure. Details have come to me in dribs and drabs from unreliable sources. But I *have* met a very interesting Highland sexagenarian. She's intimidating, taller than the tallest thistle, twice as prickly and as sharp as a honed dirk.'

'A honed dirk?'

'Yes, well. Ask Calum, he's from up this way so he'll know what I mean. Anyway, she tells me this death looks like the latest incident in a long-running, violent feud. Been simmering for years, exploding every now and then to leave an islander harmed in some way — emotionally, physically . . . financially . . . no deaths, she tells me — but now there's this, and so I thought of you. Jack Scott. Intrepid private eye.'

'I think of you,' I said, 'every minute of every day.'

'Flattering, endearing even, but definitely impossible. I, on the other hand, was thinking of you when I suggested you were getting quite a reputation as a private investigator.'

'Top of the range. Nonpareil.'

'That's your ego.'

'Like the rest of me, it has no equal. What's this prickly lady's name?'

'Peggy McBride.'

'Phone number?'

Sian gave it to me. I jotted it down. She also told me that if I wanted somewhere to stay on the island, Peggy had spare rooms in her cottage at Salen, a hamlet on the road between Craignure and Tobermory. And that the base Sian and her ex-military colleagues had established for exhausted executives stumbling down from the moors was a tumbledown bothy that just happened to be in the vicinity.

The drive north to Scotland, she told me with just the right amount of tingly seduction in her voice, was a doddle.

$\star \quad \star \quad \star$

One thing the telephone does better than almost anything else is to remove outside distractions so that a person's voice comes down the wire stripped bare. Before the irresistible, blonde-haired siren who always makes me weak at the knees upped the voltage and began singing the song that would lure me all the way to Scotland, I had been aware of nervousness, an underlying edginess in Sian's voice. She'd disguised it well. If we'd been face to face, I'd have missed it. But it was there, without a doubt, and, because Sian is usually so level headed, curiosity about possible causes gave me just one more valid reason for dropping every-thing and heading north.

The problem is, I run two businesses. The crafty one that brings in the cash is Magna Carta, a one-man firm that sees me designing and selling high quality military miniatures for collectors. Toy soldiers, and good ones. Crime investigation, on the other hand, is a sideline, and a week or more spent sneaking around in damp heather and peering through swirling Scotch mist could well mean seven days' loss of earnings.

But that assumed there were urgent orders that had to be got out. During the Creeney case, Calum had worked hard on sets of Black Watch grenadiers for a firm in Nova Scotia. In the following week we had both toiled over American Civil War figures: sets of the 1st Virginia Battalion and the 14th Brooklyn who had fought each other in the bloody Battle of Gettysburg, and had been in my workshop awaiting the fitting of their Sharps breech-loading rifles. All those sets had been completed, and despatched, which left nothing that couldn't be put on hold for a few days.

The work Calum was doing now would see the shelves filled with gleaming raw castings. With that done there would be no mad rush when we got back from the frozen north, my

Audi Quattro was parked outside, and my sidekick was available.

And Sian, my Soldier Blue, was on the Isle of Mull.

Ten minutes later I had spoken on the phone to a dour, brusque Peggy McBride, arranged two rooms in her cottage for Calum and me, and told her with increasing trepidation that we would see her later that evening. Trepidation because her voice was as dry and snappy as coarse tweed snagging on the thorns of winter gorse, her manner told me that she would not tolerate fools and, when I put down the phone, I had an address, a name, and orders to talk to the man before proceeding to Salen or 'you can be damn sure there'll be no dinner for you *or* your friend tonight'.

When I fought my way across the yard and into the workshop with my news, Calum was not impressed.

'They're all like that. Besides, she knows you're a Sassenach.'

'Yes, well, it's all right for you, you're going home.'

'Hame.'

'Right. So seeing as it's hame to you, you can lead the investigation.'

He slammed down the lid of the casting machine and leered.

'Who said I was going with you?'

'Sian insists,' I said blithely. 'She's been extolling your virtues to Peggy McBride. The poor soul's flustered, fluttering around her dressing-table after blusher and lipstick — '

'I'll go with you,' Calum said, 'if you wear a kilt.'

'Christ, in this weather — and have you seen my knees?'

'Aye, I have — so on second thoughts, we'll both wear trews. To an ignorant scouser like you, that would be keks.' He raised an eyebrow, his grey eyes glinting wickedly behind his stained John Lennon glasses. 'Now, just how old did you say this wee lass McBride is?'

*   *   *

Driving north with Calum was like a gentle soak in a barrel of warm nostalgia.

Back in my mid-thirties I had left the army after fifteen years' service in the Royal Engineers, SAS and Special Investigation Branch, disillusioned with senseless violence after a Beirut operation had gone pear shaped and left a man dead by my hand.

The following five years in Australia had got me little more than an accent with a tan, and when I arrived back in England it was to stumble — yes, literally — across a lanky Scottish stranger called Calum Wick who was fighting a bruising, losing, lonely battle in a rain swept street. Together, back to back, we bloodied our faces on the hard knuckles of three Brixton Yardies, prevailed to earn the dubious reward of an ice-cold sluicing in an evil-smelling underground gent's toilet, and joined forces permanently in a lucrative scam ferrying expensive Mercedes saloons of doubtful provenance from Germany to Liverpool.

That was more than ten years ago, but driving up the M6 with the lean and lanky Scot sprawled by my side — fast asleep as usual — brought back fond memories of those cross-channel journeys. I had turned my back on them when I took refuge in the bottle. Calum had, well, never entirely abandoned anything that was lucrative and borderline legal.

Wrapped in comfortable silence we made good time through rain that turned to a sprinkling of snow, then to sleet, and finally to dazzling sunshine slanting from beneath black clouds that had me reaching for the shades as I turned the Quattro towards the western coast. We began the run down into Oban late in the afternoon, rolled on to the Caledonian McBraine ferry at about a quarter to four, and less than an hour later Calum and I were leaning on the ship's rail as the brooding shape of Duart Castle reared out of the mists hanging beneath Duart Point. Not too long after that we were ashore, and I was in the Spar shop in Craignure buying supplies that would come in useful if Peggy McBride carried out her threat.

But first, there was a man to talk to about murder.

2

The strategy we settled on was simple: Calum would keep the bar warm in the local pub while soaking up the gossip; I would walk south up the A849 out of the village, in the freezing cold and gathering dusk, and play private eye.

The address given to me by Peggy McBride was McCafferey's Garage. I found it after ten minutes' walking, tucked back off the road on bald waste ground scattered here and there with gravel and bordered by a stand of tatty pines that tossed like frayed battle pennants in the strengthening breeze. A couple of petrol pumps that had once refuelled vehicles you started by swinging an iron handle stood on crumbling concrete. A big, battered, recovery truck was parked at the side of the building, complete with an amber light bar bolted above the cab and a rear end complete with crane and winch and enough ropes and shovels to equip McAlpine's Fusiliers. The building itself was timber and rusting corrugated iron, two storey at one end, and I guessed from the grubby net curtains covering the first floor window that the owner lived over the shop. No light showed in those quarters, but a strip of white light was leaking from beneath the garage's big double doors and I crunched over in that direction, banged on the woodwork and walked in.

I'd been in a similar workshop when working on the Sam Bone case. This was smaller, but had the same grease-blackened concrete floor, the same heavy wooden benches against the back wall littered with toolboxes and cans of WD40 and worn fan belts and rusty radiators. An oxy-acetylene welding plant strapped into a home-made angle-iron stand that could be tilted back on small metal wheels for easy movement around the workshop stood next to steel shelves holding oil filters, wing mirrors, interior mirrors, cam belts, boxes containing light bulbs and fuses and other oft-needed spares.

But they didn't interest me.

The truck that had caught my eye should by rights have been removed to the police pound for examination. Did one exist on Mull, I wondered? It was illuminated by cobwebbed neon lights hanging from rusty chains, had a crumpled cab, no front wheels, and fragments of its shattered windscreen glistened like roughcut diamonds in its rotted rubber beading. A canvas canopy bleached by

21

the weather to the colour of a clipper ship's sails was torn to shreds, its metal framework buckled. The wrecked vehicle was resting on its front brake drums. Dried mud and tufts of wiry grass from its tumble down the hillside clung to dents and jagged cracks in the metal.

Between me and the truck there was a vehicle inspection pit that ran pretty well from the doors to the back wall. Usually such facilities have thick timber planks that rest on ledges cut into the long sides to form a floor when the pit's not in use. This one didn't seem to have any. It was a dark, rectangular hole, once whitewashed, now blackened with grease and the soot from a thousand exhausts. Bulbs protected by wire cages were embedded in the walls. The bottom of the pit was filled with black, stagnant water. A couple of old plastic anti-freeze bottles floated on the oily, rainbow-hued surface.

I skirted the pit, strolled over to the wrecked truck and poked absently at the mud on the off-side front wing. The wing mirror was hanging loose, the bolts ripped out, nothing remaining but shards of blackened glass. A shovel was secured behind the driver's door by leather straps, one of which had been torn off when the truck hit the ground. The door hung open. In the gloom of the cab a near-new rear-view mirror gleamed.

The steering wheel was encrusted with something thick and dark, and on the worn rubber mat the same thick coating was imprinted with the marks of cleated boots. It looked suspiciously like dried blood.

Why? According to Sian, the man had been crushed to death beneath the truck. How had she put it? *Details in dribs and drabs, from unreliable sources.* Well —

'Can I help you?'

The man who had spoken was standing in the doorway of a ramshackle timber structure that had been thrown up against the inside of the south wall and probably used as office, rest room and a place to eat dry cheese butties washed down with black coffee. Red-bearded, red-haired, dressed in filthy blue overalls and leather boots so greasy water would have difficulty seeping in and thick socks would be forever steaming, he was eating a beef burger dripping fat and tomato sauce, held in hands big enough to crush rock.

'Doug McCafferey?'

'Dougie's out.'

I strolled over.

'I wanted to ask him some questions about that.' I half turned, nodded towards the battered truck.

'They've been asked. By the polis.' He bit

into his roll, chewed. 'Who the hell are you?'

'Jack Scott. I'm a private investigator.'

'What's your interest in this, pal?'

'Not my interest, my client's.' I could see he was about to object so I held up my hand and adopted a regretful expression. 'Sorry, client confidentiality means I can't say any more.'

He gazed towards the truck, still munching. Then he swallowed the last of the beef burger, wiped his hands on his overalls and gave me a sceptical look.

'So how much do you know?'

'Enough. The truck went off the road, the driver was thrown out and crushed.'

'Aye,' he said, 'it's as I thought — you know bugger all.'

Still absently rubbing the palms of his huge hands on his hips he said, 'I didn't hear a car, so you must have walked. Whereabouts are you staying?'

'Do you know Peggy McBride over at Salen?'

The hands went still. He frowned, probably wondering how I'd walked that far, then shrugged — which could have meant anything — turned, and went into the office.

I followed. It was a small room thick with the smell of old engine oil and the stale cigarette smoke that had impregnated the walls during the freedom years when smoking was permitted. A naked bulb hung from a dusty flex over a desk littered with catalogues, broken bits of alloy pistons, pens, invoices, stained and sticky-looking coffee mugs and an ashtray that had never been emptied. Accessory suppliers' pin-up catalogues were Blu-tacked to the walls. A small window looked towards the line of dark, ragged pines.

The bearded mechanic had gone around the desk to a filter coffee machine. He scooped two mugs off the desk, filled them from the jug with black liquid thick enough to have leaked from the wrecked vehicle's sump.

'Milk?'

The plastic bottle he held poised was a dingy yellow. I remembered the encrusted milk bottle I had seen too many times in the room above George Kingman's Liverpool club, and inwardly shuddered.

'I'll take it black, please.'

He handed me a mug, sat down, indicated a wooden chair that was lashed together with coloured cable that had probably been stripped from the inside of a written-off vehicle's loom.

'So,' I said, settling on the splintered seat, 'where did I get it wrong?'

'The driver died all right, but in the cab. The impact of the crash drove the engine and steering column backwards. Death was instantaneous.'

'Right. I noticed the blood.' I hesitated, trying to imagine the scene out there on a bitterly cold, windswept Glen More. 'I know the weather was bad, and the truck obviously went off the road because there's grass all over it so at least I got that bit right — but what did it hit, rocks?'

'One or two nasty ones in passing, then about the biggest tree it could find at the bottom of a very steep slope.'

'So if everything under the bonnet was driven back into the cab, and the driver was thrown forward — he died from, what, a crushed chest?'

'She. Her chest was crushed, yes.'

The words hung in the grubby office's stuffy air, leaving me perplexed. What had Sian said? *The truck he was driving had gone off the road . . . he'd been crushed to death.* I waited a minute, trying to work it out, then shook my head.

'I didn't get your name.'

'Jim Gorrie.'

'Mechanic?'

'And general dogsbody. Which means running the bloody business when Dougie's away. And that's most of the time.'

'Well, Jim, I was told third hand from

26

sources I admit were not all that reliable that a man was dead, crushed under this vehicle.'

'Aye, well, that's right enough. He was.'

His free hand was busy with his beard. I thought I could see a hint of amusement in his deep-set blue eyes.

I took a deep breath. 'Now I'm getting dizzy.'

'Maybe it's the coffee,' he said, deadpan. 'As winter comes on we usually add a little something for the warmth.'

I smiled. 'So I noticed — but, no, it's not that. Hell, you must know what it is: what's bothering me is the contradiction.'

'There is no contradiction.'

'Really? A woman died in the cab. A man was crushed beneath the vehicle. Are you telling me the truck careered down that slope and found not only the biggest tree in the field but a man out walking his dog miles from anywhere in a howling gale — and then rolled on him?'

'Nobody,' Gorrie said, 'would be daft enough to walk out in that weather.'

'I'm sure you're right,' I said, frowning. 'But obviously there were two deaths, and my source got them mixed up or combined the two.' I nursed my mug, waiting for a comment that didn't come. 'What puzzles me is that this truck was wrecked, written off, when the woman died. It's obvious it hasn't been moved since, so the man who died had to be crushed beneath it *before* the accident that killed the woman — yet something's telling me I've got that wrong; there's something I'm not seeing.'

Baffled, I shook my head. 'Maybe,' I said, 'you'd better give me the full story.'

But he was gone, brushing past me to answer a horn that was honking impatiently outside. I sat stoically chewing my tepid coffee and listening to the murmur of voices, the sudden grind and rattle of one of those ancient petrol pumps, the clatter of a nozzle. Then, for some reason, I stood up and walked to the door.

I could see all the way out to the tatty forecourt. A silver Mercedes convertible was parked up against the nearest of the pumps. Rain was dancing off the black canvas top, blowing like sea spray. Gorrie was bent over the nozzle with his back to the rain and his shoulders hunched. A tall man was standing with his hands thrust into the pockets of a flak jacket. He was looking towards me. His head was bare. A hand and forearm were hooked over his head holding in place long blond hair that was swept straight back. He grinned, waved his other hand, and I saw a flash of white teeth.

I thought he was grinning. Then I realized he was shouting something. The wind caught the words, carried them away like the spray that was being whipped off the top of his car . . . yet, for an instant, watching his lips from thirty yards away, I could have sworn he said 'Hi, Jack'.

Then the moment had passed. He turned away, and his tan leather boots splashed in the puddles already forming as he walked around the car and brought out one of those leather shoulder bags a certain kind of man has taken to sporting.

I watched him pay for his petrol in cash, then went back into the office. When Gorrie returned a few minutes later his beard and overalls were glistening with rain. He snapped a switch I guessed turned off the petrol pumps, threw some cash into a drawer, slammed it shut and sat down heavily.

I gave him a quizzical look.

'Local on his way home? Last customer?'

'Last, aye, and local if you stretch a point — he lives in Oban but spends time over here and in England. He was in for MOT earlier, now he's off to Oban, probably taking the late ferry,' Gorrie said with a strange, preoccupied glance towards the door. 'He'll be back in the morning, no doubt. Some ex-military types are out on the moors playing silly games with businessmen in flak jackets who should know better. Lachlan has been out there with them — Christ, he chases all over the country after them — and I'm just waiting for the flash bugger to come crying to Dougie when his pretty little Mercedes sports car gets bogged down.'

'Well, when I've gone you can lock up,' I said, 'but I really would like to hear that story.'

'It's no secret. Bridie Button was on her way home, but she didn't make it past Maddock's Switch.'

'What's that?'

'A bloody awful bend, pal. It's on the road that cuts through Glen More on its way to Fionnphort and Iona. They call it the switch because drivers must change direction very fast indeed. You're going downhill in one direction, then suddenly you're forced to turn hard left and up a steep hill. Many years ago a man called Maddock was the first to misjudge, the first to die.'

'Any clues as to where Bridie went wrong?'

Gorrie shrugged. 'She left a lot of rubber on the road just before the bend, the worst possible place. Seems she damn near stood on the brakes.'

'Why would she do that, at night, on an

empty road, in bad weather?'

'Sheep are always a bloody menace. If one had wandered on to the road . . . ' He shrugged.

'Or . . . ?'

'The steep uphill bit is quite short. It ends by going over a sharp brow. If a vehicle had been coming *towards* Bridie, it would have come over that brow and swooped down the hill. Having headlights blazing at her, appearing out of nowhere, would have been one hell of a shock.' He shook his head. 'But the road ahead of her was empty.'

'Who found her?'

'Dougie was out that way, first on the scene, but he got there way too late.'

I digested the information, knew that I could ask how it had been confirmed that the road ahead of Bridie was empty of vehicles and what Doug McCafferey was doing out that way, but decided to leave it. Instead I moved on.

'Most of that's clear enough — or clearly unclear — but what happened to the man? How did he die?'

'Now that,' Jim Gorrie said, 'is a very good question.'

It came out as 'guid'. I thought of Calum Wick, and suppressed a smile.

'Can you answer it?'

'In part. We know *what* happened. How or *why* it happened is another matter entirely.'

'Go on.'

He twisted in his chair, splashed more coffee into his mug, saw my shake of the head and turned back to the desk. He was looking down, lips pursed, staring into the coffee.

'For some strange bloody reason a man called Ray Coghlan was lying out there, underneath that vehicle.' He jerked his head towards the workshop. 'It was Saturday evening, the day after Bridie died, Ray was dead drunk — '

'That's certain?'

'Oh aye. It all came out at the post-mortem. He was way over the limit, paralytic might be the right word, probably unable to sit up never mind stand.'

I smiled and nodded. 'Sorry, go on.'

'Ray was drunk, lying under the truck, and maybe he'd wriggled under it to sober up. Or maybe it was the other way around: there was an empty whisky bottle alongside him, so maybe he slid under there sober and finished up drunk. But it's all bloody academic anyway. The vehicle was on stands, safe, so even if he had just crawled under it for a kip there should have been no problem. Christ, he could have slept off that monumental drunk and woken with nothing more than a blinding headache. But while Ray was out there, beneath that pile of scrap metal, somebody — or maybe even Ray himself before he became paralytic — fastened the end of a length of Bowden cable — wire rope, you know? — to one of the stands, fed it out underneath those double doors, then brought the other end back in and secured it to the second stand.'

'Christ,' I said softly. 'Are you saying someone seized the opportunity? Saw him there, and thought the chance was too good to miss?'

'I don't know. That sounds far-fetched, so maybe the killer got him pissed and brought him here in a vehicle using the excuse that they were taking him home. Bridie was dead. Coghlan had spent the day talking to the police or sitting in the pub; his truck was a wreck, and he'd said nothing to them about how he was going to get home. I don't suppose he knew, or cared, but he would have been open to offers.'

'However it happened, he was here, under the truck, and then . . . ?'

'Aye, well, whoever it was, and however it was begun, they fixed that cable and left a fair loop of slack outside. And Andrew Keay's 4 x 4 was there, backed up close to the doors, ready to be collected.' He paused. 'Andrew came up at about ten-thirty.'

Jim Gorrie looked up at me then, one eyebrow raised in invitation.

I finished the story for him.

'Keay came for his vehicle, jumped in, started up,' I said. 'And then he drove off. But the killer had fitted that loop of slack cable on to his tow hook. When Keay drove away, the cable snapped tight and the stands were ripped from under that truck.'

'Indeed they were,' Gorrie said. 'Keay heard them, of course. Christ, he had to, they shot out and hit the inside of those doors an almighty clout. And of course he felt the jerk; it stalled his engine, and almost sent him through the windscreen; and then he heard the bloody truck come crashing down. So he slammed on the handbrake, piled out of his vehicle and went to see what the hell was going on.'

'Poor bastard.'

'Aye, well, the collision with the tree out at Glen More had torn the truck's engine clear off its mounts,' Gorrie said, tugging restlessly at his beard. 'The whole bulk of that engine was resting there on broken metal and split rubber, ready to drop. When the stands were dragged away, that's exactly what happened. The brake drums hit the concrete with an almighty crack and the sump, with the weight of that big engine on top of it, came crashing down on Coghlan's head.' He looked at me levelly. 'It didn't do it much good.'

I met his gaze.

'Flattened it,' I said.

'Aye, you could say that.'

'The sump.'

'Of course.'

There was a terrible black humour in his eyes and in the deliberate ambiguity of his blunt statement. Either he'd known Coghlan well and was using that humour to mask his grief, or the dead man had been a casual acquaintance and his death was of no concern to Jim Gorrie.

Yet the circumstances had to be worrying. I hadn't yet discussed timings with him, but this vehicle had killed two people, within hours or days of each other, and that was either ghastly coincidence or something much more sinister.

'Same vehicle, two people dead. By sheer chance, or is there an obvious link?'

'Couldn't be plainer. Bridie Button was living with Ray Coghlan.'

'Was she now! And to get to his house means driving through this Maddock's Switch?'

'Aye, he lives in the foothills to the north of

Loch Scridain. The B8035 goes through Gleann Seilisdeir, his place is a mile or so before Bainahard.'

'So, what then? Whoever killed her did so when she was on her way home to Coghlan?'

'Nobody killed Bridie,' Gorrie said with some impatience in his voice. 'She lost control of the vehicle and went off the road. It was an accident.'

'Confirmed by the police?'

'They're not bloody needed. If it wasn't an accident it was the perfect, impossible murder — and such things don't happen outside crime books.'

'All right, so let's say it was an accident. But what about Coghlan? Is suicide likely? If Bridie was living with him, I suppose it's possible her death so grieved him that he got drunk and took his own life. Using, as a weapon, the vehicle that had killed the woman he loved.'

'Aye, that's one possibility.'

'But . . . what? You prefer the idea of murder? A clever one. Difficult to solve. Not impossible, but close to perfect.'

'Bridie had only recently moved in with Coghlan. Before that, she lived here.' His thick thumb jerked towards the timber ceiling.

'Here? Her own room? Or with you?'

'Bridie Button,' Gorrie said, 'was Doug McCafferey's wife. She was married to him two years, only she never did take his name. Then maybe a couple of months ago there was a terrible row and she walked out to live with Coghlan.'

He waited for that to sink in, then went on, 'And here's something else that might be of interest to a private investigator. The woman you've taken a room with was married twice, both husbands dead a long while now. Her first husband was Tom McCafferey: Peggy McBride is Doug McCafferey's mother.'

* * *

As I began the walk back down the road towards the haloed lights of Craignure, head bent into the cold drizzle, I was forced to narrow my eyes against a pair of dazzling headlights that came rushing up the hill towards me. It was a Land Rover. As it drew level I saw the shadowy figure inside, the paler flash as a face turned towards me. Then it had rattled by in a cloud of spray, and I turned briefly to watch it swing on to McCafferey's forecourt.

Doug McCafferey?

Jim Gorrie had told me that when

37

McCafferey was away, he ran the business — and that was most of the time. So where had Doug McCafferey been, I wondered, on the night Ray Coghlan was crushed by a three ton truck balanced precariously on stands in his garage?

3

I took those thoughts with me all the way down the hill into Craignure. Those, and the realization that complications, like the truck driven by Bridie on that terrible night, were threatening to career out of control — and so far I'd been on the island for less than two hours and spoken to just one man.

But that was all about to change. When, with rain dripping off my eyebrows and trickling icily down the back of my neck, I stumbled into the mustard-coloured pub on the outskirts of Craignure, it was to find Calum Wick sitting on a scarred settle at a table in a cramped corner of the room looking with longing at his unopened packet of Schimmelpenninck cigars.

Not too far away a large woman sitting on her own, holding what looked like a half-pint of whisky, was straining the seams of an XXL Adidas shell suit as she twisted to watch two girls in short skirts bouncing darts off the whitewashed half tyre encircling the pocked dart board.

The man talking to Calum had hair like wire wool and grey eyes sharp enough to pierce armour plate. I knew the type: in less than an hour my clued-up colleague had found, and was breaking bread with, a plain-clothed member of the local constabulary.

★ ★ ★

DS Hills, a stubbled Scot in a plaid shirt, was sitting back in a Scottish pub drinking Irish whiskey as he eyed an Englishman without too much animosity and listened idly to a track by Guns 'N Roses — an American band. Did his apparent disdain for tradition, I wondered, hint at a lack of respect for authority and leave him open to . . . persuasion? Offers of help? The making of mutually beneficial deals?

'Gorrie was right on all counts,' Hills told me, sipping his double Jamesons. 'Bridie Button's death was pure accident, Ray Coghlan's is still being looked into.'

'With the odds on what?'

'There's a history of strife between various factions on the island as you'll discover if you hang around for long enough.'

'Was that some kind of an answer?'

'The only one you'll get.'

'But you've no objection to us, er, hanging around?'

'I'm all in favour of tourism.'

Calum Wick chuckled. 'Give it up, Jack, it's like trying to catch fog in a fishing net.'

He'd done the introductions, gone to the bar for an ice-cold Holsten Pils for me as soon as I walked in, and while he was away I'd let DS Hills know that from Jim Gorrie at McCafferey's garage I'd got nothing more than the bare details of the two deaths. Calum had returned, I'd downed half the drink and now, in heat generated by bodies and a couple of Calor gas heaters that were causing the stone walls to glisten, I was gently steaming.

The pub was small, crowded and noisy, the bar all gleaming brass and glass, the walls bedecked with crumbling driftwood, stringy nets holed like a raddled tart's tights and cracked ships' running lights of red and green that shone weakly from fake bulk-heads and transformed bonnie drinkers into the living dead. The effect was of sitting in the forecastle of a fishing vessel sunk between the wars and only recently hauled to the surface complete with ghostly crew.

I glanced sideways at Calum, caught his eye then looked away.

'As tourists,' I said, 'we make pretty canny investigators.'

Hills shook his head. 'You'll not get the

chance while I'm around.'

'Ah, but we've already got a contact smack in the middle of those rival factions.'

He said nothing, but interest stirred behind the sharp grey eyes.

'Name?'

'Peggy McBride. We're renting two rooms in her Salen cottage.'

Hills grunted dismissively. 'A bitter woman, with no interest in what's been going on.'

'That's hard to believe. She's Doug McCafferey's mother, which makes her Bridie Button's mother-in-law. Bridie left her husband, McCafferey, to go and live with Ray Coghlan — and now she and Ray are dead.'

I was talking for Calum's benefit, slipping him information while letting Hills know I'd been busy.

'You're looking for conspiracy where there is none. They died in separate, unrelated incidents,' Hills said.

'Same potent weapon — a three ton Bedford truck — and both deaths suspicious.'

'You're becoming tiresome. I told you, Bridie Button died in a tragic accident.'

'But McCafferey was there. Doesn't that cast the tiniest bit of doubt?'

'Why the hell should it? And, no, he wasn't there, he arrived too late at the scene of a fatal accident that had already happened. The driver was his wife. She was dead. The poor man stood there cradling her bloody body in his arms while he waited for the emergency services.'

'But then another coincidence: Ray Coghlan, the man who'd stolen McCafferey's wife, dies in his garage.'

'Again, when McCafferey was many miles away.'

'How do you know?'

'Because we're the police: we investigate these things, and so it's our bloody job to know.'

A new voice. Strong, throatily feminine. The burly woman in the shell suit had taken her eyes off the girls bouncing handfuls of wild arrows off walls and furniture, and now she dragged her chair close to our table.

'I'm DI Vales,' she said. 'Your colleague's been here a while. I couldn't help overhearing him say that you're some kind of private investigator.'

'The better kind,' I said, and held out my hand. 'Jack Scott.'

'A better kind of PI?' She took my hand, but her eyes dripped amused contempt. 'If there is such an animal, it's news to me.'

'Better to be a PI of any kind at all and out in the open,' I said, 'than an undercover cop poorly disguised as Mull's only steroidal

43

female caber tosser — '

'Off duty, not undercover,' Vales cut in coldly, 'and the only tosser in here is you and I can assure you I'm not talking cabers. As it happens I could take you apart with or without the aid of that anabolic crap, and if this is your idea of ingratiating yourself with the local fuzz, it's failed miserably. I'm warning you now: keep your noses out of a Strathclyde Police investigation.'

'Do I sense the cream of the Argyll, Bute and West Dunbartonshire Division turning a wee bit curdled?' Calum Wick said, grinning at me as Vales threw him a warning glance.

'And is that really how they see us?' I said innocently. 'Scott and Wick, two annoying clouds floating on high o're Vales and Hills?'

'For Christ's sake,' Vales said irritably, 'can you imagine how bloody boring that gets?'

'Maybe you two should stop seeing each other,' I said, 'and remove temptation.'

'We see each other on a daily basis and in an official capacity,' Vales said, 'and if there are clouds of any description interfering with the progress and smooth running of an ongoing police investigation they're bloody soon blown away.'

'Tough and tetchy,' I said approvingly. 'But what if information that accidentally comes our way could be useful in your ongoing investigation? Be good little tourists and keep our traps shut, or — ?'

'Ring this number.'

DS Hills, who had stayed out of the childish slanging match, had downed his Jamesons and was on his feet. He flipped a business card on to the table. DI Vales was also ready to go, her bulk casting a huge shadow over the corner of the room as she pushed back her chair.

As she did so, and prepared to leave, one of the girls trying to play darts actually did hit the board — the wire on the top edge of double twenty. The dart rang like a spear striking a shield, bounced high enough to scrape the blackened beams, flew in an artistic parabola as everyone ducked out of the flight path and, with a solid thud, neatly pinned the card left by DS Hills to the table.

Vales grinned. 'Welcome to Mull,' she said. 'Have a nice stay.'

⋆   ⋆   ⋆

The rain had eased when we finished our drinks and walked out into a dank night thick with wet mist and the rank smell of the sea. We sat for five minutes while I brought Calum completely up to date with what I had learned from Jim Gorrie. When I'd finished I realized he was looking reflective.

'I like that big lassie's style,' he said, 'and she certainly had you sussed. From where I was sitting it sounded as if you were deliberately rubbing her up the wrong way. If you get my meaning.' He grinned. 'Was there a point to your boorish behaviour?'

'Misdirection,' I said. I edged the Quattro out of a tight cluster of cars cowering under weak overhead lights like primal beasts with sightless eyes and fogged shells, skilfully drifted out of the pub's gravel car-park and headed north on the road out of Craignure. 'She now thinks I'm a brainless, misogynistic slob.'

'DS Hills wasn't fooled.'

'No, and DI Vales won't be when she cools down.'

'So there *was* no point.'

'Well, it got us noticed.'

'Incognito is more fun.'

'I'm talking about the baddies, not the police. Mull's a small island. Word will get around and they'll realize what they're up against.'

'*Two* brainless, misogynistic slobs?'

'Right. Lull them into a false sense of security, hit them when they're looking the other way.'

'When we track them down.'

'The dream team. We never fail.'

'Be nice if we knew what we were looking for,' Calum said. 'And for whom.'

'For whom?'

'There's no crime to investigate, as yet no client to come up with the dosh. And no dosh means the best we can hope for is a couple of weeks on job seekers' allowance.'

I chuckled. 'You wouldn't pass the means test.'

Peggy McBride's cottage in Salen was probably twenty minutes' drive away. On the Isle of Mull, on a filthy November night, I was not expecting to meet any traffic. Yet, understandably, what had happened to Bridie Button on Glen More was a fiery red gremlin capering a silent warning in the shadows at the back of my mind. So I kept the mighty Quattro reined back to a steady fifty; watched the road for adverse camber that might send the unwary slewing into the ditch; diligently kept my eyes on the road ahead for the dazzle of approaching headlights behind which a tired driver might be fighting to keep his eyes open.

It was as well I took those precautions.

As I took a long flat turn and sent spray hissing from glistening black tarmac and into the trees, the Quattro's headlights picked out a dirty white shape standing stock still on the

47

crown of the road. Calum grabbed instinctively for the handle above his door. I swerved around a sodden sheep that stared unblinkingly at us with glowing yellow eyes, then eased into a straight ribbon of road that seemed to unreel endlessly as the headlights bounced back off the mist.

It was at that point that Calum yawned, jerked a thumb over his shoulder and told me sleepily that we were being followed. He was up to his usual trick of pulling down the passenger side sun visor and using the vanity mirror for covert surveillance — PI jargon for being nosy.

As it turned out, he was both right and wrong. There were headlights fifty yards behind us. They were travelling in our direction. Technically, we were being followed. But that following was not a sinister pursuit: an innocent driver sick and tired of squinting ahead had latched on to us and was using the Quattro's glowing tail-lights as convenient beacons to pull him along through the mist.

The lights in my mirror winked out a few hundred yards before I pulled into Salen, and for a brief moment I wondered if the driver had turned into a side road or concentrated himself dizzy and finished up in a ditch.

Two minutes later we were knocking on Peggy McBride's front door.

★ ★ ★

The woman who rattled the iron latch as she pulled open the heavy black door was tall and slim and as straight as Galahad's lance. Long hair like pure white gossamer swirled about a slender neck encircled by a band of black velvet above a cerise dress whose hem swept the floor as she smiled like an angel and invited us to enter in tones bearing the accent and cadences of Malcolm Rifkind but dripping with the raw femininity of a sixty-year old vamp. As she glided away and left two stunned PIs to close the door behind them I was reminded of the Edinburgh portrayed by Alexander McCall Smith in *The Sunday Philosopher Club*; and when, after exchanging disbelieving glances, we followed her up a narrow, thickly carpeted hallway, the original oils hanging on walls of damask rose did nothing to dispel that image.

Talk about a conflict of impressions!

During the drive up from Wales I had been looking forward to meeting a tall sixty-year old with a snap like a Pekinese. Jim Gorrie's revelation that Peggy McBride was the twice married mother of the man who owned McCafferey's Garage had turned the mental image into a crude stereotype: I'd driven apprehensively to Salen expecting to be

49

greeted by a harridan with dirty fingernails who chain smoked roll-ups and wore a frayed woolly cardi reeking of Old Holborn and petrol.

Those thoughts said a lot about me and very little about Peggy McBride. As if in a dream we were led through a cosy living-room into a kitchen-diner by a woman of impeccable manners who shook hands over the introductions, sat us at an oak refectory table set on a tiled floor fit for the London Hilton and watched over us with amusement as we polished off a meal that could have been cooked in that hotel's kitchens.

As prickly as a thistle, as sharp as a honed dirk — that's what Sian had said. DS Hills had talked about *a bitter woman, with no interest in what's been going on.* Both assessments could be close to the truth, because a person's character can appear very different as circumstances change — not just from day to day, but hour by hour. A snap judgement would be based on first impressions, which in our case was a warm welcome and a meal fit for the gods — and therein lay the danger. The way to a man's heart may be through his stomach, but the food that leaves him happily replete can just as easily dull the brain.

I pushed back my plate with a sigh of satisfaction. We waited for Peggy McBride to finish, then followed her through to a room now lit by a single standard lamp standing in front of an uncurtained window and sank with the sighs of tired old men into easy chairs flanking the living room's blazing log fire. I watched with admiration as the slim, white-haired woman crossed gracefully to a cabinet and returned to hand us crystal glasses containing the inevitable wee dram that tasted like bottled smoke and set the throat on fire, helped herself to another glass containing a dram that was even less wee, and settled like a Persian cat on to a leather Chesterfield that time had polished to a rich sheen.

A sophisticated meal had been accompanied by conversation that sank from lively to lethargy and eventually stalled — but now the light in Peggy McBride's eyes had changed.

'Did you talk to Dougie?' she said.

'I must have spoken to someone,' I said slyly, 'or, according to our earlier chat, we wouldn't have been fed.'

She chuckled. 'That seems to imply that you've been tracked every step of the way, and each scrap of information passed to me, ever since you drove off the ferry.'

'It wouldn't surprise me. And I'll bet it was

Jim Gorrie who phoned to tell you I'd called at the garage.'

'Maybe he did, in which case I know you didn't meet my son. And here's a bet *I'll* win: you got very little from Jim.'

I shrugged. 'Enough. Facts that set me straight. Before I came to Mull I had Ray Coghlan dying out there on the moors, and no knowledge of a dead young woman.'

'And you got the information from that tall, fair-haired young woman?'

I smiled at the richly rolled Rs. 'Sian Laidlaw. Yes, I did.'

'Then perhaps, when I spoke to her, I was a wee bit misleading.' She paused to let me mull over various implications, then said, 'And am I right in thinking that Miss Laidlaw is out there now in the rain with those daft office boys?'

'Mm. IBM executives, and others from local businesses. When she's finished with them they'll still be office boys, but not quite so daft.'

'And what about you? What do you want here on Mull? What are you here for?'

'Ahah.'

That was Calum. He was stretched out, feet close to the flames, ankles crossed. For some reason he'd put on the John Lennon glasses he used mostly when painting toy soldiers. They were perched on the end of his nose. His grey eyes were dancing above the smeared lenses, and he was holding the crystal whisky glass in one hand and tugging at his grey-streaked beard with the other.

'And what exactly does 'ahah' mean?' Peggy McBride said sweetly.

'Cut to the chase,' Calum said.

'I was merely asking a polite and perfectly reasonable question.'

'Aye, but you posed the question already knowing the answer.'

'Which is?'

'Jack investigates, I assist,' Calum said. 'It's what we do. You know that from the, er, fair-haired young woman, so you already *know* why we're here.'

'And now I've got a question,' I said when she parried Calum's accusation with a haughtily raised eyebrow. 'If that young woman told you all about us, where exactly did you meet — and what else went on?'

'She sat where you are sitting. Drank what you are drinking. Thought' — she smiled enig-matically — 'the very thoughts that I've no doubt are consuming both of you this very minute.'

'And they are?'

'That here on the island there is a mystery you cannot pass up, Mr Scott. One you would dearly love to get your teeth into. If I can inject a little black humour into the situation, here we have a mystery to die for.'

'I wonder,' I said, 'if that's an invitation, or a threat?'

For a few moments conversation again faltered as we sipped our aged whisky and, one by one, placed our empty glasses on the oak occasional table. The silence was comfortable, but it masked disconnected thoughts that were as difficult to grasp as wind-blown chaff. Peggy McBride touched a simple gold locket with her fingers; settled a watch that had slipped down on her wrist, and adjusted her long skirt. She had strong hands, big hands, yet the overall impression she gave was of fragility and she moved as weightlessly as a bird. Calum removed his glasses and there was a soft click as he slipped them into his shirt pocket. The fire crackled; a log settled in a shower of sparks as three people looked anywhere but at each other with eyes that gave away no secrets.

I thought of Sian, getting it all wrong — which was unprecedented. Of this woman being misleading, which was possible but unnecessary, unless it was done deliberately and with intent to deceive. Why had she, through Sian, allowed me to believe a man had been driving the truck out there on Glen More, when the driver had been a young woman? Why had she hinted at murder, when the police were convinced it was an accident? And why, when there had been a second death that *did* look like murder, had that gone unmentioned?

From Jim Gorrie I'd got the impression of a tragic love triangle. When talking to Sian, Peggy McBride had spoken of a long-running, violent feud that had been simmering for years. Now she was watching and waiting (pointedly ignoring my remark about a threat), Calum was giving his effortless, eyes-closed impression of a dying highland chief, and I was searching for inspiration.

'Someone was murdered out on Glen More,' I said, the sudden words like tossed pebbles disturbing the waters of a still pool. 'That was the false impression you gave Sian when, in your words, you were 'a wee bit misleading'. Why did you do that? Mislead her?'

'Because I was guilty of jumping to conclusions. Today is Friday, so it must have been last Friday that I got news of the death. Within the hour your young lady had called here — the precise reason escapes me, but in any case it matters not. The point is that during our conversation I told her what I thought must have happened. What I was only *assuming* must have sounded to her like pure fact.'

'And the man you thought had died out there was Ray Coghlan?'

'Of course.'

'Why of course?'

'My son owns a garage, and I knew fair well that Ray's truck was in there that day. Something was being fixed. It always was a rattling death trap of a vehicle, so perhaps some welding was being done, something to patch the bodywork ... ' She shrugged, suggesting insignificance but all the while watching me closely.

I had the strange feeling of being played like a fish.

'But the weather that day,' I said, 'made an accident the most likely conclusion. Why would you immediately assume murder?'

'Because there was no love lost between Ray Coghlan and my son.'

That made me blink, not so much at the idea of animosity, but at what she was suggesting.

'Are you saying your son, Doug, hated Coghlan enough to resort to murder?'

'He had made threats publicly. But why not? Any reasonable man would have been pushed to the very limit of his endurance by what Coghlan had done.'

'What was that?'

Her dark eyes were reproachful. 'I said you

got very little from Jim Gorrie, Mr Scott. I did not say you came away with nothing.'

I contrived a faint, guilty smile, then gazed for a moment into the glowing coals as I followed a train of thought that led to one obvious contradiction.

'Jim Gorrie did tell me about your son's troubles,' I admitted, turning my gaze back to Peggy McBride. 'I know your son's wife had left him and gone to live with Coghlan, and that would certainly drive a man close to the edge, give him the urge to break bones. Yet I still can't understand why you jumped to the wrong conclusion. You've just told me Coghlan's truck was in for repairs. I know from Gorrie that Bridie Button was driving home — to Coghlan's house — when she ran off the road. She was in Coghlan's truck. This island's marvellous grapevine obviously keeps you abreast of events, so why would you assume Ray Coghlan had died out on the moors when you must have known his truck was picked up by Bridie Button?'

'But it wasn't.'

I frowned. 'I don't understand.'

'The plain facts are that on that particular day Ray Coghlan's truck was in my son's garage for repairs, and at some time around six o'clock, the repaired vehicle was collected — and it was collected *by Ray Coghlan*. My

57

son Dougie was there, and so was Jim Gorrie. They saw it all, saw Ray walk up the hill from the village, saw him climb into his truck and drive away — but on that tragic day, then or at any other time, neither Dougie nor Jim Gorrie saw hide nor hair of poor Bridie Button.'

4

Peggy McBride slipped upstairs to bed, leaving behind her a puzzle with no reasonable solution. On a filthy night, with a fierce gale roaring in from the Sound of Mull and whistling eerily through the island glens, a young woman had driven to her death off a lonely moorland road. Yet the last person seen climbing into that vehicle, by reliable witnesses, was her lover. As far as anyone knew, Bridie Button was at home cooking Ray Coghlan a supper of stuffed, seasoned trout with baked potatoes and buttered sweetcorn.

At least, that was what we were told.

'Where else could she have been?' a flushed and pink dressing-gowned Peggy McBride had said as she stood in the living room doorway. 'It was a Friday. It was Bridie's invariable habit to take the bus to town in the morning, do some shopping for the weekend then catch the midday bus back home. That bus roared up the hill and passed the garage as usual. Dougie watched it as he worked on Coghlan's truck. There is absolutely no doubt.'

'What about Coghlan?'

'I've no idea what he said to the police. I do know that he was here the very next day, after he'd answered their questions. He was in Salen, visiting one of his cronies. Mistakenly believing that I, as mother-in-law, would be distressed by Bridie's death, he called in.'

'If he'd been seen by the police,' I said, 'then he would have got here quite late?'

'Shortly after dark.'

'And he was wrong, you weren't . . . distressed?'

'There was a sadness within me for that poor young girl,' she said with a quirky smile, 'but if there was pure distress it was not because of the death that had occurred, but the one that had not.'

She had come down from the bathroom to make herself a steaming mug of cocoa, poked her head out of the kitchen to offer us some — with buttered toast — which, still dazed by developments, we politely declined. Before she made for the stairs, Calum did ask her if it was all right for him to smoke; she gave her permission, announcing with a saucy glance that the rich aroma drifting up the stairs would no doubt send her to sleep with a pleasurable smile on her lips.

'She'll need something stronger than that to send her off,' I said now as Calum fired up

60

a Schimmelpenninck and stood with his back to the fire. 'Either she's as puzzled as we are, or she knows something and is laughing gleefully up her sleeve.' I grinned. 'Maybe what she took up with her is strong enough to knock her out. I should have followed her through and caught her red-handed lacing that cocoa.'

'The cocoa on its own will finish off what those wee drams started. She'll probably keep us awake with her snoring.'

'That's later. Right now I could do with something cool, liquid and strong enough to strip paint.'

'I know there's wine to spare in the kitchen,' Calum said, starting across the room. 'I'll fetch the decanter, you find a couple of glasses — and while you're at it, do some serious thinking about buses and trucks, what sweet Peggy McBride said, and what she thinks we're gullible enough to believe.'

His Timberland boots squeaked on the kitchen tiles. In the living room I rummaged in cabinets, glasses clinked as I carried my find to the occasional table, and I must confess I was casting apprehensive glances at the ceiling as I sat down. I shared his feelings. Peggy McBride was up to something, and I had visions of her in the bedroom immediately overhead with some kind of listening device pointing in my direction. Paranoia? Well, maybe — but if I'd had those same forebodings in an earlier case, a murderous woman called Georgie might have been prevented from planting her electronic bugs and been caught much sooner.

Calum returned. Wine gurgled into glasses. The decanter, still one third full, was placed within easy reach. My Scottish colleague sank into his fireside chair, glass in one hand, cigar in the other. He looked across at me enquiringly.

'Spotted the deliberate mistake?'

'Not even close.'

'Before Peggy went to bed she told us Bridie Button took the bus into the village of Craignure every Friday, caught the midday bus back home. She told us that on that fateful day, her son watched the midday bus chug up the hill.'

'Right, got that.'

'However, just a wee while earlier, she told us that throughout that same day neither Doug nor Jim Gorrie saw hide nor hair of Bridie Button,'

'Christ,' I said softly. 'They saw the bus, but they don't know if she was on it.'

'They saw the bus,' Calum said, beaming, 'but not the girl. Maybe she *was* on it. Who knows? But if she wasn't, where was she? Still at home, where she'd been all day? Or in the village, where she'd stayed when she got off the morning bus?'

I sipped wine, contemplated possibilities.

'What difference does it make? At around six o'clock, Jim Gorrie and Doug McCafferey saw Ray Coghlan climb into that truck and drive away from the garage. Doesn't matter where Bridie was. In the village or at home means she couldn't have been near the truck — yet, what, twenty minutes later she *was* in that truck. She hammered down the road to Maddock's Switch and went crashing to her death in the pines.'

'The only plausible answer,' Calum said, 'is that, somewhere between McCafferey's garage and Maddock's Switch, she and Coghlan swapped places. She got in, he got out. But that would mean that out there on the moors, in a roaring gale and driving rain, she was waiting at the side of the road.'

'And what happened to Coghlan afterwards?'

'Walked home?' Calum shrugged. 'Maybe. But what was the point of the exercise? What the hell were they trying to do that somehow ended in tragedy?'

'There is another possibility. Another plausible answer to how Bridie got behind the wheel.'

'Aye, and I'm way ahead of you,' Calum said. 'Bridie Button had been murdered by her lover before he left home that morning. She was at home all day, lying in a pool of blood on the kitchen floor. Ray Coghlan took his truck in for repair, hung around the village, then drove home from the garage. In the darkness he carried his wife's dead body out to the truck, drove back to Maddock's Switch, wedged her behind the wheel and set the truck rolling off the road and across that field.'

'And *then* he walked home.'

'Plausible,' Calum said, 'but absolute, utter bollocks. Any number of much more reasonable possibilities could be arrived at by intelligent or perhaps inventive minds. The simplest is that Peggy McBride is lying through her teeth.'

I pulled a face, sipped wine, watched the ribbon of smoke twisting above the tip of Calum Wick's cigar. Did I trust Sian's judgement? If so, then Peggy McBride was a delightful sexagenarian and as bright as a button. Calum had already pointed out that unlimited stories could be dreamed up by inventive minds. Peggy McBride had sprayed unreliable information like a demented crop duster, but she hadn't touched on the bit about the death — Coghlan's — being the latest incident in a long-running feud. Was that a deliberate omission, or simple absent-mindedness?

'Let's look closer at the delightful Peggy McBride,' I said. 'What do you think she's up to, Cal?'

'I haven't a bloody clue. I'm pretty certain that tomorrow morning she'll put us on the payroll — after all, didn't Sian tell you the old girl was interested in your talent? But the purpose of all this misdirection . . . ?' He shook his head, clearly perplexed.

'She's obviously bothered by the thought that her son made threats against Coghlan,' I said. 'That was at the back of her mind, then came the death on the moors, she jumped to a conclusion — and I think she's scared she got it right first time.'

'Except that it wasn't Coghlan who died.'

'No, it was Bridie. So . . . what then? Doug murdered Bridie Button? It's possible — though Christ knows how he managed it. The motive would be the same. She ran out on him, presumably went willingly.'

'Aye, and then, after a wee break of just twenty-four hours to recover his nerve, he lured Coghlan to his workshop.'

'Sadly, those theories won't work,' I said. 'The death out on the moors was an accident, pure and simple, and when Coghlan died

— surely murdered — Dougie McCafferey was miles away.'

'All may not be as it seems,' Calum said. 'Remember, it's been proved time and time again that there are no limits to man's ingenuity.'

I chuckled. 'Are you including DI Vales and DS Hills in that?'

Calum rolled his eyes. 'They'll see what's staring them in the face: that's accident and murder, same as you.'

'No finer testimony to my acumen.'

'Pity about the name.'

'Hm? What, mine?'

'Hills. Have a guess what he was christened.'

I thought for a moment, then started to grin. 'You're kidding! Not . . . Beverly?'

'As I live and breathe,' Calum said.

And then, with a crash of breaking glass and a blast of searing hot air, the living room window exploded in a sheet of flame.

5

With a sudden dazzling blue flash the standard lamp went out. Transformed by the flickering glare of the flames into a jerky marionette, Calum flopped awkwardly out of his chair, hit the carpet on his behind and shunted away from the terrible heat. I dived for the Chesterfield, ripped the beautiful embroidered throw from its back and cast it like a net over the pool of fire. The cloth seemed to recoil, writhing like something alive but in agony. Then, blackened, knotted and glistening, it sank, twisting as in the throes of death, and was swallowed by the flames.

Peggy McBride had left the living room door partly open when she went up to bed. Calum had done the same with the kitchen door when he came in with the wine. Somewhere at the back of the house and upstairs, windows were open. Through-draught from the shattered window was now sucking the flames into the house. Tongues of fire licked across the room towards both exits. The stink of petrol was carried on air hot enough to sear skin and hair.

Calum spun on hand and foot, came up off the floor and headed for the living room door at a crouching run.

'Get out,' he roared. 'Then use your phone.'

Then he was gone, gallant Lochinvar, pounding up the stairs to his frail Ellen.

Fire had consumed the curtains and was lapping across the ceiling. At the same time it was advancing at ground level, hissing and roaring. Calum's chair burst into flame. I fell back, arms up shielding my face as I felt my hair singeing. Twisting away, I saw the leather Chesterfield bubbling, blistering, as black smoke billowed ahead of the fire. Then I made a dash for the door. I burst through, slammed it shut, for an instant rested my back and head against the cool wood.

Above the angry roaring and crackling I heard voices upstairs. Calum was snapping orders. Peggy McBride was replying in a voice that was sweetly defiant. I wondered if Calum intended to frogmarch her down the stairs before flames cut them off, or drop her from bedroom window to soggy lawn.

Unbeknown to him, the decision was being snatched from his hands. The cool timber at my back was suddenly hot enough to blister skin. Smoke was issuing from every crack in and around the door and catching at my throat. I leaped away as one of the panels split and flame spurted. Another panel burst with a loud crack, scattering fragments of flaming timber across the hall. At once the thick carpet began to smoulder. My nostrils twitched at the animal stink of burning wool.

'Calum,' I shouted up the stairs, 'stay inside, shut the bedroom door and go to the window.'

Then, ducking away from the blast of smoke and flame gushing through the remains of the living room door and licking towards ceiling and stairs, I ran down the hall, wrenched open the front door and leaped out into the rain.

The Quattro was parked on a bumpy gravel patch under a stand of oak trees alongside the village shop. There was a police station in Salen, but I had no idea if it was manned and no time to find out. I splashed along the road fumbling for my keys and ducked inside, dug my phone out of the door pocket and quickly keyed in 999. Gentle Scottish voices informed me that appliances were already on the way, and when I looked back at Peggy McBride's detached cottage I saw that my hasty exit had been witnessed by villagers who had emerged from neighbouring houses where lights gleamed warmly through the steady rain.

One front window of Peggy's double-fronted cottage had been demolished when the petrol bomb smashed through and exploded. Smoke was now gushing from all the ground-floor's front windows. Behind the smoke, fire raged. I pocketed the phone and ran back towards the cottage as an upstairs sash window banged up and Calum poked his head out. Behind him the room glowed. Smoke was curling around his grey hair and beard, giving him the appearance of an evil satyr cloaked in swirling woodland mist.

Eyes flashing, he shouted something I didn't catch. Two men ran across the road, carrying a wooden ladder. They crossed the small lawn and drove one end of the ladder into the soft soil of a flower border, then swung it up to slam against the wall. Calum ducked back into the smoke. Seconds later the soles of a pair of pale, naked feet appeared, then a slender rump covered by a cotton nightdress. Helped by Calum, Peggy had climbed up and was kneeling painfully on the window sill.

A grey-haired man with a wet crinkly beard and a green vest tucked into worn jeans shinned quickly up the ladder. He braced himself, hands gripping each side of the ladder. Peggy came out backwards, steadied by Calum's strong hands. The bearded man let her inch her way down, guiding her naked feet to each rung until she was safe in the circle of his arms. Then he let her lean back against him as he walked her the rest of the way down. As soon as her bare feet touched the wet grass the man swept her into his arms and carried her across the road to where a woman waited in a lighted doorway. And only then did Calum throw a leg over the window sill and use the ladder to make his escape from the burning cottage.

When he stepped off the ladder and turned to look at me, it was with sharp blue eyes staring out of white sockets set in a smoke-blackened face.

Grinning with relief, I said, 'Your mascara's a mess.'

The wail of a siren approaching rapidly from the direction of Tobermory was loud enough to cut off his unprintable reply, but well before the fire engine reached the outskirts of the village a metallic silver vehicle came tearing down the hill opposite, bounced across the road spraying mud and water and skidded to a gravel-crunching halt alongside the Quattro.

It was a Mitsubishi Shogun.

There was a sudden, aching silence as the wailing siren died away and the big fire engine cruised smoothly into the village. The Shogun's door opened. Sian Laidlaw, togged out in combat gear, stepped out into the rain, placed hands on hips and looked across at me.

'What the hell,' she said, 'have you two done now?'

★   ★   ★

It was after midnight, the blaze was out of control and spewing sparks and burning embers in all directions, but Peggy McBride's cottage stood on its own in small lawned gardens and in the pouring rain the inferno was of no danger to other properties in the village. As we watched through the rain-spattered windows of the Shogun the firefighters got to work unreeling hoses, connecting up and turning on the water, but it was clear they were doing it to flex their muscles and make the journey worthwhile; they were never going to put out a fire in which accelerant had been used in a house that was all oak beams and lath-and-plaster ceilings that had been drying out for 200 years.

'Gone,' Sian said at last, staring miserably out at the dripping, blackened mess of charred beams and blackened stone walls. 'All gone. But I wonder where *she'll* go now, where she'll sleep tonight?'

'The people who took her in will certainly ring Doug, and then it'll be up to him.'

'Doug McCafferey?'

'That's right. You've been on the island a while, so at risk of going over what for you may be old ground, let me bring you up to date.'

I expected the telling of my tale to take no more than ten minutes, but five minutes after I'd started, a police car drove into the village with blue light flashing and Calum and I were called out into the slackening rain to give brief statements to Vales and Hills. While pencils were scribbling, the fire crew from Tobermory departed, and when the Mull detectives snapped shut their notebooks and drove out after them, the village returned to its former calm. The narrow main road, glistening in the rain, was lit by a single yellow street light and the gentle glow from the dying embers of the fire.

Damp and dishevelled, Calum and I returned to the Shogun. I picked up where I had left off, and at the end of what turned out to be a full half-hour, Sian knew everything that had happened or been said since Calum and I arrived on Mull. Her blue eyes were smoky as she listened in the dim light seeping through the Shogun's windscreen, but I saw the brightness of understanding flicker as I mentioned the relationship between Peggy McBride and Doug McCafferey, the brightness of something that might have been anger flare dangerously when I told of watching the blond-haired man called Lachlan grinning and mouthing something to me as he stood in the rain alongside his low-slung Mercedes.

'That just about wraps up all I know,' I said, 'but I've got a horrible feeling that the blond-haired character with the fast car is going to loom large in this investigation. What about that, Sian? Who is this Lachlan?'

'Ah.' She looked slightly disturbed, definitely embarrassed and, as I was to discover, infuriated by her own failings. She caught my eye, flushed slightly and said, 'He's an old . . . acquaintance of ours, Jack. A man we've discussed, a man we once argued about in a pub out Hale way; a man, dare I say it, who has threatened to come between us.'

She smiled, her eyes suspiciously bright. 'But that's old stuff, isn't it? Of more interest to us now is his second name. He's Lachlan McBride, and that woman Calum helped on to the ladder like a bundle of rags is his mother.'

6

We left the Quattro in Salen and Sian drove us four miles along dirt tracks slick with mud to the bothy she and her fellow instructors were using as a base. It was a sagging stone shack set back in an isolated stand of straggling black pines on mist-shrouded moorland. As we bounced towards it we were guided to a gravel hard-standing by one square window lit by lamplight that spilled out to shine on wet stones, and I could see the dark shape of two LWB Land Rovers at the far side of the building. When Sian parked, drips from the pines rattled like hail on the roof of the Shogun. Stones crunched underfoot. Door hinges creaked like coffin lids in a gothic horror movie. The long room we entered reeked of mildew and damp socks, and the darkness was alive with heavy breathing.

Sian pulled a blanket aside and led us through an opening in the thick interior wall and we found ourselves in a small, crude kitchen that turned out to be the room with the oil lamp. Walls glistened with condensation. Straight chairs stood around a rough scrubbed table. Sian filled a kettle from a huge plastic bottle of water and set it on a portable gas stove that began hissing like an unremittingly angry cat. I dragged out a chair and sat down. Calum, ever restless, reached up to a shelf over which cobwebs drooped like clusters of dirty butterfly nets and began taking down tin mugs and a box of tea bags.

'I counted very few bodies occupying those camp beds,' I said.

'Four when I left,' Sian said, 'and two of those are instructors. This course is dying the death.'

'But one of those hanging on is Lachlan McBride?'

'Yes — but he's not here now. His sister's ill. He was given permission to go to Oban for the night.'

'Ah, yes.'

Something in my voice drew her attention as she sat down.

'You knew.'

'That he was going, yes, but not the reason. I told you I watched Jim Gorrie filling Lachlan's Mercedes at McCafferey's garage. Apparently he was in for MOT, then petrol, and rushing to catch the ferry.'

With a tea bag poised over a tin mug, Calum said, 'What *is* all this about Lachlan

McBride, anyway? Who is he? What's he done?'

I took a deep breath. 'Sian saved his life on an earlier course up at Cape Wrath when he was suffering from hypothermia.'

'Ah ha,' Calum said, tossing me a knowing glance. 'So Lachlan is the young executive on whom she practised standard survival techniques, such as sharing bodily heat and all that intimate stuff?'

'That's right. After that he tried to keep in touch with her, but was rebuffed.'

'Keep in touch,' Calum said, grinning at Sian. 'And was rebuffed.'

'And during the Joe Creeney case,' I said, 'he actually kidnapped her to try and prove a point.'

'I thought that man's name was Mark Deeson?'

'It was,' Sian said. 'But now it's not.' She shook her head irritably. 'Forget Lachlan, Jack. I instruct on survival courses. Other people do the advertising in corporate magazines, and take the money from those who swallow the bait. I train those who turn up, and Lachlan happens to be hooked on what he would like to be vicarious adventure — '

'Through a certain instructor — '

'Who has rebuffed him yet again.' She cast

77

a wan smile in Calum's direction. 'He propositioned me at the beginning of this course, Jack. Told me to get rid of the private eye, the toy-soldier man; that we — Lachlan and I — had *much* more in common.' She met my gaze. 'I told him to get lost.'

'He was mouthing something at me down at McCafferey's. At the time I thought he was being friendly, but wondered how he knew my name. Now I think he was up to no good, so if you want me to talk to him — '

'No. I said drop it.'

I raised my hands, palms out.

'It's dropped,' I said, smiling at her to banish the ghost that for too long had been haunting us. 'Gone for good, unless he crops up again in our dealings with his mother. Because that's what we should be worrying about, the maniac who sneaked in out of the rain to toss a Molotov cocktail through her cottage window. What was he trying to do? Murder Peggy McBride? Or was he after the two visiting English investigators?'

'Now just hold on a wee minute,' Calum said.

'Sorry. Investigators from England.'

Sian's grin was fleeting. 'The answer seems obvious. Peggy McBride's been here all her life, and come to no harm. You arrive on the island and start asking questions and someone lobs a firebomb.'

'Yes, but that could be subterfuge. The killings happened recently. The bomb-thrower could have been biding his time, waiting for the right moment.'

'What, to kill the elderly McBride?' Calum was frowning. 'Why would he do that? What's she done?'

'She's also Doug McCafferey's mother, you know that.'

'We both know that,' Sian said. 'What we don't know is where those husbands are now.'

'These are all questions I'm itching to ask,' I said, 'but the point I was about to make was that Ray Coghlan died in Doug's garage, Coghlan would have friends, relatives, many of them anxious to get even.'

Sian nodded agreement. 'Anything to go on?'

'Not yet. No suspects. No client — though that should be settled tomorrow. Not much idea of what we'd be investigating, either — though, again, tomorrow should change that when our host for this evening takes us into her employ. She admitted to misleading you, by the way, and the reasons she gave were very convincing — but of course, liars usually are. Tomorrow I'll head back to McCafferey's garage, where I'm pretty certain I'll find Peggy McBride living over the shop. If she is, I'll ask her some very awkward questions.'

'Like which crime we're supposed to be investigating on her behalf,' Calum said from the stove.

'There is only one crime: the deliberate killing of Ray Coghlan. Bridie Button's death was accidental.'

'Until proved otherwise,' Sian said. 'Peggy believes that — or says she does — but as she's misled us once — '

'Be very careful.' I nodded agreement. 'But to get back to your question about what we've got to go on, well, the story as we know it has dead bodies, one wrecked vehicle responsible for two deaths, a troubled marriage and a local bad lad businessman who ended up as one of the corpses. There's a death that we'll say *looks* accidental. Another that certainly *looks* like murder, and a man with an excellent motive. But someone got wind of this long before we stepped off the ferry at Craignure — '

'Me, and my inquisitive mind,' Sian said, putting up her hand.

' — and I'm hoping my informant will have been using her womanly wiles — '

'Innate curiosity.'

' — to dig up some interesting background information.'

'Actually, no,' Sian said. 'Yes, I have been enquiring, and yes, islanders have been forthcoming. Unfortunately, everything said by everyone I've spoken to — or eaves-dropped on — leads to just one conclusion.'

'The late Ray Coghlan,' she said, as Calum planted three steaming mugs on the table and sat down, 'was the kind of man who took what he wanted, trod on everyone's toes and ruffled lots of Highland feathers. But the man who suffered most sorely at his hands was Doug McCafferey.'

'You mean Coghlan luring Doug's wife away from him wasn't the start of it?'

'Lord, no. A few years ago, Ray Coghlan won most of Doug's money from him in a marathon poker session in the back room of that pub in Craignure. Doug clawed his way back up through sheer hard work, only for Coghlan to kill his younger brother by driving his truck off a mountain road — and he got away with it. Doug's also nursing a seriously damaged knee. I don't know the details, but apparently once again Coghlan was to blame.'

A match flared as Calum lit a Schimmel-penninck. Blue smoke drifted across the oil lamp. An empty jerry can pinged as he flicked the dead match.

'Too pat,' he said. 'Christ, with all that animosity and resentment burning inside him, McCafferey's as good as convicted.'

Sian shook her head. 'His alibi's watertight. He was in Oban when that truck fell on Coghlan's head.'

'And *that*'s too bloody convenient.'

'But true. He kept the tickets in his wallet. And the ferrymen all know him well. From deckhands to captain, they back up his story.'

'You see?' Calum squinted one eye at me through the smoke drifting from his cigar. 'Who the hell keeps old tickets? Doesn't that suggest he was expecting someone to check his story? And if the ferrymen do know him that well, isn't it possible at least one of them would bend the truth?'

'One, yes,' Sian said, 'but not the whole crew.'

'Why not? If one trusted man swore Doug was on board . . . '

'The others might be pulled along,' I said, as Calum left the thought hanging. 'If they were all looking the other way and couldn't swear to seeing or not seeing McCafferey, they just might back their friend. But you called it too pat, and I think you're right. Nevertheless, although motive seems to make McCafferey the obvious suspect, he's not been charged. DS Hills said Coghlan's killing's being looked into, DI Vales calls it an ongoing investigation, and I think they're following other leads.' I looked at Sian. 'You said Coghlan ruffled feathers: surely that suggests other suspects out there?'

'Just the one that I know of.'

'Oh? And what had Coghlan done to him?'

'I'm not sure he'd done anything. But this man was definitely seen near the garage at the time Coghlan died.'

'If he was seen there,' I said, 'someone must have been there to see *him*. And report the sighting. That makes two suspects.'

'The man who reported seeing him was Andrew Keay. He told police he saw a man coming away from McCafferey's garage when he was tramping up the hill to collect his 4 × 4.'

For a moment there was silence. It seemed that as we sipped our tea we were all recalling that this was a killing in which the man who pulled the trigger was already known. Andrew Keay had driven away the vehicle that wrenched away the iron stands and caused the truck to fall on Ray Coghlan's head.

'Keay's an obvious suspect, and his report about sighting another man could have been deliberate misdirection,' I said. 'Was Keay one of Coghlan's victims?'

Sian shrugged. 'I think you'll find that few people were untouched.'

'What about the man Keay says he saw? Did he come up with a name?'

'Oh dear,' Sian said. 'I hate to tell you this — but it was Lachlan McBride.'

7

Saturday

It was early when Sian drove down the drying roads to drop me alongside the Quattro in Salen. The rain had drifted over the sea to the west and late autumn midges stubbornly refusing to die were out in force, attacking in swarms from the hanging mist like Mitsubishi Zeros of the Japanese Air Force swooping out of thin clouds over the Pacific.

Calum and I had slept on camp beds vacated by miserable, mud-caked executives who had slunk back to the cities with their tails between their camouflaged legs leaving Sian to clean up. The plan was for me to seek out Peggy McBride at the garage in Craignure. Cal, when he eventually rolled out of bed, would amble down to Salen where, authorities permitting, he would poke around in the blackened ruins of the cottage then talk to the locals. That, of course, was the object of the exercise, and as a Scotsman he would have a measure of rapport that should loosen tongues.

Although there were just three people left

on the survival course, Sian still had to continue as if she and her fellow instructors had a full complement of executives eager to break limbs and bruise egos — their own, of course. Her thoughts on the matter were very clear.

'We'll be taking both Land Rovers,' she said. 'Those office boys are going to be practising their map reading on the slower slopes of Ben More, so, what with wet maps, compass-reading skills below Boy Scout level and a complete lack of common sense we could be out for, well — '

'Days?'

She rolled her eyes towards an unsympathetic heaven, we hugged warmly, and I watched her drive away up the slope before ducking into my car and slamming the door against the invading hordes.

As I slipped the key in the ignition it occurred to me that I hadn't yet discussed with her the disquiet I had detected in her voice when she phoned me at Bryn Aur. It had again been there when her troubled relationship with the man I now knew as Lachlan McBride came up in last night's conversation, and it would have been reasonable to suppose that was the cause. But, despite his being a pain in the neck, McBride had never been much more than a minor irritation. Yes, he harassed Sian and, no, he wouldn't go away — but something was telling me the cause of her troubles lay much deeper.

This, after all, was a woman who had seen her Scottish seafaring father lost overboard in an Arctic gale when she'd been ten years old and illegally aboard his ship, had returned to nurse her dying mother in the Cardiff slums and, years later, with a university degree under her Shotokan karate black belt, move north to become something of a legend among the high peaks of the Cairngorms.

She had come into my life in Norway where she'd been taking a break from military duty and I had been stepping gingerly on to skis for the first time since my own lengthy stint in uniform. That first meeting had brought together two people who considered themselves misfits, so we were shocked and delighted to discover that even misfits can have soul mates. Fairly glowing, we went on to share a holiday that had very little to do with skiing but a lot to do with intimate moments, romantic music and heady cocktails, all in a thickly carpeted chalet warmed by crackling log fires where we spent endless hours dreaming by candlelight as we looked ahead to a future filled with promise.

Now, more than two years on, the promise

was, well, still not fully realized. My blonde Soldier Blue had left the armed forces, shared my home and, occasionally, my bed, but as I started the Quattro and pulled on to the road to Craignure I knew that she had never fully taken me into her life. Oh, she had moved into Bryn Aur on what was intended to be a permanent basis during the Danny Maguire case, and though we had jokingly referred to it as me taking her into sheltered accommodation, it was working well. And yet — she was holding something back. There were dark shadows I hadn't been allowed to look into, and instinct was warning me that the cause of her present unease was locked away in that cold, impenetrable darkness.

As always happens, I was to discover that I was only half right.

★   ★   ★

The same Land Rover that last night had passed me on my wet walk down into Craignure was this morning parked in front of McCafferey's garage. I pulled on to the barren forecourt where the ancient rusting petrol pumps stood like sentinels frozen by time, splashed the Quattro through a couple of puddles to the side of the building closest to the black pines and stepped out to listen to them rustling in the now stiff breeze. Cold droplets showered down from their branches. I shrank into my collar and noticed the stairs leading up the side of the building. A black Volkswagen Golf was parked at the foot of the stairs — Peggy was obviously strong enough to have driven herself over from Salen — and light was shining through the half-glazed door at the top of the flight. I debated going up, thought better of it then locked the car and jogged around to the front of the building where bearded Jim Gorrie stood watching from the open double doors.

'Morning, Jim.' I rubbed my hands. 'Cold today.'

'It's November, pal. And this is Scotland, not your balmy south.'

I grinned. 'Yeah, I know, puts hairs on your chest. Speaking of which, is Peggy here?'

Something stirred in the deep-set blue eyes. I looked at his big fists, and took a mental step backwards while heroically holding my ground.

'Aye, she is — and Dougie's up there with her.'

'Good. Like to let them know I'm here?'

'Why would they be interested?'

'My colleague saved Peggy's life. I've come to collect the reward.'

'Jesus Christ,' he said softly.

He went into the office and as he telephoned upstairs I looked again at the wrecked truck. A battered hulk. Blood in the cab, blood underneath. Two people dead. I was sure that the woman I was about to see would hire me to find out how they died, because that was the only reason she had brought me from North Wales. But could I trust her? Already she had changed her story, and while forgetfulness sometimes comes unbidden with old age, deviousness usually takes practise.

Out of the corner of my eye I caught the flicker of dull blue. Jim Gorrie was gesturing from the office, pointing to the flaking ceiling. I nodded my thanks, walked around the outside of the building and climbed the shaky timber stairs. The door was open. I walked in. My breath was almost snatched away by a blast of hot air from a portable Calor gas heater. The ambience finished the job, delivering a killer blow created by a lifetime's scruffy living overlaid and enhanced by Old Holborn tobacco and last-night's curry and chips.

Peggy McBride was sitting by the front window on a double-wide seat taken from one of Mull's single-decker buses and set on four house-bricks. The slender, elegant lady Calum had rescued from the flames wore expensive jeans and a green hand-knitted sweater. Her white hair hung down the front of one shoulder in a plait as thick as rope. Thin fingers plucked at it nervously, the loose wrist watch I had noticed last night slipping down her arm, but there was fire in her eyes and I knew my first impression had not deceived me: this was no ordinary woman, and I was well aware that description could be applied to a lady who was a consummate actress. Had she for some reason been concocting a web of deceit as she led me gaily up the garden path with a performance that almost ended in death?

I had walked straight past Doug McCafferey.

The door clicked shut. A tall man smelling of stale sweat limped away from the door, gestured to a chair alongside a plastic garden table still littered with breakfast dishes and ran his hand through dark curly hair as he bent to turn the heater's controls and two of the glowing panels began to fade.

'You're Jack Scott,' he said, as if it was news that would excite me. 'Let me say at once that you're here at my mother's bidding, not mine. But now you are, maybe you'll enlighten me: what the hell can you do that I cannae do for myself?'

'He can find proof that Bridie died in a tragic accident,' Peggy McBride said. 'He can

91

find proof that you did not murder Ray Coghlan.'

'We don't need bloody proof. Everyone knows what happened to Bridie. Everyone knows I was miles away when Coghlan died.'

'Someone tossed a Molotov cocktail through a window and burned down your mother's cottage,' I said. 'Are you saying that wasn't linked to either of the deaths?'

'Bridie Button was an orphan,' Doug McCafferey said, 'brought up in some religious home or other in darkest Edinburgh. Christ, the name Button was given to her by nuns because from the very start that's how bright she was — and I'd say that anonymous upbringing rules out vengeful relatives toting rusty cans of petrol, wouldn't you?'

'Coghlan died in your garage.'

'Aye, and I'm telling you some bastard arranged that purely to point the finger at me.'

'Which proves my point, doesn't it? You're linked to a murder, your mother's cottage gets razed. Doesn't that suggest someone's out to get you?'

'Crap.' McCafferey's voice was scornful. 'Her house got torched because she was daft enough to put up two private-bloody-investigators — '

'And clever enough to hire them to sort out

this mess,' Peggy McBride said.

McCafferey glared. 'You'd do that?'

'It's done — right, Mr Scott?'

'And dusted,' I said and, with my head averted from Dougie, I gave her a conspiratorial wink.

'All right, then you two get on with this madness, because I'm having no bloody part of it, not ever — you understand?'

The thin door slammed behind him; the loose doorknob rattled; his footsteps hammered down the outside stairs, and Peggy McBride and I exchanged impassive glances as we heard a thud followed by a muffled curse as he slipped on the wet timber and finished the descent in a rush.

'Thank you, Mr Scott, for playing along.'

'It's Jack,' I said, 'and it was nothing.'

She dipped her head, and gazed at me from under arched eyebrows.

'Perhaps more than you think. You heard me talking to Dougie, so you know exactly what I want you to do. The trouble is,' — she pursed her lips — 'my straitened circumstances have been made so much worse by the disastrous fire that remuneration will be a headache — '

'If you mean you're broke,' I said, 'don't worry about it. That makes it business as usual, because I rarely get paid — and didn't you say this was a mystery to die for?'

'I think I did,' she said gently, 'but doing that will get you nowhere.'

'Which is probably what our mysterious firebomber had in mind when he lobbed his Molotov cocktail through your window.'

'Didn't work, though, did it?'

'It was a close run thing,' I said, and her appreciative chuckle was a rich gurgle. Then suddenly she was serious, her thin fingers again toying with the twisted rope of white hair.

'Last night your colleague said something about cutting to the chase, Jack. He was right then, and that's what we should do now. The first point I want to make is this: I know you can understand why I'm asking you to prove Dougie did not murder Ray Coghlan. He's my son, he's innocent, and I want the world to know. But here's the second: you're probably wondering why I want you to prove Bridie Button's death was accidental.'

'Calum and I discussed that last night. The conclusion we reached was that her death *was* an accident. But along the way we did linger over an interesting and probably workable alternative.'

'Involving Ray Coghlan?'

'That's right.'

Her smile was almost gleeful. 'Well, there

you are, now didn't I go and pick the right man for the job? You see, all that talk of accident was for Dougie's ears. The truth is, Jack, I want you to get out there and prove beyond any shadow of doubt that poor wee Bridie Button was murdered by Ray Coghlan.'

8

'My first husband, Tom McCafferey, died a natural death. He was taken by something of a vaguely coronary nature, and has been gone almost thirty years. My second, Stuart McBride, disappeared without trace a couple of years ago. So does that mean he's dead?' Peggy spread her hands. 'I'd say yes, but that's just my opinion based on intimate knowledge of a man who always lived on the edge. Stuart was a hunter, an excellent shot; he took risks in every aspect of his life. What that means is I could see him dying in some violent incident, but I could not see him taking his own life.'

We were drinking coffee out of thick mugs she had first rinsed with boiling water then dried on that coarse, pale-blue tissue paper garages hang alongside petrol pumps. I had moved my plastic chair close enough to Peggy's old bus seat to bask in perfume that was faint, but a welcome alternative to Calor gas fumes. Her answers were in response to my request for background information. Both her sons could be linked to the garage murder; I'd thought it not beyond the bounds of possibility that the respective fathers might be involved. McCafferey senior was now ruled out. I made a mental note to get up to date information on Stuart McBride.

But first I needed to find out more about the sons.

'Losing his wife to Ray Coghlan gives Dougie a strong motive for murder,' I said, 'and the trouble between the two men goes back much further than that, doesn't it?'

'More than ten years,' Peggy said. She'd drawn up her slender jean-clad legs, and the thick braid of hair falling across one shoulder, combined with fine-boned features and a graceful posture, gave her the air of a delicate oriental figurine. She was watching me with speculative dark eyes; waiting, I thought, to see how much I knew.

'Sian's been doing some digging,' I explained. 'She told me Dougie got involved in a card game with Coghlan and ended up bankrupt; that his damaged leg can also be blamed on Coghlan.'

'Dougie was flat broke, yes, but he came roaring back the better for the experience. And he never again played cards with the man. As for the other . . . well, Ray Coghlan was a rich man who'd acquired wealth through property but liked to pose as a self-sufficient Scottish landowner who was at one with nature. He wore shabby clothes. Drove clapped-out vehicles. Amongst other daft notions, he fancied himself as a lobster fisherman. He placed dozens of pots in Loch Fuaran — more likely paid someone to do it for him — and then forgot all about them. It was left to Dougie to sort out the mess when they got entangled with his own pots, and a slip while clambering about on jagged rocks left his right knee shattered.'

'And then,' I said, 'he lost a brother, with Coghlan again involved. Was that more recent?'

The coffee mug trembled slightly in her slender hands.

'Two years ago. Dougie's thirty-nine now, so that would make Alec thirty-three when he died. An accident is how Coghlan described it, at the inquest in Tobermory. He'd been on his way home, he told them, fighting the wheel of his old truck as it bucked and slewed in the wind swirling across the icy road. He must have nudged my Alec's Land Rover as he tried to go past him at Wilson's Gap, and in those conditions the bump had knocked it clean off the road. Didn't hear him, didn't feel the nudge, Coghlan said, straight-faced, telling bald lies to the Procurator-fiscal. He'd have stopped, he said, had he known — and now, so help me, there was a tear in his eye

— but it had been impossible to hear anything above that shrieking westerly gale. And so he drove on, unaware, and when they found my son he had bitten through his lip in agony; he was pinned beneath a pile of twisted metal that had been a Land Rover, and bled his life away into the purple heather of Glen More.'

I watched her close her eyes in remembered grief, and said quietly, 'And that truck Coghlan was driving then is the same truck that's down there now, in the garage?'

Her smile was bitter. 'Ironic, isn't it?'

I thought for a moment. 'If your husband, Stuart McBride, *is* alive — is that something he could have done? Murdered Coghlan? You said he disappeared a couple of years ago. Do you believe he went because the tragedy was too much for him to bear, his grief so terrible that he had to get away?'

'Alec was his stepson; Stuart didn't have strong feelings for my boys. No, if he was going to murder Ray Coghlan, it would have been in revenge for the suffering he'd endured at the hands of that blackguard.'

'Over and *above* the death of his stepson?'

'Stuart lived on the edge, as I've mentioned. That meant dabbling in get-rich-quick schemes, and Ray Coghlan had those in abundance. Unfortunately, they were intended to make just the one man rich, and that man was not Stuart McBride.'

'So the motive was there.'

'Indeed. But if he was going to murder Ray Coghlan for any one of those reasons,' she said, 'why would he have waited? His money's been gone a full decade, his stepson two years already.'

'And what about Lachlan?'

Her head tilted like a bird's as she frowned. 'What about him?'

'He's Stuart's son, isn't he? That makes him much younger than his half-brothers.'

'He's twenty-eight.'

'And your daughter?'

'Nellie? Why, she's twenty-eight too. She's Lachlan's twin.'

I'd never heard her name mentioned and, watching Peggy as she waited a little less serenely for my next question, I knew I'd prodded a nerve.

'I know about Nellie because Lachlan went across to Oban to see her last night, didn't he?'

'I believe so. I've heard she has a bungalow just outside the town. I've never been invited there.'

'Lachlan told Sian his sister was sick, and he asked for time off. Was her illness genuine?'

'I really have no idea. My daughter left me the day after Stuart walked out. I've not seen her in all that time.'

'I'm sorry.' I hesitated. 'Is Stuart with her, do you think? Is he, too, in Oban?'

'What I said was that Stuart disappeared without trace.' She smiled as if at a child. 'What do you think that means, Jack?'

'It means I'm not listening — '

'Or trying to trap me.'

'Or a little of both.' I returned her smile, then changed tack.

'Andrew Keay told the police he saw a man coming away from the garage, on the night Coghlan died. He was on his way up the hill to collect his 4 x 4. He's pretty sure that man was Lachlan. So I'll ask the same question I asked about Stuart: could Lachlan have draped that cable, that wire rope, over Keay's tow bar? Is your son capable of murder?'

'For your answer, you get the very same question,' Peggy said.

'You mean why would he wait two years?' I nodded. 'Sounds reasonable, but it's the *wrong* question. The correct question is, why do it now?'

'Or why do it at all?' Clearly flummoxed, she said, 'Jack, isn't this a rather strange way to go about proving Dougie's innocence?'

I shook my head. 'Proving innocence is

another way of saying eliminating guilt. In the eyes of the police, Dougie, Lachlan and your missing husband will be prime suspects, and we've got to change that. Trouble is, we all know that Bridie Button was found dead, and she was found in Ray Coghlan's old truck. You've asked me to find proof that Coghlan murdered her. What if Stuart, Lachlan or Dougie couldn't wait for proof? What if the killing of Bridie was for one, or all three of them, the last straw?'

'If it was,' she said, 'then you will discover that in your investigations.'

'At the moment, Dougie has an alibi; I don't know about the others. If one of them is guilty, is that something you're prepared to face?'

'Preparation is unnecessary. It won't happen.'

'Do you think Lachlan knows what happened to his father — perhaps knows where he is?'

But she was no longer listening to me. Her eyes had drifted towards the filthy window overlooking the front of the building, and I realized her attention had been caught by the throaty sound of a car being driven on to the forecourt. Then she smiled.

'That's Lachlan now,' she said, as a door slammed. 'He'll have come from the ferry, it gets in just before ten . . . '

She was looking at her watch. I glanced at mine, then at the cracked railway clock hanging on the wall. That was ten minutes slow.

'I wonder what he's doing here now?' Peggy said softly.

'Well, he was in yesterday so he shouldn't need petrol — '

'By the way, I told him about your young lady's visit,' she said in a sort of tangential aside. 'He was upset.' She frowned. 'Perhaps that's the wrong word. I think he was quite angry.'

'Tough. I'm sorry if that sounds harsh, but it's something your son will just have to put up with.'

'Lachlan McBride,' Peggy said softly, 'is not the kind of young man to put up with anything he doesn't much like.'

★　★　★

A weak sun had broken through the high clouds, and on fields, dark pine trees, petrol pumps and the untidy gravel stretching out to the road the lingering wetness of overnight rain glistened brightly.

Lachlan McBride was talking to Jim Gorrie when I preceded Peggy down the slippery stairs. When he saw us he said something to the mechanic, clapped him on the shoulder and watched him jump into the car and drive the low-slung Mercedes into the workshop.

Then he turned with a grin to his mother.

'To put your mind at rest, I was talking to Alan on the way back. He's absolutely certain Dougie went across to the mainland that afternoon and did not come back until the next day.'

'Not the evening? Because there's one at nine forty-five on Saturday?'

'No, it was the four o'clock boat.'

Peggy took a deep breath. 'Alan's a deckhand on the ferry,' she said, to nobody in particular but for my benefit.

I nodded understanding, at the same time wondering if some signal had passed between them, and this spoken confirmation of an alibi was for my benefit. Wondering, too, why Lachlan McBride was not, at the very least, enquiring after his mother's health. Her house had burned down, for God's sake. He was acting as if nothing had happened, yet even if the news hadn't reached him in Oban it would surely have been the first bit of gossip to greet him as he stepped off the ferry.

Then Lachlan was in front of me, dark eyes dancing under the shock of blond hair, hand thrust forward.

'I've heard a lot about you,' he said as we shook hands.

'Dib, dib, dib.' I smiled, and raised two fingers in the Scout salute. 'Won't Sian be wondering where you are? Shouldn't you be out there squelching through a bog, or clawing your way up a crag?'

'She let me off for the night, but unfortunately something's gone wrong with the Merc's charging system. I think the alternator's packed up. So, if she wants me — '

'She'll have to come and get you.'

I nodded absently as I reached for my brightly trilling mobile and glanced at the readout.

'You're in luck, that's her now,' I said, and, excusing myself, I walked a few yards away in the direction of the tattered black pine trees.

'Jack, I've had some bad news, from Liverpool. My sister's badly injured. Don't ask me why, or how, but I *must* go and see her.'

'Where is she?'

'The Royal.'

'Drive down to the ferry. It's Saturday, so there's one at ten o'clock. I'll pick you up there. We'll go to Liverpool in my car.'

'Jack — '

'Just do it.'

I switched off, put the phone in my pocket; stared at the pines' ragged, trailing fronds, beyond those to the fields of short grass being moulded by the soft breeze into the rippling surface of a sea.

Well, I'd sensed unease, hadn't I? And now I had the reason — or a part of it. I'd always known the story of Sian's life, but she had never, ever, mentioned the existence of a sister. If that was deliberate deception, then it could have caused her considerable disquiet. But her sister must have been there, in the background and without my knowledge, for as long as I had known Sian, and as far as I could tell it had never seriously troubled my Soldier Blue. So why now? When she had phoned from Scotland with news of a mystery on the Isle of Mull, I had noticed the difference in her voice and wondered what was troubling her. In the Shogun and, later, in the bothy, I had seen the unease in her eyes when Lachlan's name cropped up and thought with relief that I had stumbled on the cause — then quickly realized that her troubles went much deeper than irritation with a pathetic stalker.

And now I knew instinctively that even the fact that she had kept her sister a secret, on its own, could not be the underlying cause of her distress. There had been a sequence of

106

events: Sian's unease had been new, and palpable; within days, her sister was lying badly injured in hospital.

Had Sian, in some way, anticipated the accident? If so, how — and if she had, then surely it *was* no accident.

It was time for the truth to come out.

★   ★   ★

I phoned Calum from the ferry terminal.

'I'm heading back to Liverpool with Sian,' I said. 'Her sister's been injured.'

'I didn't know she had one.'

'No. It was sprung on me, and now's not the time to ask questions.'

'Right, well, you've got a key,' Calum said, 'so phone me when you get to the flat.'

'Thanks, Cal. I don't know what to expect. Sian mentioned an accident. I think she's hiding something.' I thought for a moment. 'I'm not going to get deeply involved. Even if Sian stays on in Liverpool, I should be back late today, or early tomorrow — but that leaves you stuck, doesn't it?'

'In what way?'

'Transport. I want you to keep the investigation moving. And, by the way, our brief has changed. Our instructions now are to prove that Ray Coghlan murdered Bridie Button.'

'Getting to the bottom of that death on the moors is going to be fiendishly difficult whatever the brief.'

'Particularly as you don't drive and, if you did, you haven't got a car.'

'What did you ask me to do this morning?'

'Nose around. Ask questions.'

'Aye, well, by so doing I've made one or two good friends. Both of them have got cars.'

'And wear skirts.'

'In Scotland that's very likely, regardless of gender.'

I chuckled. 'Did you learn anything?'

'It appears,' Calum said, 'that there was something not quite straightforward about the death of one Tom McCafferey.'

'Peggy's first husband,' I said softly.

'The same. There was a suggestion that death by coronary was, in his case, what you might call an assisted passage. One of the obscure poisons was mentioned. Leaves no trace in the body, of course. Names were bandied about. Eventually, opinion seemed to settle on one man; it was thought likely that the administrator — if that's the right word — was Peggy's second husband, Stuart McBride.'

PART TWO

9

The driver hoping to head south from Oban
is not exactly spoilt for choice. Most roads
tend to meander more than a little, picking
up mist and peat along the way. The route
I've always chosen when heading back to
England from the Western isles takes me
inland along the A85 through Taynuilt,
Lochawe and Clifton, and at Crianlarich I
turn south on to the A82 for the long run
down Loch Lomond which brings me,
eventually, to the city of Glasgow. After that
it's all plain sailing: the M74 then A74 all the
way of Gretna, where very quickly it turns
itself into the M6. Liverpool is reached a few
hours later via the dying reaches of the M62.

It would be nice to report that, on the
journey south, prolonged periods of intense
brainstorming resulted in dramatic inspiration and illumination that transformed both
investigations and made quick solutions
inevitable. In fact, the reason for reciting
those interesting but hardly riveting details of
the route we took is because, during that
journey, Sian and I exchanged few words.
Three hundred miles of complete silence

would be exaggerating a little, but by the time I rolled the Quattro into the Royal's car-park in Liverpool I would willingly have started a conversation with a stray cat.

There was none around. I walked in silence with Sian into the central Liverpool hospital but there, as arranged, she went her own way. She'd used her phone on the drive south and discovered that her sister, Siobhan, was still in intensive care. I watched her walk — a little stiff with apprehension — towards the lifts, then strolled outside again. It was early afternoon, and sunny. I dug out my mobile. DI Mike Haggard picked up on the first ring.

When he realized who was calling, his pleasure was obvious.

'Jesus Christ,' he said, 'an' here was me havin' a good day.'

'Would a good day mean you've found out what happened to Siobhan Laidlaw?'

There was a moment's silence in which I could almost hear the oily clicking of mental cogs. Then Haggard grunted, either in satisfaction or shock.

'Are you tellin' me that bird's related to Sian?'

'Her sister.'

'Brilliant. So while we've been combin' the city and beyond for relatives — '

'When the bad news reached her, Sian was

in Scotland, Mike.'

'Directing another of those corporate outward bound courses for, er, bankers?'

'That's right. She got the phone call early this morning. We caught the ferry almost at once, and drove into Liverpool fifteen minutes ago. Sian's just gone up to the ward.'

'Right, well, when she's finished there, bring her in to Admiral Street for a cosy chat. And listen: her bein' related to the victim doesn't mean you're on the case. Keep your nose out, got it?'

'You said 'victim'. Does that mean a crime was committed?'

'It means there was an incident, and Siobhan Laidlaw is the injured party. If you want to know more, talk to Sian when she comes down from the ward — and have smellin' salts at the ready. Then both of you come and talk to me.'

★   ★   ★

I've already mentioned DI Mike Haggard and the Gerry Gault case, but my dealings with the Liverpool detective have extended far beyond my successful search for a missing knife-thrower. Haggard and his side-kick DI Willie Vine — an elegant police officer with genuine literary aspirations — are the sides into which the thorn of my unwelcome interference regularly pricks: I have harassed them through cases involving a female killer called Sam Bone; a photographer called Frank Danson who was reunited with his children twenty years after they went missing; and Joe Creeney, a man released from prison who apparently committed the perfect murder, then accidentally killed himself.

It is against Haggard and Vine that I have been unfavourably comparing Vales and Hills of the Strathclyde Police. And it was Haggard and Vine who were there to greet us when Sian and I waltzed upstairs to their office in the police station located in Admiral Street on the fringes of Toxteth.

★   ★   ★

'Siobhan Laidlaw was walking home from her local in Garston,' Haggard said. 'She'd been somewhere else, God knows where, an' it really doesn't matter. Anyway, it was late, and pouring with rain. She was making for the house she rents in Darby Road — '

'What, Darby Road *Grassendale*?'

Sian glanced at me. 'She's been living there for two years.' She smiled absently, weakly. 'I know. It's just five minutes' walk from Calum's flat, we've stayed there so many times, you and I, and I had no idea . . . '

I wasn't quite sure what she meant by that, but Haggard was watching impatiently, anxious to get on. I nodded at him, spread my hands.

'She was on her way home,' the DI repeated, 'in the rain, at about one in the morning. She turned into Garston Old Road. An old feller livin' on his own had just switched off the tele and was at the window, drawin' the curtains. He saw a tall, lean-lookin' feller spring out of an entry and knock Siobhan to the ground. Then he was bending over her, hittin' her repeatedly — the police surgeon reckon he must've been using a short iron bar of some kind, maybe a car's wheel brace — '

He broke off. I felt Sian trembling in the chair next to mine, and I reached out and grasped her cold hand. She squeezed hard. Her eyes were closed, her lashes moist.

Haggard waited. She opened her eyes and smiled at him, and I swear the burly detective went pink. He cleared his throat.

'Anyway, as I was sayin', this old feller opens the front door on the chain and yells across the road, and through the crack he sees the attacker sprint off for fifty yards or so and jump in a car. There, then gone.'

'What kind of car?'

'Too far away, street lighting too bad so the witness couldn't say. Light colour's the best he could do.'

'Any CCTV?'

'Not at the scene. The attacker drove off in the direction of Long Lane. If he turned right the car might've been picked up, there's a small shopping crescent where Long Lane joins Woolton Road and Horrocks Avenue. Those cameras are being looked at.'

'What we need to know,' Willie Vine said from his desk across the room, 'is who would be likely to do this to her.' He was looking directly at Sian.

'The stalker,' she said emphatically.

Haggard sat back in his chair, frowning. His jacket was swept back from his broad chest, his tie loosened, crumpled shirt-collar unbuttoned.

'This is someone we know about?'

Sian shook her head.

'Why not?'

'She didn't report it.'

'But she told you. So what happened. Did you and Ill Wind there do some more amateur sleuthin'?' He glared at me. 'Because if you did, the two of you made another right balls — '

'Jack didn't know about him.'

'That makes three of us,' Haggard growled.

'So let's hear about him, this stalker. When did it begin? How bad did it get?'

'Siobhan met him at a party, and went out with him for a while. Clubs, pubs, the occasional show. He seemed nice; they had shared interests, she liked him a lot. But then the attraction faded, as it can, and she wanted to end the relationship. Apparently he was quite young, much younger than Siobhan. She told him it was over. He turned nasty.'

'What, verbal abuse, physical abuse?'

'Harassment. She'd catch sight of him, in the supermarket, watching her. There were persistent phone calls; as soon as she put the receiver down, it would ring again, on and on. She'd look out of the window and see him hanging around outside her house, at all hours of the night.' She shrugged. 'You know the kind of thing.'

'And still she didn't report it?'

'No. Instead, she plucked up courage and had it out with him. He was lurking outside her house, one night, wearing one of those horrible hooded jackets. She opened the door and invited him in. They talked. Argued. She was terrified, she could smell drink on him and at first he wouldn't listen. Then, suddenly, he changed. And when he left, well, that was it. The harassment stopped, just like that; she hasn't seen him or heard from him since.' She grimaced ruefully. 'Until last night.'

Willie Vine had been listening, and looking ever more thoughtful. Now he held his hand up to Haggard.

'Sian, how long is it since your sister broke off the relationship?' he said.

'About twelve months.'

'And how long after that did she call this man into her house, have it out with him, and see a miraculous end to the stalking?'

'About three months.'

'Have you any idea why he stopped so suddenly? Has your *sister* any idea?'

'None at all.'

'All right,' Haggard said, coming back in, 'how about this. If he stopped stalking her three months ago, why, last night, did he come back and beat the shit out of her? Half kill her? What provoked him?'

'I don't know. I've been seeing her regularly' — she flashed a glance at me — 'and I know she's had no contact with him. She hasn't seen or heard from him — but I've already told you that. He disappeared off the face of the earth. And Siobhan's kept herself to herself, she's not seeing anyone . . . '

Sian shrugged helplessly in the heavy silence.

After a moment, Willie Vine said, 'Well, at least we've got something to go on.' He reached for his notebook and said, 'If you give us this man's name and address — '

'I can't. I don't know anything about him. Not his name. Not his address. I've no idea *where* he's from.'

Haggard was visibly sceptical.

'You mean your sister didn't tell you anything about him?'

'That's exactly what I do mean. She told me nothing. And that's not at all surprising.'

She looked at me, and now she was smiling sadly and the expression in her eyes told that she was looking, not for forgiveness, but for understanding.

'You see, until twelve months ago,' she said softly, and for nobody's benefit but her own, 'I didn't even know I had a sister.'

10

That night we had an escort back to the Isle of Mull, a rusty white van that hung on to the Quattro's tail like one of those tin cans that bounce behind beribboned wedding cars at the end of a long piece of string. Its presence was strangely comforting — but of course, I'm getting ahead of myself.

From Admiral Street police station I drove to Calum Wick's flat in Grassendale. Watched through dirty net curtains by Sammy Quade, the scruffy occupant of the ground-floor bed-sit, we crossed the road from the car then climbed the stairs and let ourselves in. The familiar ambience washed over us like balm. Under the light of an Anglepoise lamp with a paint-smeared metal shade, glittering toy soldiers waited patiently on Wick's work table for their glossy enamel uniforms. A leather settee and easy chairs glistened with an expensive sheen. The air was rich with the aromas of Humbrol enamels, strong coffee and Schimmelpenninck cigars. One wall, in deep shadow, would have given a psychologist a field day. I had often watched my Scottish painter cut illustrations from military books, articles from newspapers, poetry from library books he returned minus their clear plastic covers that were removed and used to protect his own paperbacks, and display alongside those items photographs of people or scenes he considered of unusual interest. The wall was a vibrant history of Liverpool, from one man's selective view-point. Blu-Tack held his wilting art gallery in place. Age turned the exhibits curly and yellow. Space was running out.

In that room, still with conversation kept to a minimum, Sian and I dined on Dr Ottaker pizzas washed down with hot black coffee, balancing plates and mugs precariously, Sian, as always, with her legs stretched out on the settee. And we were sitting in semi-darkness, stuffed to capacity and wondering who would be first to tackle head on the subject we had both been circling like wary picadors goading a dangerous bull, when Jones the Van came thumping up the stairs in search of Calum Wick.

Stan Jones is the middle-aged, vaguely Welsh, white-bearded scally who, the first time I saw him, had a cigarette dangling from his lips as he was picked up and bounced on the bonnet of his own rusty white vehicle. We were in the middle of the Gerry Gault case. Calum had been doing the muscular bouncing and it had been some time before I learned it was all an act. Since then Jones the Van had, with Calum, wriggled out of a stolen car handling charge, been close to involvement in a Toxteth car-jacking, and on more than one investigation had assisted harassed PIs with sterling work as a mobile surveillance unit: one rusty white van, one mobile phone, one bottomless reservoir of patience.

The door slammed behind him, propelled by the sole of one off-white trainer. He stood with hands on hips and looked at us with contempt, roll-up dangling, flakes of ash clinging to his white stubble.

'Nothin' to do?'

'Work is three hundred miles away, Stan. We're recharging the batteries before setting off for distant climes — '

'Lazin' around. Yeah, right. So where's the tall feller with specs an' a funny accent?'

'He's back home in Scotland. Sorry, *hame*. We're deeply involved in an intriguing mystery on the Isle of Mull.'

'OK. What d'you want me to do?'

So when he put it like that, what could I say?

★   ★   ★

Six hours and three hundred miles later the bothy's kitchen was again alive with the sound of heavy breathing drifting through from the long room where executives and instructors slept, the drum of rain on the tin roof, the plink from the tin can standing under one of the many leaks, the faint hissing of the portable gas stove. The walls still glistened with condensation, heat still rose in waves from the stove to form a hot canopy under the tin roof, but, this time, four people sat in that damp room in various attitudes of relaxation or total exhaustion.

I was at the table with Sian, leaning forward, arms folded on the rough timber surface, my hands cupping a steaming tin mug of coffee. Sian was sitting back, looking droopy. Her blue eyes were heavy-lidded, her pale face peeking out from the sweeping veil of blonde hair which she had untied as soon as she stepped out of the Quattro into the wet, gusting wind. I knew her obvious weariness had nothing to do with physical exertion or the strain of the long drive. My Soldier Blue was in fine condition, but in the past eighteen hours or so she had been confronted by unexpected, shocking mental challenges. I don't think she knew how to deal with them.

Stan Jones had been brought fully up to date with events before we left Calum's Liverpool flat. Now, in tatty jeans and a brown T-shirt bearing the logo *Aged to Perfection*, he was slumped on a crate close to the stove, smoking a roll-up. Calum Wick had dragged a chair away from the table and across the pitted concrete to the other side of the stove. He was sitting with his long legs stretched out and crossed at the ankles. From time to time he would stroke his greying beard, and look wise. Smoke rose pencil-thin from the cigar held in his steady right hand. His bright eyes were constantly on the move, wide awake and alert.

'If Sian decides to classify this kitchen as an office,' I said, deliberately narrowing my eyes against the fug, 'your smoking becomes illegal.'

'She can classify and be damned,' Stan Jones said, and bared tobacco-stained teeth as he flashed her a grin. 'An' in case you're wonderin', that's paraphrasin' the Duke of Wellington *and* puttin' the boot on the other foot.'

Calum was perplexed, but not by Stan's verbal convolutions.

'If your sister's that badly hurt,' he said to Sian, 'surely the other instructors would take over so you could be by her side?'

Sian shook her head. 'I'm army barmy, like Jack,' she said. 'Assess the situation, then act accordingly and without hesitation: Siobhan's in good hands, I'd be in the way, so leave everything to the professionals.'

'Which is exactly what super sleuth did when he headed south,' Calum said, curling his fingers and ostentatiously examining his nails.

'Yes, but you're a professional Scotsman,' I said, winking at Sian, 'and blowing hot breath into one bag while another dangles between your legs isn't the best training for a private investigator.'

'Aye, well, when I wasn't tootling *Scotland the Brave* on those damn bagpipes or tripping over that bloody sporran,' Calum said, humouring me, 'I did manage to discover something interesting about Ray Coghlan. Something that puts some of what we've been told into an entirely different light.'

'In that case I take back everything I've ever said — '

'Please, not everything,' Calum said. 'I distinctly remember a day in January of 2005 when I was paid a rare and unexpected compliment — '

'For Christ's sake gerron with it,' Stan Jones growled.

'Ray Coghlan,' Calum said, 'never did drive out of Craignure on the night Bridie Button died.'

'Oops.' I took a deep, slow draught of now

lukewarm coffee, my mind racing. 'So either Gorrie and McCafferey were lying when they said they saw Coghlan climb in his truck and drive out of the garage, or Peggy McBride was lying when she said they said that. Because we heard it from her, didn't we, not them?'

Calum pulled a face. 'That someone's lying is the obvious conclusion but, at first glance, it doesn't gel with what Jim Gorrie told me. Remember, it was Doug McCafferey who was first at the scene of Bridie's accident. One of my new friends took me from Salen down to the garage at Craignure, and I asked Gorrie how that came about. He told me Coghlan's truck was in for repairs that involved oxy-acetylene welding to the interior. For safety, McCafferey had removed Coghlan's battered old briefcase from the cab, but when the work was done he forgot to replace it. As soon as he saw Coghlan heading for home, McCafferey realized what he'd done and took action to make amends.'

Calum was watching me closely. 'Did you get that?'

'All of it. Which bit do you mean?'

'I think some of the wording might be important. *As soon as he saw Coghlan heading for home* — that's what Gorrie said. So, McCafferey was watching Coghlan's truck, he saw the briefcase, grabbed it, and then he jumped in his Land Rover and *chased after Ray Coghlan.*'

'After Ray Coghlan's truck?'

'Right.'

I shook my head. 'We've already been over this. Something's wrong. It couldn't have been Coghlan in that truck. When it went off the road at Maddock's Switch, Bridie Button was driving.'

Calum smiled brightly. 'Absolutely. It makes nonsense of those words, doesn't it? If McCafferey chased after Coghlan's truck, never let it out of his sight, and was there at the crash to take his estranged wife's dead body in his arms — he couldn't possibly have seen *Coghlan heading for home.*'

Stan Jones, the Liverpool scally who reads *War and Peace* in his rusty van when doing surveillance work for us and takes the *Daily Telegraph* for the cryptic crossword, had been listening intently.

'This Bridie bird died that night, Friday, wasn' it? So when did Coghlan get crushed under his truck?'

'Twenty-four hours later,' Calum said. 'Saturday night.'

'Then the police had bags of time to begin the investigation. It was Coghlan's truck killed her, and he was supposed to be in it.

They'd've been straight on to him, Friday night or Saturday mornin', bombardin' him with questions. They must know, from Coghlan 'imself, where he was if he wasn't in his truck — an' how he worked it so it looked as if he was.'

'Or how others,' I said, 'came to the mistaken conclusion that he was driving.'

'That's it exactly,' Calum said. 'I said that at first glance it didn't gel with the way Doug and Jim Gorrie described events. But that's because both men left out the bits they didn't think were important. From what I've pieced together, what actually happened seems to have been a simple family arrangement that nobody else happened to pick up on. Which is entirely understandable: the arrangement was between Coghlan and Bridie, nobody else needed to know.'

'What bothers me,' I said, 'is why Peggy McBride said nothing about this.'

'Good point,' Calum said. 'She told us Coghlan called at her cottage the very next day. Bridie was dead. He must have explained, told Peggy of the terrible mistake that had been made and how it came to happen.'

'Not necessarily,' I said. 'He was grief-stricken, probably fresh from exhaustive questioning by the police. And, as Calum said, the arrangement was between Coghlan and Bridie, there was no need for anyone else to know about it.'

'Except us,' Sian said, stirring. 'So what did go on? What was this family arrangement?'

Her eyes were brighter, and I knew the talk, the gradual involvement in an intriguing mystery, was banishing weariness and lifting her out of the doldrums.

'Ray Coghlan had made plans to spend the evening and most of the night playing cards in Craignure,' Calum said. 'Not an uncommon occurrence. Anyway, it seems that when he drove his repaired truck out of the garage he turned right, not left, and went down the hill into Craignure. That's what McCafferey and Gorrie saw, and that's the bit they missed out. The bit they thought unimportant. Because what they saw next was the truck coming back up the hill and roaring past the garage. They assumed that Coghlan had simply gone into Craignure on some sort of errand; that it was Coghlan, errand completed, belatedly heading for home.'

'As they would,' I said. 'The assumption came from force of habit: it was a Friday, and Peggy McBride told us that it was Bridie Button's invariable habit to take the bus to town on Friday morning, do some shopping for the weekend, then catch the midday bus back home. McCafferey and Gorrie knew that; they'd watched the midday bus heading out of Craignure and *assumed* Bridie was on board.' I flashed a sharp glance at Calum, who was nodding. 'We know it must have been an assumption, because Peggy's already told us they hadn't seen Bridie that day. So they made that assumption, and if Bridie was on the midday bus, and they knew nothing of the card game, then it had to be Coghlan driving the truck home that evening.'

'Only this Bridie bird wasn't on the bus, was she?' Stan said. 'She stayed in town all afternoon, then in the evenin' her old man collected the truck from the garage and handed it over to her. She was takin' it home.'

'When Doug McCafferey grabbed that briefcase and jumped in his Land Rover, he was chasing the right truck, but the wrong driver,' I said.

Sian was frowning. 'But surely it doesn't matter who was driving the truck. If Dougie was that close, he must have seen what happened out there on the moors. He *must* have *some* idea what caused the accident.'

'Aye, but it was a dark and stormy night,' Calum said, grinning at the cliché. 'Wind, rain, ice on the road. He'd have been attending to his driving, intent on keeping his own vehicle on the road.'

'Or maybe not,' Sian said. 'If we're taking it for granted he was close enough to see something, then maybe he was deliberately *very* close — close enough to *do* something. Isn't it possible Doug McCafferey forced the truck off the road?'

'Because he thought it was Coghlan?'

'Of course. Remember what I told you: the man who suffered most at the hands of Ray Coghlan was Doug McCafferey.'

'Yes, and the most recent incident was remarkably similar to the accident that killed Bridie: two years ago, Alec McBride, Doug's brother, was driven off the road by Ray Coghlan.'

'If it can be proved that Dougie did murder Bridie Button — and I think you'll find that's highly unlikely — it would explain why Peggy McBride wants us to prove the opposite: she wants her son absolved from guilt, or blame, and we achieve that if we prove the crash was Ray Coghlan's doing,' Calum said. 'After dinner last night she admitted she'd been guilty of jumping to the wrong conclusion: her first thought on hearing about the crash was that Dougie had gone after Coghlan. We now know he did, even if wanting to return a briefcase seems to make his reason for doing it perfectly innocent.'

'Innocent accordin' to him,' Stan pointed

out. 'That story of a briefcase comes from him and a bloke who works for him, an' knows which side his bread's buttered.'

I nodded. 'It makes you wonder why Vales and Hills are adamant that it was an accident. That road was deserted, so they must be taking McCafferey's word for what happened — and that's surely not enough.'

'They're actually relying on two witnesses who saw pretty near everything,' Calum said.

'Witnesses? On the same road, at the same time? Come on, we've been saying all along there was no traffic on that road.'

'No, these two are a couple of old codgers who were all nice and cosy preparing for their bed,' Calum said. 'They live in an isolated cottage a couple of miles away, high up, with a wonderful clear view of the road across open moorland. Apparently they were drawing the curtains when they saw the truck's lights, and very shortly afterwards they saw the Land Rover's lights quite close behind it.'

'Why shortly afterwards? If the two vehicles were that close together on a deserted road, surely they would have seen them both at the same time.'

Calum shrugged. 'That's a question we'll have to ask them. Amongst others. Because I can tell you now that those two stayed glued to the window and saw everything that happened.'

'Trustworthy?'

'Churchgoers, I believe — though I'm not sure if that's a guarantee of probity.'

'And they're not close friends of Dougie McCafferey?'

'From their tone, they don't think very much of him. Or Coghlan, for that matter, who has stepped outside the religious pale by running off with McCafferey's wife. I believe they know Dr Andrew Keay very well indeed. Apparently he comes to their cottage regularly and they play games of Booby — which, if you are not acquainted with it, is a game of bridge for three players invented during the World War II blitz by a feller called Hubert Phillips.'

'And you knew that?'

He grinned. 'I do now — as do you.'

I grimaced. 'And these two creaking old card sharps are the reason why it'll be difficult to pin the murder on Dougie.'

'That's right. Dougie's Land Rover never got closer than close, if you see what I mean. They're willing to swear he was still, I don't know, fifty yards behind maybe when Bridie somehow and for some reason caused that truck to leap off the road and roll down towards the trees. And there was nothing coming the other way: no vehicle coming down the slope into Maddock's Switch from the other direction.'

Stan Jones was up off his chair, stretching and yawning. Like Calum, he'd tossed a sleeping bag on to one of the empty camp beds on his way in through the long room, and now he headed for the door. I looked at Sian, saw that she was struggling to stay awake and decided enough was enough.

'There are questions to be asked of several people,' I said, 'but we'll get around to that tomorrow. We'll also take a much closer look at the wrecked truck, then drive out to the scene of the accident.'

'Who's that,' Stan said, standing in the opening in the thick stone wall with the mildewed blanket that served as a door draped across his bony shoulders. 'You and him, you and her, me and you, me and him — '

'Keep your voice down, you dope,' Sian said, as soft snoring in the other room broke off and a bed creaked.

'I'll go down to McCafferey's garage and look over the truck,' I said quietly. 'Sian's still busy instructing the remaining executives and office boys. I want you, Stan, to take Calum out to the crash site and take a general look around. I'll meet you there.'

Calum was on his feet.

'We'll try not to contaminate the scene,' he said, also heading for the other room. Then he turned. 'And as I'm not entirely sure that young Stan's capable of driving in these severe conditions, I may just decide to take over the wheel.'

He let the blanket fall, leaving behind him a stunned silence.

11

Sian used her mobile to call the hospital in Liverpool and check on Siobhan's condition. I was watching her from the depths of a plump sleeping bag laid out on one of those canvas camp beds. The kind with spring-steel legs that threaten to dislocate wrists on assembly, and stubbornly refuse to come apart.

When she switched off, it was with a tremulous smile of relief.

The previous night, after the cottage fire, Calum and I had kipped in the long room with the instructors and those adventurous souls Peggy McBride called daft office boys. Tonight I wanted to be close to Sian, and I'd joined her in the small room at the opposite end of the bothy where she had her camp bed and some privacy. My Soldier Blue was sad and lonely. I had a sneaking suspicion she was also feeling guilty. She wanted to explain, to wipe clean a slate I hadn't known existed.

The room was lit by one of those small paraffin hurricane lamps they make in China and sell in the UK for about three quid. Sometimes smelly, but always silent and efficient. It stood on a sweet-smelling orange-box between our two beds. With the wick turned halfway down, the light it cast was akin to wan moonlight weak enough to leave the cobwebbed walls and dank corners of the room in deep shadow.

When Sian had stripped to her underwear — executing a painful barefoot dance on the cold concrete floor — and wriggled shivering into her sleeping bag, I reached across and took her icy hand in mine. The light from the oil lamp was smoothing the lines of tension in her face, softening her blue eyes. She sighed deeply, and squeezed my hand.

'Go on,' I said, 'tell me about it.'

'I met Siobhan for the first time . . . I think it was a few months before you got involved in the Gault case and I went off to Cape Wrath — '

'And your first meeting with Lachlan McBride.'

'Jack,' she said, a warning in her voice.

'Sorry.' I released her hand and ran my fingers through my hair. 'But he is here, and he is a witness in a murder case — '

'Yes, but he's got nothing to do with what I'm talking about. I'm talking about my very first meeting with a sister I didn't know existed. Can you imagine what that was like? I was down town, in Liverpool, enjoying a latte in a coffee bar somewhere — I think it was Whitechapel — and suddenly, there she was. I didn't know her from Adam, but she recognized me at once — '

'How?'

'She's got a photograph from somewhere that she had framed and now keeps in her living room — from the army, I would imagine or, oh, I don't know. Anyway, she saw me, and came over to my table. Jack, she's ten years older than me, but looks a lot younger than that. When I was out on the stormy seas with my dad, she was twenty, and long gone from the family home. She'd moved to London, certainly lost touch, of course, but somehow she'd traced me — '

'So why didn't she pick up the phone? You're the young sister she's never seen.'

'Oh, she'd seen me. She had to, didn't she? When I was born she was only ten years old. She was probably a convenient babysitter, though I don't remember it — she must have left home when I was very young, because I don't remember *anything* about her.'

'So why *didn't* she get in touch sooner?' I pursed my lips. 'Would she have got in touch at all if she hadn't run into you like that?'

'I don't know. She's mixed up. Pushing sixty, living alone; I think she's been in trouble; possibly been in prison.'

'Which would explain her reluctance, I suppose.' I nodded. 'So after that first meeting you went to see her from time to time?'

'That's right.' She smiled wanly. 'I saw no reason to tell you, told myself I would eventually, but never got around to it.' Inside the sleeping bag she shrugged, and again I reached out and she wriggled her arms free and gave me her hand, hot now, and I gave it a reassuring squeeze.

'Doesn't matter. All that matters now is that she makes a complete recovery. Then, well, maybe we'll both go and see her.'

'Mm.' She nodded agreement, but was obviously thinking along different lines. 'I'm worried for her. You were there when I was talking to Mike Haggard. Even if she does make a full recovery, the stalker's still out there, isn't he?'

'But surely realizing it's now too dangerous to take up where he left off. He'll have moved on, selected another victim. And, talking of stalkers, what *about* the one who's become an important witness?' I said, keen to take her mind off Siobhan and her troubles. 'Lachlan's fancy Merc was in McCafferey's garage when you phoned with the bad news. Something wrong with the charging system. Did he make it back here?'

She smiled. 'I think I saw his blond hair poking out of one of those sleeping bags.'

I hesitated. 'I was going to say that, as he's here, he'll be the first person I interview tomorrow. But I'll leave that to another time. Tomorrow's already arranged with Calum and Stan.'

'He's the reason I was down at Peggy's, you know, before I phoned you in Wales,' Sian said.

'I know. She told me.'

'Did she tell you why?'

'No. But she did mention that Lachlan was angry.'

'I'm not surprised. Remember I told you he propositioned me at the start of this course? Well, I knew Peggy was his mother, so I stormed down there and told her to buckle the reins on her naughty child, or I'd really hurt him. I meant it, too.'

'And you're more than capable.'

'Yes, well.' She grinned. 'As of a couple of days ago, he's out of our hair, because I'm sure Peggy will have used her sharp tongue to good effect.'

Which was, I suppose, one way of drifting to sleep in an optimistic frame of mind — but I couldn't help thinking, as I dozed off, that we'd not heard the last of young Lachlan McBride.

12

Sunday

In the event I did tackle Lachlan McBride, plucking him from the tiny kitchen crowded with men eating bowls of steaming porridge (salted for the Scots, sugared for the English) and taking him out to Sian's Shogun. We sat in the back. The sun was not yet up, the skies clear and blue and endless, the moorland white with frost.

I got much more than I'd bargained for, after a brief preamble that netted me information of dubious worth.

'Nice car I saw you with,' I said. 'What's the story, a rich uncle in Australia?'

'Almost as far fetched. I make money making games that make people into cabbages.' He let me puzzle over that, then relented. 'And give them RSI of the thumbs.'

'*Computer* games?'

'That's right. I'm a talented programmer, with a vivid imagination. Two of us run a small company in Oban. The office overlooks the harbour. A single game made us rich, now we're coasting.'

'That's almost as bad as me. I make toy soldiers — '

'And run an Audi Quattro.'

'Mm, a rich man's toy I really can't afford.' I paused, dropped the small talk and said, 'Andrew Keay reported seeing you close to McCafferey's garage on the night Ray Coghlan died. He was on his way up to collect his vehicle. What were you doing there?'

'So that's what this is about.' He spread his hands. 'When Keay saw me, I was leaving.'

'What, leaving after setting up Coghlan's murder? After knocking him out, placing him under the truck, fixing a steel cable to the stands?'

He was bigger than I'd realized, tall, with shoulders built for scrum or ruck and the neck of a prop forward. His long blond hair kept flopping over his forehead. He brushed it back absently with a hand like a garden fork. His dark eyes were devoid of expression; his lips fixed in a curl of amusement for which there was no obvious source.

'You should stick to painting kid's toys. Ray Coghlan wasn't there. He was still down in the village getting tanked up. The murder set-up came later.'

'Yes, and you should stay with your computer games and virtual reality. Coghlan

142

couldn't have been in the village at that time. The trap was sprung by Keay driving his vehicle away from the workshop doors. Coghlan *must* have been there, in the workshop, and the cables *must* have been in position, because Keay had almost reached the garage when he saw you — he might even have been crossing the forecourt — '

'We passed on the road.'

'Close to the garage?'

'Very.'

'Well there you are. Coghlan was already there, and if the cable wasn't in place the only way it could have got there is if Keay put it there.'

'If it was in place, I didn't see it. Why should I? It was pitch dark.'

I took a deep breath, let it out. 'What *were* you doing there?'

'I was talking to my father, Stuart. He came across on the ferry.'

'Wasn't Dougie leaving on that same ferry?' Lachlan nodded. 'So wouldn't he have spotted Stuart coming off?'

'Maybe he did. You'll have to ask him.'

'I thought Stuart McBride was officially missing.'

'Everybody did, and does. That's what my mother still believes.' He smiled. 'Or perhaps not.'

'What were you and Stuart talking about?'

'Attempted murder.'

'Whose?'

'His. Why do you think he disappeared?'

'He went two years ago, after Ray Coghlan killed your half-brother, Alec, in a road accident. If murder was on his mind, it would have been Coghlan's, for revenge. But who would want to murder your father?'

'His wife.'

'Your mother? Peggy?' I thought of Calum telling me it was possible Tom McCafferey, Peggy's first husband, had been poisoned; that Stuart McBride was a suspect. Maybe that was true. If that was the way it had happened, and Peggy was his partner in crime, would she have decided to murder Stuart to ensure he couldn't talk, ever? But if Stuart had twigged what she was about to do in the nick of time, and made a swift exit — why had he now come back?'

There was only one reason that came instantly to mind.

'Did Stuart McBride,' I said softly, 'firebomb his wife's cottage?'

'Goodness, I really have no idea. I was away last night. My sister — '

'Yes, I know. Have you told any of this to the police?'

His expression was blank. 'I've told *you*.'

'The police must have questioned you about the night Keay saw you, the night Coghlan died. What did you tell them?'

'Dougie was away. I told them I was up in his rooms, picking up a CD he'd borrowed.'

'Why would they believe that story?'

'Because there was nothing to disprove it.' He grinned. 'Also, I told my mother I was going there, and so she was able to back up my story.'

'But that story could have been camouflage: collect the CD, set up Coghlan's murder.'

'It wasn't.'

'So if you're sticking to your story — which one is true, the CD or your father?'

'The choice,' Lachlan said, still with that fixed smirk, 'is yours.'

★ ★ ★

We left the bothy in a two-vehicle convoy, me leading in the Quattro, Stan Jones following in his rusty white van. Calum was in the passenger seat. It seemed he'd chickened out, or Stan had refused to let him take the wheel. I didn't blame him. The road from Salen to Craignure was slick with black ice, a cold mist drifting across the flat fields to curl like smoke across the glistening tarmac. The waters in the Sound of Mull were like glass, and a fishing boat was trailing blue smoke as it cut through the mirror-like surface on its way to the open sea.

Both vehicles pulled on to the forecourt of McCafferey's garage behind Dougie McCafferey's Land Rover, and I jumped out to get the exact location of Bridie Button's fatal accident from Jim Gorrie. Then, arranging to catch up with my colleagues within the hour, I banged on the roof and waved Stan on his way.

I was watching the white van rattling its smoky way up the hill into the mist, when Dougie McCafferey crunched up behind me.

'If they've gone to poke about at the site, what the hell are you doing here?'

'Keeping you out of prison, according to your mother.'

'Aye, well, I've told you what I think of that.'

'Nevertheless, it doesn't hurt to humour her. If you had nothing to do with your wife's death you're in the clear anyway. And if somebody did kill her, wouldn't you like to know?'

'It was a bloody accident,' he growled, and made as if to swing away.

'Did you know your stepfather's back on the island?'

He stopped, staring. 'Who told you that?'

'Lachlan.'

'Then you can take it with a pinch of salt.'

'You haven't seen him? Lachlan reckons Stuart disembarked from the same ferry you were taking to Oban.'

'That boy likes to make up stories with a lot of detail.' He grinned fiercely, and now he did turn and walk away. 'Reckons it lends them a degree of verisimilitude,' he called over his shoulder.

'Mind if I take another look at that wreck?'

'Help yourself.'

As I approached the mangled truck he cast a final, glowering glance in my direction, then stormed off into the office.

What was I looking for? I had no idea. I did know that on the day Coghlan died, the truck was in McCafferey's for repairs, and I could have asked Dougie for details of the work he'd done. But if he was going to be as truthful as his half-brother, then I'd be wasting time and clouding my thinking and judgement. Far better to do it my way.

I'd first set eyes on the truck when I walked up the hill the night Calum and I arrived on Mull. The impression then had been of a crumpled cab, shattered glass, tufts of grass, here and there smears of dried mud and blood. On my second visit I had paid it less attention, though my impressions had been confirmed. But now it was time for more than a cursory examination.

Peggy McBride had told me Coghlan's truck was a rattling death trap requiring welding. The oxy-acetylene welding plant I'd noticed on my first visit was still standing up against the shelves, close to a door set in the back wall probably leading to an open area behind the building.

Jim Gorrie was by the welding plant, preparing to work on a split silencer resting on a nearby bench. As I watched, he used a metal key to turn on the acetylene and oxygen at the tanks. He opened the acetylene control and snapped a flint lighter close to the torch's nozzle. A flaring yellow flame burst from the nozzle as the acetylene ignited. Black smoke spewed from the flame's tip. Particles of soot floated lazily towards the roof.

Then a strange thing happened. Standing there with the blow-torch pointing away from him and black smoke gushing upwards to form a spreading cloud under the roof, Gorrie seemed to slip into a trance. He stood for long seconds, staring into space. Seconds stretched to half a minute; then a minute. At last he moved. A hand lifted. He dashed particles of soot from his beard, looked at the black smears on the back of his hand. Then, becoming aware of the black smoke, the lowering cloud, he reached down and opened the oxygen control. The flame turned an icy blue with a white cone at the nozzle's tip. It began to roar. The smoke and soot disappeared.

He looked across at me, opened his mouth and half lifted a hand. Then he shook his head.

'Talk to you later,' he called, and with another shake of his head he turned to the bench and began welding.

What, I thought, was all that about?

Well, I'd been thinking about welding, he'd obviously been thinking about welding — and, OK, so the welding equipment *was* available and had, presumably, been available when Coghlan's truck was in for repair. But although it looked as if Peggy had been right in some respects, in a five-minute close examination of the wrecked vehicle I found not a single sign of any fresh welding. And Doug certainly hadn't disguised the job with a neat coat of paint; the only paint that vehicle had seen, spray or otherwise, had been at the time of manufacture.

So if he wasn't welding, what repairs had Doug McCafferey been carrying out? Were they repairs — or something much more sinister?

I wandered outside, deep in thought, glanced up at the living accommodation and saw Peggy McBride looking out at me. I gave her a wave. She smiled, then allowed the filthy net curtain to fall. I remembered Lachlan telling me that on the night of the murder he'd been here to pick up a CD, and tried to recall if I'd seen a stereo or hi-fi of any kind in Doug's room. For the life of me, I couldn't remember.

If a killer planned to use a vehicle to kill its driver in what appeared to be an accident, you would expect to find hydraulic brake pipes sawn through, a nut left off a steering arm — something like that. But this vehicle had negotiated many miles of twisting road with the driver wrestling with the steering, and when the brakes were applied fiercely, they had worked with devastating efficiency.

Bridie Button had, for some reason, applied those brakes. And, according to Calum, two elderly witnesses who had watched from the high ground were willing to swear that the only vehicles on the road at that time were Coghlan's truck and Doug McCafferey's Land Rover — and he was at least fifty yards behind Bridie.

Jim Gorrie had mentioned the possibility of a sheep straying on to the road causing Bridie to apply the brakes. I'd seen how easily that could happen, on the drive to Salen. Unless we made a startling discovery at a soggy site that had already been trampled over by investigating police and the vehicle recovery team, I knew we were looking at a tragic accident, or the perfect murder.

13

As I drove out of Craignure on the Fionnphort road it was difficult to envisage the conditions Bridie Button had faced on the night she died. The bright winter sun, still low in the sky, was casting long shadows across endless moors glistening with melting frost. Without a breath of wind to disturb it the thin mist filled dips and hollows and hung like tattered shreds of white gauze in the skeletal branches of leafless trees. The road was empty of traffic. I drove fast, taking the sweeping curves and tighter bends at speed, trying hard to imagine how it must have been in Coghlan's rattling truck with the wind buffeting the smoking vehicle, worn tyres sliding on the icy road, the young woman's gloved hand scrubbing at the condensation fogging the inside of the unheated windscreen while the loose windscreen wipers scraped uselessly across the outside frost and she tried desperately to see the road ahead in the yellow light from weak, dirty headlamps.

Visibility must have been down to fifty yards or considerably less — when she was able to see *anything* through that windscreen

— yet she *had* seen something, and what she had seen had caused her to stab at the brake pedal with a frantic right foot then sit helplessly gripping the steering wheel as the vehicle ran out of control, dropped sickeningly off the road and carried her into the dense pines where she died.

But what? *What* had she seen? And could what she had seen and the consequences of that sighting have been carefully and cleverly orchestrated by a man or woman intent on murder?

I didn't know. But when I took the Quattro over one final rise and saw the roof of a rusty white van poking out of the mist in the dip and realized that at last I was looking down on the infamous Maddock's Switch where the terrible skid marks left by Bridie Button scarred the road I knew, with absolute conviction, that I would find out.

★ ★ ★

Calum and Stan had walked across the sloping field, following the deep furrows gouged out of the grass and earth by the rolling, careering truck, and were waiting for me by a huge scarred pine in the stand of the trees sixty yards or so from the road. I parked behind Stan's van, climbed through the wrecked fence then, without wasting time, jogged across the bumpy field towards them: if we were going to discover any evidence missed by the police it would be back on the road, in the timber where Coghlan's truck had come to rest, but not in the open grassland between those two points.

Calum was watching with amusement as I approached. I thought he'd noticed the puzzled expression on my face, but he was looking at my feet, clad in ordinary casual shoes by Rieker and now soaking wet. He, of course, was wearing his Timberland boots and looking superior. I glanced at Stan Jones, huddled against a tree with a smouldering roll-up cupped in his hand, and immediately recalled the John Cleese, Ronnie Barker and Ronnie Corbett sketch: Calum might be looking down on me, but Stan was certainly looking up because my shoes, even when wet, were outperforming his rotting discount-store trainers. Which put me neatly in the middle.

Of course, if I'd remembered to wear the posh green wellies I always carry in the boot of the car . . .

'Anything?'

Calum waved a hand. 'Smashed timber, lots of oil, traces of blood.'

'Clues?'

'Like what?' Stan said. 'If there is a dead

sheep, it'd be on the road.'

'Yes, and a dead giveaway — but it's not there and never was,' I said. 'I hereby stick my neck out: after vacillating between accident and murder I'm going to plump firmly for the latter and say Bridie Button was murdered. All we've got to do is find out how.'

'No sweat then,' Stan said, sneering.

Calum was lighting up a cigar. The match flared, he flicked it on to the wet grass and blew smoke, eyes narrowed in thought.

'Stan may have gone a wee bit heavy on it, but there's more than a smidgeon of truth under that sarcasm. Working out *what* happened is easy. Working out *why* it happened is going to be much more difficult.'

'Jim Gorrie said more or less the same,' I said, 'but about Ray Coghlan's death.'

'Yes, well, we know Bridie applied her brakes sharply near the bottom of the hill. The skid marks make that clear. We know what the weather was like, and wicked reverse or adverse camber exacerbated the effect of that sudden braking.'

'He means she lost control and the truck smashed through the fence,' Stan said, rolling his eyes.

'By the looks of the furrows ploughed across the field,' Calum said, undeterred, 'I'd say the truck rolled once, slid on its canopy

155

— which didn't do it much good — and had bounced back on to four wheels when it ploughed into the trees. Less than thirty seconds, start to finish. We've got Dougie McCafferey behind her in his Land Rover: he saw nothing unusual. Two elderly witnesses saw the truck and Dougie's Land Rover from a distance, but nothing else, nothing out of the ordinary until the truck slid down the hill and went off the road. So if this was murder . . . '

'You've spotted nothing obviously unusual here, so far, but that night there was something *very* unusual,' I said. 'When Dougie McCafferey came running across this field in darkness, rain and wind, adrenalin pumping, heart pounding, he expected to find Ray Coghlan in that truck; instead, he found his wife.'

'An' if you forget about lookin' for the unusual and look instead for the suspicious,' Stan said, 'how about the fact Dougie was workin' on the truck minutes before it took off from the garage?'

'Ah, but forensics must have examined the truck,' Calum said. 'If Dougie had done something to cause the accident, they would have spotted it.'

'We've already been over this,' I said. 'There was nothing wrong with brakes or steering.'

'So if this was murder, forensics missed something.'

'Yeah, but how can you knock up something in a garage that ends up forcin' a driver to apply the brakes on a deserted road?' Stan said. 'An' at that exact spot — what's it called, Maddock's Switch? Because it had to be there, didn' it, or somewhere very like it?'

'Why? Because the slope and the camber helped take the truck off the road?' Calum thought for a moment, then nodded. 'You're right. And I think we'd be wasting our time trekking back up the slope to look for clues.' He squinted at me through a thin veil of cigar smoke. 'I think Stan's right. If we *are* looking at murder, it was plotted and worked in McCafferey's garage.'

'I agree. And Jim Gorrie does want to talk to me,' I said. 'I wonder why?'

Calum studied the tip of his cigar, then sat down on a tree trunk that must have been ripped from the earth by a storm when Coghlan's old truck was still a three-foot long pedal car. The sun was as high as it was going to get that day. The field was gently steaming. Stan had strolled away and was looking back up the twin grooves scored across the grass like a farmer weighing up how much he could

157

claim for manoeuvre damage from the British Army.

'I was wondering about Jim Gorrie,' Calum said. 'Why haven't we considered him as a suspect?'

'I don't know. Maybe because we've been sucked in by the McCafferey clan's tale of woe. Maybe because Jim Gorrie's just there, in the background, the stolid, overlooked, overworked and unremarkable Mister Dependable. Gorrie told me Doug McCafferey's away a lot, so he just about runs the place. And we know for a fact he was there on the night Bridie died. We also know the truck was in for repair, but all Peggy McBride said was that something was being fixed. So who did the fixing, I wonder?'

'I spoke to Gorrie, as you know,' Calum said. 'He told me the truck was in for repairs that involved welding and, for safety, McCafferey took Coghlan's briefcase out of the cab and forgot to replace it. But again that doesn't make it clear, because it's possible McCafferey removed the briefcase before *Gorrie* started on the work.'

'I've been over the truck again, and whatever that work was,' I said, 'it wasn't welding.'

'That's as maybe, but this is all talk and no

action,' Stan Jones said, walking back as Calum stood up and ground his cigar under his heel. 'Instead of freezin' our balls off out here, why don't we go back to McCafferey's and ask those two Jocks outright who did the work, which one of them fixed the truck so it killed the girl.'

'Maybe we'll do that,' I said. 'But as the truck stopped here, we're going to take a good look around before we make wild accusations.'

We went over the site for a good fifteen minutes, and at the end of it we were no wiser. Besides the oil and blood Calum had mentioned we found an awful lot of what you expect to find at a crash site: shattered glass. There was glass from the windscreen, glass from both doors, blackened glass that was much thinner and could have been from a smashed wing mirror, thicker curved glass with a pattern that had obviously come from the headlights.

There was nothing there to help us understand what had occurred on the night Bridie Button died. I knew Calum was right: the answer had to lie, not in this half frozen field, but back at McCafferey's garage.

'Come on,' I said, 'let's go and talk to Jim Gorrie.'

★ ★ ★

Low cloud had swept in to cover the late morning sun by the time I drove back on to McCafferey's forecourt ahead of Stan Jones and his white van, and the light had faded badly. A true November chill had crept over the land. The branches of the black pines bordering the site hung without lustre like the ragged wings of dead ravens, and the distant waters of the Sound of Mull were like grey steel plates reaching as far as the steel-grey skies. I couldn't see the join.

As I walked away from the Quattro a helicopter came clattering in from the direction of Ben More, flying low under the clouds, and moved swiftly out over the bleak waters. It appeared to be heading for Oban. I watched it dwindle until it was no bigger than a dragonfly, wondered idly if it had taken police officers out to complete their investigations at the crash sight or, much more likely, if it was connected with the courses Sian was working on the moors.

My Soldier Blue's quite a girl I thought, with an illogical feeling of pride. Then the sound of the rotors thrummed into silence and I turned my attention to the garage.

Dougie's Land Rover had gone. The

160

workshop's doors were open, and I could see the welding plant as I climbed out of the Quattro. There was no sign of Gorrie. He'd finished working on the silencer and, if he had any sense, would be in the office with his big hands clutching a mug of hot coffee.

I walked towards the workshop, then stopped as Stan's van bounced on to the bald forecourt, swung in a wide half-circle and pulled up with a squeal. A stone popped up and caromed off one of the petrol pumps. I guessed that after the long drive from Liverpool his engine was running on fumes. Stan wanted petrol. For that he needed Jim Gorrie.

'Toot your horn,' I told Stan, as he and Calum got out of the van.

He did so, leaning his skinny frame in through the van's open door that had swung wide against a non-existent stop. A honk that sounded like an old moose blowing its nose disturbed a huge crow that flapped away from the pines, screeching in anger. Nothing else happened. Stan tried again, blowing the horn three times as Calum ambled towards me with a grin then went on by and wandered towards the workshop.

'The Land Rover's gone, so McCafferey's

not here,' I said to his back. 'I can't see Gorrie, so maybe there's no work and he's finished for the day.'

Stan slammed the van's door.

'That net curtain up there just twitched. Just like Liverpool and Cal's grotty neighbour.'

'That'll be Peggy McBride, McCafferey's mother.'

'Give her a shout, then, she'll know where those fellers are.' Then he looked towards the workshops. 'Or maybe,' he said, 'we won't need her after all.'

Calum had been looking down into the pit. Now he took a hasty pace back, as if recoiling from a nasty smell. He waved us over.

'Saying he's finished for the day may have been a wee bit of an understatement,' he said, as we walked past him and approached the edge of the vehicle inspection pit. 'I've only met the man once, so I can't be too sure — but if that is Jim Gorrie down there, I'd say he's finished for good.'

I looked down, my throat constricting with horror, and knew that somehow, in some way, the wrecked vehicle that loomed large in the background was once again party to a ghastly murder.

On the oily waters of that filthy sump, the plastic anti-freeze bottles I'd seen earlier had been pushed out of the way like plastic ducks bobbing in a bath to make room for something much bulkier and heavier, a dead weight like a soft sack of grain that must have created curling waves of filth as it hit the bottom with a tremendous splash.

Jim Gorrie lay face down, half submerged. The black water was level with his ears, leaking in to fill them with its oily chill. The back of his head was a soggy pulp in which fragments of hard dry soil were embedded with splinters of white bone. Blood had trickled from his broken scalp, and a filthy scum lapped at the gore matting the curling red hair at the nape of his neck. His arms were bent at the elbows, forearms floating in the water alongside his head. His big mechanic's hands were like claws, clutching the black water as he reached for the life that had been snatched away.

Calum Wick nudged gently with one of his tan boots, pushing an object that lay on the floor. Metal grated on concrete.

I met his eyes and nodded, sickened, as Stan Jones went outside and spat thickly.

The shovel the killer had ripped from the rotting leather straps on the wrecked truck and used to smash Jim Gorrie's skull lay on the greasy concrete floor at the side of the pit. The soil the shovel had picked up in the road accident that had killed Bridie Button and which now, more than ever, I believed had been murder, was stained with Jim Gorrie's blood.

14

Calum rang the police from the grubby little office at the side of the workshop, carelessly clearing mugs and papers away with a sweep of the hand to get at the phone. He spoke anonymously. When he emerged, he told me DI Vales was racing over from Tobermory, picking up the police surgeon on the way. With luck, they would arrive within twenty minutes.

'Right, you and Stan buzz off. You've seen nothing, know nothing; I found the body after you'd gone.' I thought for a moment. 'We didn't learn anything at the crash scene, and you're going to put distance between yourselves and this place. So, is there anything useful you can be doing?'

'Not a lot without petrol,' Stan said.

'Damn, I'd forgotten about that. OK, start filling the van now. Put twenty quid in, leave the cash on the desk. I'll nip upstairs and tell Peggy what's going on — though God knows you'd expect her to have heard something.'

'Wait till we've gone,' Stan said. 'The old girl knows me 'n Cal're here, so it's best you duck in and find the body when we're well out of the way.'

'And when we're all fuelled up,' Calum said, 'the most useful thing we can do is head back to the bothy and regroup. Another murder's been thrown into an already confused mix. Your two loyal aids will put their heads together, see if we can come up with anything by the time you're finished here.'

I nodded agreement. 'That shouldn't be too long. Vales is going to take my statement when she gets here, then make damn sure I'm on the side of the police tape that puts me well away from Coghlan's body.'

I waited with growing impatience while Stan pumped twenty quid's worth of unleaded into his van and jogged inside with the cash. He was back in a flash, and I waved them away as he bounced the van off the forecourt and roared away down the hill. Then, glancing up at the curtained windows and seeing no movement, I went back into the garage.

It was treading a thin tightrope, wanting to get up to see Peggy before the police arrived, but also keen to have one last swift look around. This was sure to be my last chance before the whole workshop was designated crime scene and put out of bounds.

Unfortunately, apart from the bloody murder weapon which was, to put it crudely, bloody obvious, nothing leaped up to punch me on the nose and scream at me that this latest twist in an increasingly puzzling mystery would be the bit that was easily solved. The best I could do as I walked around the pit with my eyes averted was to remember my brief moments with the burly, bearded mechanic, wonder why the hell he'd been murdered, then cross to the bench and look down with some sadness at the job he had never known was the last he would ever do.

He'd finished welding the silencer. I remembered the gush of black smoke when he'd fired up the acetylene, and knew from the look of the metalwork that at some time that yellow flame must have flared again. Perhaps the oxygen had begun to run out, and he'd tried to push on to the end rather than stop to connect a new cylinder. Anyway, part of the silencer's tin-can shaped body was coated with soot, suggesting that he'd waited too long, but elsewhere the bright seams of metal testified to the dead mechanic's welding skills.

Enough time had passed. Twisting my face into a frozen grimace of horror for the benefit of anyone watching, I ran outside, raced round the end of the building and pounded up the slippery stairs.

When I burst into Dougie McCafferey's scruffy room, Peggy was sitting on her bus seat near the gas heater reading the *Daily Telegraph*. Her white hair in a neat chignon, gold pince-nez perched on the end of her nose. A police siren was wailing like a midnight cat, yet she seemed not to have heard it. She looked up at me with a warm but absent smile, then took the shocking news of Gorrie's death with astonishing equanimity. In reply to my question she told me that Dougie was down in Craignure, probably indulging in a liquid lunch. I suggested she phone him and get him back up to the garage pronto. Then, fleetingly wondering at her state of mind, what had caused it, and the effect it would have on me as her employee, I left her to her newspaper and went back down the stairs to face the music.

I had taken the time, while talking to her, to look around the room. I saw no sign of a stereo system, or even the simplest, cheapest of CD players.

My mobile phone stopped me halfway to the petrol pumps as a police car raced up the hill and swung on to the forecourt. I pressed it to my ear as the car slid to a halt and DI Vales stepped out dressed in a patterned dark-green trouser suit she probably thought was the height of fashion for a female detective but which made her look like a burly squaddie dressed in camouflage gear.

Then whatever flippant remarks I had stored within me ready to launch in her direction were banished in an instant as, in soft Scottish accents, the caller identified herself. Feeling a cold hand grasp my heart, I turned my back on Hills, the civilian I took to be the police surgeon, and the two police officers — all of whom had arrived with Vales — and found myself gazing straight through the garage's open doors at the wrecked hulk that was Ray Coghlan's truck.

That chance look turned out to be portentous.

'Mr Scott?'

'Yes?'

'Mr Scott, this is Sister Jackie Green at the Lorn and the Islands Hospital in Oban. We have a Miss Sian Laidlaw here in the ICU. She was brought in by helicopter. Apparently she was involved in a road accident on Mull. She's conscious, able to talk, and' — there was a moment's silence as a hand went over the mouthpiece — 'ah, well now, I've just been told that she's already been moved out of the ICU and into a general ward. Would you like me to take a telephone to her?'

'Indeed I would. Thank you very much.'

Heart thumping, I waved away DS Hills as

he strode towards me, saw him frown and turn uncertainly back to DI Vales. Blindly, seeing nothing, I wandered away towards the tall pines. What the hell, I thought wildly, what the *bloody hell* — ?'

'Jack?'

'Christ, Sian,' I said throatily, 'what have you done?'

'Wrecked the Shogun, for starters.'

'Never mind the bloody car, what about you?'

'Well, apart from assorted cuts and bruises and a broken collar bone, I'm as good as new.' She paused, and I could hear her breathing; picture her bruised face, the pain in her blue eyes. 'They suspected internal injuries,' she said, 'perhaps some bleeding, but apparently all the soft stuff's OK.'

'Which includes the head?' I heard her chuckle, then wince. 'I can't believe it, I really can't. You *and* your sister, battered and bruised — '

'Yes, but, weird as it is, we're both going to be fine. I got through to the hospital in Liverpool from up on the moors, and was able to speak to Siobhan. She's spoken to Mike Haggard, given him the stalker's name and his description. She also knows he worked in Liverpool city centre, although she can't say where — and she didn't tell me what he does. Anyway, they're on to it now . . . '

'What *is* his name?'

'Oh, Alan Spence, or Spencer, something like that. It means nothing to me.'

She sounded tired. I could hear a nurse in the background, and Sian said something to her. Then she came back on.

'They want me to rest, so I'd better go — '

'What about your accident,' I said quickly. 'How did it happen?'

'My brakes went.'

'Went?'

'Yes, you know, silly: they didn't work. I started down the hill, put my foot on the brake and it was like treading on water; it went straight to the floor.' She laughed softly. 'And guess what? I finished up hanging upside down from my seat belt in that field at Maddock's Switch.'

15

I was sitting in the back seat, near side, of DI Vales's black Volvo, adopting an air of bland insouciance. Vales was in the driving seat, her broad back against the door, one arm on the steering wheel and the other doing its awkward best to hang on the squab so that she could fix me with a darkly menacing stare. Our opposing personalities collided in the air above the centre console — roughly a foot back from the gear stick — and hovered there in fragile impasse.

I had told my tale, which didn't amount to much: I had discovered a body, informed the police (I let her believe I had done the phoning), and they had moved in swiftly. Two constables had strung the crime-scene tape. Vales sent DS Hills off to talk to Peggy McBride. Dougie McCafferey had not yet returned from Craignure, but Vales was quite sure the sirens howling past the pub would bring him running.

As for me, well, apart from the dark stare that was already turning from menacing to thoughtful, she was being strangely solicitous. I quickly discovered the reason.

'We knew of the accident involving Miss Laidlaw,' she said, 'but I had no idea you and she were . . . connected.'

'Oops,' I said, looking prim, 'isn't that sort of . . . lewd?'

'Bollocks — and don't bother to pardon my French,' she said. 'The story I've got is that Miss Laidlaw lost traction on a very tricky slope and wound up in the field where Bridie Button died — a place you'd know all about, wouldn't you, having been there yourself just recently?'

'Lost traction doesn't accurately describe what happened. When you saw me on the phone I was through to the Lorn and Islands Hospital in Oban, talking to Sian. She told me her brakes went. The way she described it suggests complete loss of brake fluid. I'd like to know where it went.'

'No problem. We'll get Dougie to look at the vehicle when he brings it in. One of my officers will be present.'

'There may *be* a problem. With Jim Gorrie taken from him, Dougie's a man down. When he eventually gets here, he'll need help recovering the Shogun.'

Her smile was cutting. 'Why don't you go with him? You seem to like it out there, and now you've got two accidents to investigate.'

'No, not even one. Sian's was probably

attempted murder; Bridie's *was* murder.'

'Any idea how that was done?'

'Not yet.'

'But you're not going to give up?'

'I never do. And I've got a high success rate. If you want testimonials, get on the phone to a Merseyside DI named Mike Haggard, his sidekick, DI Willie Vine, or several — '

'I know Haggard. We both attended an Association of Police Officers meeting in London a couple of years back.'

'And?'

She pursed her lips. 'Hard but fair. Doesn't suffer fools, gladly or otherwise.' She waited for me to work out that she was paying me a compliment, then said, 'Tell me about your successes.'

'A knife-thrower missing for twelve months: found. Two boys missing for twenty years: found. A man who broke out of jail and committed what looked like the perfect murder or an impossible crime: mystery solved.'

'And now you've got another impossible crime, haven't you?' she said. 'Two witnesses have convinced me Bridie's death was pure accident. If you hope to prove otherwise you'll need to rubbish a statement made by two very religious pensioners. I really don't believe that can be done.'

This was a problem already presented to me by Calum, but it was worth hearing again, perhaps in greater detail, from the official source. I frowned at Vales, as if confronted by something unexpected.

'Two witnesses? Where were they, and what did they see?'

'Gregor Neill and his wife Janet live in a cottage out in the country close to . . . well, let's just say they can see the heights of Corra-bheinn out of their back window, quite a lot of the A849 Fionnphort road from the front. According to Gregor, he saw two sets of headlights on that road, and there was always a gap of at least fifty yards between the vehicles. He watched them for no more than two minutes, because at the end of that time the lead vehicle's lights were all over the sky as it left the road and rolled down to the trees. And then, of course, they were extinguished in a horrible shattering of glass and metal. Which, thankfully, Gregor and his wife could not hear.'

This was essentially the same story I'd got from Calum — but not quite.

'So Gregor went to the window carrying his cup of steaming cocoa or Ovaltine, pulled the curtain to one side — and there they were? Two sets of lights?'

Vales eased her position. The seats, door

and suspension creaked as the centre of gravity shifted. There was a glint of amusement in her dark eyes.

'Why are you asking questions and expecting me to go over it if you've already heard the story?'

'Sorry.' I grinned sheepishly. 'It's just that Calum Wick gave me a slightly different version. According to his source — and I've no idea who or what that was — Gregor looked out of his window and saw one set of headlights, then *shortly afterwards* he saw the second set.'

'Aye, well maybe that's the way it was, but why make a big issue of it? Dougie McCafferey set off in his Land Rover, chasing a truck that had a few minutes' start. He had to catch up. I think that explains the slight time lag in Gregor's story, don't you?'

'Possibly. Probably.' I shrugged, knowing I was missing something important, but willing to move on and return to it later.

'What about Peggy's house? Any idea who tossed the firebomb through her window?'

'A couple of local bad lads have been pulled in. One of them's acting very shifty.'

'If he did do it, what was the motive?'

'I'd say I'm sitting quite close to one of them.'

'If the bomb was intended for Calum and

me, the motive lay elsewhere. This local thug was probably recruited to do the dirty work.'

'That sounds reasonable.'

'And Ray Coghlan's murder? Before I went out to the accident site I called here for another look at the wrecked truck. Jim Gorrie was welding. Something seemed to occur to him — something of great importance, because he appeared stunned. He recovered, but because he was busy he said he'd talk to me later. But when I came back, well, it was too late, wasn't it? You know, I think he remembered something he'd seen on the night Coghlan died.'

'Like what?'

'Well, Lachlan McBride had already been seen near McCafferey's garage only minutes before Keay drove away and sprang the deadly trap. If one person could see him acting perfectly innocently . . . '

'Unfortunately,' Vales said, 'we'll never know.'

I nodded, grimacing. 'Do you believe Lachlan's story of picking up a CD Dougie had borrowed?'

'Who told you about that?'

'He did. Lachlan.'

'You've been busy. But why should I not believe him?'

'Because, as far as I could tell from a swift

glance, Dougie hasn't got anything to play CDs on.'

'But you didn't believe Lachlan before you took that swift glance around Dougie's room, did you? Why was that? What did Lachlan say he was doing?'

'He told me he was talking to Stuart McBride.'

Her laugh was an incredulous snort.

'Stuart went missing two years ago. If he was back, we'd know about it.'

'Why? Because after all these years — and I'm talking thirty, going all the way back to Peggy's first marriage — you still want to question him about the death of Tom McCafferey?'

'Jesus Christ,' Vales said, swivelling her head as a Land Rover came roaring and smoking on to the forecourt. 'Working like a beaver isn't going to pay off if you start believing wild rumours. That story of mysterious poisons administered by Stuart McBride was probably circulated by a rejected suitor who wanted Peggy for himself. It never happened.'

'So McBride is not under suspicion?'

Vales turned from watching Dougie McCafferey climb out of his vehicle and walk over to meet DS Hills, back from talking to Peggy.

'I didn't say that.'

178

'Erm, yes, I think you did.'

'When I said it never happened, I was referring to Stuart. You merely said McBride — and there's more than one. Stuart never was under suspicion. Most people realized that if anyone was going to do away with Tom McCafferey, it would have been his loving wife, Peggy.'

★ ★ ★

For the second time that day I found myself struggling to climb through a wrecked fence where snapped wires lay coiled in wait like rusty snares, then dropping into long wet grass and setting off across a field with thick mud sucking at my feet. This time I'd had the sense to don my green wellies before leaving the Quattro, but the feeling was still one of sheer unreality. The wrecked vehicle I was approaching was Sian Laidlaw's silver Mitsubishi Shogun. My indomitable Soldier Blue had slipped up, put much more than a foot wrong and come within a flattened roof of crushing failure — and it was unprecedented.

Her 4 x 4 had rolled and bounced some thirty yards into the field before coming to a stop with all four wheels spinning in the damp air. As I walked towards it I could see crumpled metalwork, deep scratches running the full length of the body from its passage through that broken fence, the bright glitter of shattered glass.

Upside down, I thought, was the best way it could have ended up — for me, if not for Sian — because it would make it so much easier to examine brake pipes and cylinders.

I had almost reached the wreck when Doug McCafferey's breakdown vehicle came roaring across the field. He'd dropped me off, then used the gate through which he had recovered Coghlan's wrecked truck. Now he swung wide, halted, and came reversing in to stop with the rear of the truck some twenty yards from the Shogun's off side.

'We need to hook up a cable and pull it right way up,' he called, as he jumped down.

'Not yet. I want to look at the underside.'

He came over, running fingers through his dark curly hair, already sweating, his pores leaking beer. His face was flushed, his eyes dark and unfriendly.

'You know the driver? Wasn't she the woman instructing on those daft outward bound courses?'

I smiled absently. 'Sian Laidlaw. I've spoken to her. She's in hospital in Oban.'

'Did she say how it happened?'

'The brakes went. Her foot went straight to the floor.'

He'd gone past me and was stretching to lean over the upturned Shogun, looking at the wet, muddy underside. Starting at the front, using eyes and hands, he began working his way slowly towards the rear. He stopped with a grunt.

'Here.'

I went forward to look where he indicated. He ran a finger through a colourless liquid that was coating a pipe and the section of chassis to which it had been clipped. He rubbed wet finger and thumb together, testing the viscosity, put finger and thumb to his nose and sniffed.

'That's it. Brake fluid. That section there is where it was lost.'

A foot long section of the pipe had been ripped away from the chassis and bashed up against the floor panels hard enough to split the pipe and dent the panels — although the split in the pipe wasn't visible. A fine jet of leaking fluid had squirted up against the floor panels each time Sian's right foot depressed the brake pedal. On that last steep run down to Maddock's Switch, she had depressed the pedal in vain: by then, the brake master cylinder and its reservoir were both empty.

'What did the damage — a hammer?'

'Christ, no.' Dougie's tone was contemptuous. 'Can you not see the roughness and irregularities caused by the impact, the fragments of moss, the tiny flecks of white? Those are chips of rock. Whoever drove this vehicle across country did so with a reckless disregard for safety — '

'She's an experienced instructor, a fine driver.'

'That's as maybe. But she either bottomed out on a ridge, or dropped into a bloody deep pothole where the chassis came down hard on a protruding rock.'

'So it was an accident?'

'Bad driving.'

'But not attempted murder?'

He stepped back, planted his hands on his hips. His eyes were ugly.

'Is that your idea of a joke?'

'Far from it. After what's been happening around here — '

'Look, pal, what's been happening around here has been affecting me, not you. In the past couple of weeks I've lost my wife in a tragic accident, a man was bizarrely murdered in my garage, and today I got back from the pub to see a good friend lying dead at the bottom of my inspection pit — '

'I found him, it was shocking, I can understand how you feel.'

He flapped a hand, waving away my sympathy. 'Balls to that, too. You have no bloody idea. Listen, your lady friend got off light. She hit something hard out there on the moors, must have heard the impact but didn't even bother to stop, and when her brakes failed she as good as walked away from the wreck. But it was not attempted murder, my friend, it was pure bloody stupidity — have you got that?'

As far as an enraged Dougie was concerned, the discussion was over. He stormed back to his vehicle and began muscularly paying out a cable. He took it all the way over the upside-down Shogun, fed it back underneath and hooked it on to the roof. Then he climbed into his truck and drove away. The cable snapped tight. The Shogun jerked, then rolled over neatly to finish up rocking on four wheels.

Five minutes later we were done. The cable had been unhooked and rewound, the front end of the Shogun had been lifted for the short suspended-tow to Craignure — and all I'd done was prowl helplessly and watch an angry man with jaw muscles bulging as he held his tongue and did his best to ignore me.

But I couldn't ignore him. I didn't know when I would next get the chance to talk to him on his own. This was an opportunity that could not be missed.

He was wiping his hands on an oily rag

when I walked over and made my mistake.

'I know you were there when your mother asked me to prove that your wife died in an accident — '

'Aye, and I pointed out then that I don't need proof,' he growled. 'The night it happened, there was nobody closer to that truck than me. Bridie made one mistake, and she paid for it with her life — '

'I think she was murdered.'

His lips clamped into a thin line. He took a step towards me.

'Jesus, have you not been listening to a word I've said? There were just two vehicles on that road and one of them was mine — '

'I know where you were — '

'Aye, right; so if you say Bridie was murdered and I was the only man out there — where does that leave me?'

'Tell me what work you were doing on Ray Coghlan's truck — '

His big fist came swinging up from nowhere. I felt a mighty blow on the side of my jaw. Then I was weightless. The cold wet grass was soaking the back of my head. There was a roaring in my ears. I was looking up at sullen grey skies, and in my mouth there was the salt taste of blood.

I turned my face to one side and spat, rolled over, hoisted myself up on to my elbows and shook my head to clear it. The roaring wouldn't go away. I squeezed my eyes shut, opened them again, and saw what was happening.

Dougie McCafferey was leaving in a hurry. The roar of the big diesel engine intensified as he took the recovery vehicle in a wide half circle to swing it perilously close to me. Mud squirted from beneath the big cleated tyres, spattering my face. I ducked as a stone popped, narrowly missing my eye.

He was hanging out of the window as he went by, one hand gripping the big steering wheel, his teeth flashing in a savage grin.

'Find your own bloody way back,' he yelled, 'then make damn sure you book yourself and your pals on to the next Oban ferry.'

In a cloud of blue diesel fumes he bounced the truck and the wrecked Shogun across the field, damn near demolishing the gate as he roared on to the road and turned towards Craignure.

16

In green wellies that over thin socks were much too big for me I walked what felt like half of the twenty miles between Maddock's Switch and Craignure before my mobile registered a signal and I was able to get through to Stan. He picked me up after another blistered mile had been trudged, and dropped me at the garage where I crossed the forecourt, changed into my shoes and climbed achingly into the Quattro.

The breakdown vehicle with the wrecked Shogun still suspended was parked as close to the workshop as it could get without snapping the crime scene tape. One or two police officers were visible, shoulders hunched, faces long. There was no sign of Dougie, and my eyes automatically drifted to the upstairs windows where light glowed behind drab net curtains.

What was I to make of her, the devious Peggy McBride? A couple of words from DI Vales had altered all my perceptions. I was having to face the disturbing possibility that I was being wound tightly around Peggy's little finger, a compliant dupe unwittingly aiding a fading island matriarch in some complex plot that was leaving the landscape of Mull littered with corpses. But if she was conning me, what was her aim? And where did the others fit in: Dougie, Lachlan and his twin sister Nellie, and the ghost that was Stuart McBride?

I turned away, bemused. Trying to get my teeth into a problem when there was little to chew on was a waste of time, and there was no reason for me to hang around. I would have reported my findings on Sian's Shogun to DI Vales, but her Volvo had gone and I guessed she was back at the police station in Western Road, Tobermory. So, that could wait until tomorrow.

Keeping a face as rigid as stone so as not to disturb my pummelled countenance, I drove out of the garage and stopped in Craignure to buy a bottle of Islay single malt. Then, after a long moment's consideration which was strongly influenced by the pain in my jaw but even more so by my desire to interview the man at the very heart of the Coghlan murder, I went looking for the local doctor.

★   ★   ★

Andrew Keay turned out to be a man in his forties who would have been classed as anorexic if seen on the catwalk modelling something by Armani, but was cursed for being superbly fit by those people he finished ahead of in the many marathons he had run.

There was no surgery on Sunday but, although it was his day off, he was perfectly willing to see me. When I walked into his surgery — the best place, he had said, for a chat — he greeted me like a long lost friend. Why, I thought, gripping his bony hand, does that make me deeply suspicious?

'The facial damage is obvious,' he said, frowning but with a very definite twinkle in his eye as he gazed at my swellings and bruises, 'but for you to be here at all I'm sure there must be something much more serious that I cannot see.'

'Snapped bits and pieces,' I said, managing a wince as I gingerly touched my rib cage. 'That's what it feels like, anyway, and I'd like you to have a look and either send me to hospital, or out the door with a flea in my ear.'

'Likely to be the latter,' he said, 'from the ease with which you walked in here. And if somebody punched you on the chin, as seems very likely, why would that have caused a broken rib?'

'I fell heavily.'

'Aye, well, take off your coat and shirt and see if you can manage to climb on to the bed.'

Within moments I was flat on my back and, with hard fingers, he was probing what he and I both knew was a perfectly sound bony framework. After a few moments of that, me lying down then sitting up, breathing in then breathing out, he took hold of my wrists and hauled me upright and told me to get dressed. Once I was on my feet he gave my face a cursory examination but, just like me, by this time he was deeply suspicious.

'All right,' he said, his fingers trailing from my jawbone to linger ominously at my throat while he looked with feigned concern into my eyes, 'perhaps you'd now like to tell me the real reason you are here, Mr Scott.'

'The first was genuine, and you've dealt with that. The second and ulterior motive stems from Peggy McBride having heard of my expertise in the field of private investigation. I'm working for her, and when Ray Coghlan was murdered, the killer chose you to pull the trigger. I'd like to talk to you about that.'

'I have been talked to exhaustively, Mr Scott.'

'But not always,' I said, 'by experts.'

'Perhaps not ever.' He chuckled, and flapped a hand. 'I can give you a few minutes. Take a seat.'

I took the patient's chair, he sat behind his

desk and the inevitable computer, prescription pads and medical bits and pieces, and swivelled to face me.

'What happened is quite straightforward, and has been noted by the police,' he said. 'I walked up the hill to collect my car. A cable had been looped over the ball that usually pulls my caravan. When I drove away, I brought a wrecked truck crashing down on poor Ray Coghlan.' He raised an eyebrow. 'What do you hope to add to that?'

'You're right, everybody knows what happened. I'd like to delve a little deeper. For instance, I'd like to hear your comments on how Ray Coghlan came to be under the vehicle.'

'Haven't really thought about it. I suppose he crawled there, or someone put him there.' He shrugged, waited.

Hadn't really thought about it? No, that wouldn't wash. Keay drove the vehicle that snapped a cable tight and crushed a man to death. In the hours and days since then he must have agonized over every moment leading up to the tragedy, cursed himself for not checking all round his vehicle before driving it away, heaped much stronger curses on the person who had cynically used him to commit murder.

So what was Keay? A man extraordinarily

capable of emerging from stressful situations unmoved, someone with a limited imagination — or a cynical liar?

'I don't like the idea of Coghlan crawling under the truck,' I said. 'Oh, he might have done it if he was drunk enough, but that then makes the murderer's coming across him serendipitous: this unknown person walks into the workshop for some innocent reason, sees the man he hates lying there under the wrecked vehicle and thinks, wow, here's my chance, now how can I drop that truck on his head?' I pursed my lips. 'No, I can't see it. And if it didn't happen that way, then someone put Coghlan there.'

I looked hard at Andrew Keay.

He said, 'Go on.'

'If he was put there, when did the putting begin? I mean, we know Coghlan was drunk, so where was he doing his drinking? If it was in the pub in Craignure and he was so drunk he had to be assisted out of the door, that would have been noticed — and the killer couldn't risk attracting attention.'

'I agree, but you're asking the impossible,' Keay said. 'If I had any thoughts on the matter they'd be worthless. Conjecture. Guesswork. I'm not a detective, Mr Scott.'

'I am, in my own small way, and that's the way I work and probably the way the police work: we look closely at a number of hypothetical situations, any one of which would fit the circumstances. Then we rule them all out, all except one — and that one usually turns out to be what actually happened.'

'And you're ruling out the pub as a starting point because it would have been too risky for the killer?'

'No. I'm ruling out Coghlan being helped out of the pub.'

'And . . . what? Are you saying he wasn't too drunk to have walked up the hill unaided?'

'Jim Gorrie told me there was a whisky bottle under the truck with Coghlan. That leads to another possibility.'

'Coghlan crawled under the truck and *then* got drunk.' Keay shook his head. 'I don't like it. By suggesting that, you're letting serendipity sneak back in, and even I can see that idea of the killer coming across Coghlan by chance is preposterous.'

'So we have to come up with another hypothetical situation.' I thought for a moment. 'How about this. Gorrie told me Coghlan spent most of that day after Bridie Button's death talking to the police, sitting in the pub, and . . . ' I was about to say he'd also gone to see Peggy McBride, but something made me stop. 'Well, that's about it. He was probably too shocked by what had happened to do very much at all. So, what if the killer was watching him? He was in no hurry. Very patient, he bided his time and watched this shocked and disorientated middle-aged man take on a lot of strong drink. And when Coghlan decided to leave the pub and start up the hill — '

'Why would Coghlan do that? His truck was wrecked, he'd want to go home.'

I smiled. 'Hypothetical, remember? Which means I can't tell you why he went up there. Who knows? Maybe in the depths of depression or maudlin intoxication he wanted another look at the truck that had killed Bridie Button.' I shook my head. 'What I was *going* to say was that perhaps the killer followed him up the hill, but with your talk of Coghlan wanting to go home you've now opened the door to yet another possibility. Coghlan was drunk and had no transport. The killer knew this, and he used that knowledge: he offered to take Coghlan home. Coghlan accepted. He got in the car, the killer drove up the hill, but instead of heading off into the hills he turned into McCafferey's garage.'

'Possible but unlikely. The killer couldn't risk his car being recognized.'

'Mm, I don't know. Dark night, late, not

many people about. But let's ignore that for a minute. Let's just say that somehow, under some pretext, the killer has managed to get Ray Coghlan into the workshop without being seen. Now, let me digress for a minute. What about you, Keay? Why did you walk up the hill to collect your car when you did? Why so late? Had you been enjoying a sociable evening in the pub, were you working late — ?'

'I was working, yes, in my surgery.'

'Anyone know how long you were going to be there?'

'My receptionist knew I was going to be there. She didn't stay behind. I told her I was unlikely to get away before ten.'

'Right, so now back to the killer. He's managed to talk to your receptionist and find out from her what time you're likely to be heading up to the garage — '

'Quite possible. I know she had a swift drink before heading home.'

'There we are then. The killer's in the workshop with Ray Coghlan, who's either drunk or very drunk. But the killer has got to get Coghlan under the truck, set up the cable from stands to your tow ball, and then make sure Coghlan stays put until you arrive and pick up your . . . ?'

'Suzuki.'

'Right, you're going to pick up your Suzuki, probably a little after ten. So how does the killer keep Ray Coghlan under that truck?'

'A bang on the head would be risky,' Keay said. 'Too light a blow, and he'd be conscious within minutes. Too heavy, and he could easily kill the man.'

'Isn't that what he wanted to do?'

'Yes, but — '

'A truck fell on Coghlan's head. A fatal blow delivered earlier, however messy, is not going to be noticed amid the greater trauma caused by the truck. And worries about time of death?' I shook my head. 'A police surgeon's estimate is always going to allow four hours or so either way, and with cause of death clearly the massive injuries caused by the truck — '

'So you think that's it? The killer took Coghlan to McCafferey's in his vehicle, killed him with a blow to the head, then put him under the truck to hide what he had done?'

I hesitated, but not for long.

'No, I don't.'

'Then why make it sound so plausible?'

'Hypothetical scenarios, remember? Dream them up, look closely, eliminate most. Like serendipity: the killer could have come across Coghlan by chance, but it's highly unlikely.

And so it is with a killer blow. The blow would work, the man would die — but why then put him under the truck?'

'You said it yourself. The truck falling on his head would hide what actually happened.'

'Yes, I know. But there's no point to it. And the complicated set up, the stands, the cable, your Suzuki . . . ' I shook my head emphatically. 'No, the killer wanted Coghlan to die by being crushed to death under that vehicle. He arranged it that way, so he must have worked out some way of keeping the drunken man in position under the truck until you came along and drove merrily away.'

And suddenly there was a wariness in Andrew Keay's eyes that increased my suspicions.

'How would he do that?'

'The easiest, surest way,' I said softly, 'would be to inject Coghlan with a suitable drug.'

In the sudden silence I could clearly hear brittle dry leaves blowing across the nearby road, the faint moan of a fog horn out on the Sound of Mull.

'You really think I'd do that to a drunken man?' Keay said, rocking slightly in his chair.

'I didn't say that.'

'It's what you meant.'

'I've been thinking on my feet. Drugs never

196

entered my head until you asked that question: how would he, the killer, keep Coghlan in position under the truck. We'd talked about a blow, decided it could be too risky — especially if the killer wanted Coghlan to die in a certain way. Short of tying him up — which he could have done, I suppose — drugging him seemed the logical way to go.'

'Then perhaps, in the circumstances, I should come clean.'

If my hopes surged in anticipation of an amazing confession, they were quickly dashed. And I knew, from Keay's face, that he had couched his remark in just such a way to send me tumbling headlong to the wrong conclusion.

'If Ray Coghlan was drugged before being pushed under that truck, it certainly wasn't done by me. I told you I was working in my surgery, as indeed I was. But not all evening. Shortly after I sat down, I received a call from Peggy McBride. She was unwell, and wanted to see me. I arranged a lift with a friend. He took me out to Salen.'

'And you stayed there how long?'

'Long enough. Peggy always was sociable, she liked a wee dram and she hated drinking alone. I attended to her, then she attended to me, as you might say. We whiled away several pleasant hours. So you see, when all that skulduggery — '

197

'Murderous activity.'

'If you wish. But the point I'm making is that when a murderer was setting the stage at McCafferey's garage, Mr Scott, I was many miles away — and Peggy is a reliable witness who will cheerfully verify my story.'

17

What a difference a day makes.

I drew the Quattro to a halt outside a bothy from whose windows and doors light was flooding. Bright light, too. Someone had replaced Chinese paraffin lamps with hissing gas monsters that turned night into day, and when I stepped into the long room that I had seen only in darkness I was met by a B.B. King blues standard howling from Jones the Van's portable CD player and the nose-twitching smell of hot food issuing from the small kitchen.

Instructors and office boys and programmers had gone, taking with them their equipment but leaving naked camp beds behind in a room that looked like one of those army huts they called spiders waiting for the next 1950s National Service intake. Stan was holding back the blanket in the kitchen doorway and grinning at me, a scruffy, unshaven corporal with the light behind him as he watched with glee the arrival of the latest raw recruit. This one limping, and with a badly bruised jaw.

I brandished my bottle of Islay single malt.

'What's cooking?'

'Your choice, from the Salen bothy's unique à la carte. Chicken curry an' rice, chicken curry an' chips, egg an' chips, curried egg, chicken an' egg, chicken an' chips with no curry, curry on its own with sod all else — '

'What's the speciality of the day?'

'Chicken curry an' rice.' He grinned. 'Everythin' else is off.'

'I'll have that,' I said. Then, gingerly testing my jaw, 'But tell him to make it tender.' I waved the bottle again. 'And see if you can dig up three glasses.'

What he found were three empty jam jars, the small ones made for preserves of the special kind. We drank out of those in preference to tin mugs, whisky and water in lieu of wine, eating from tin plates in a section of the long room that had been made reasonably cosy by tipping camp beds on their sides to form low walls that enclosed the table we'd dragged from the damp and dingy kitchen and left us encircled by shadows. All lights had been extinguished but for the one standing in the centre of the table which had been turned down low. The CD player's volume had also been turned down and, as we worked our way through a curry that looked like a sloppy cow pat but had a wonderful fiery piquancy, B.B. King was telling us over a wailing guitar that he wanted to give up living and go shop-ping. Something to do with a note he found on his pillow that morning. Which took me inevitably to thoughts of Sian lying in a hospital bed, a drift into a maudlin couple of minutes' reverie from which I emerged with the realization that the level in the whisky bottle was dropping alarmingly — and I hadn't seen Stan move.

I grabbed it, topped up our three recherché wine glasses and placed the half-empty bottle on the floor.

'Right,' I said, pushing back my plate, 'the food's gone, the booze is out of reach, so let's get down to brass tacks. Instead of conducting a murder investigation, we're sitting in a cold, damp hovel acting like Curly, Larry and Moe — and in case you're too young to have heard of them, Stan, they were an American trio known as The Three Stooges and at the moment we're making those film comics look positively intelligent.'

'Yeah, an' I can give you a good ten years — '

'Give me some ideas instead. Vales and Hills must be laughing up their sleeves because, after promising all, we've delivered nothing — just the opposite. My employer's been firebombed out of her home; I can't work out who beat up Sian's sister; Sian's in hospital after driving her Shogun off the road; I've been thumped on the jaw by one of the suspects, and the murderer has struck again.'

I spread my hands beseechingly, looked across the table at two grey-haired men peering at me across tin plates stained with curry, and rolled my eyes.

'OK, before you confound me with your brilliance, let me tell you that I've talked to Andrew Keay and my knowledge of human nature gained through years of experience as a PI warns me that he was probably involved in Coghlan's murder.'

'Now that is bloody brilliant,' Stan Jones said, 'seein' as it was Keay that fuckin' killed him.'

'Killed him unwittingly,' I said. 'I think he was involved in the positioning of the man prior to death: he helped put him under the truck.'

Calum grunted. 'Why Keay?'

'Between us, as we chatted, we came to the conclusion that the best way of keeping Coghlan in place was to drug him.'

'Both of you decided?'

I grinned. 'All right, I decided.'

'Aye, it came to you in a flash of

inspiration. You were in a doctor's surgery, doctors deal in drugs, ergo . . . '

'Exactly. In response he came up with something he thought would be acceptable as an alibi: he's a doctor, remember, and he told me he was called to Peggy McBride's house because she was feeling unwell. As his Suzuki was at McCafferey's garage, a friend gave him a lift to Salen. He stayed at Peggy's for some time. We know from experience she likes a drink, and Keay stayed there for a while, indulging in the local tipple — local in the broad sense, as in Scotland and whisky.'

'Went out there, stayed for some time.' Calum shook his head. 'Too vague for an alibi. The times would need checking.'

'How'd he get back?' Stan said. 'Did his friend hang around as well?'

'He didn't say.' I nodded slowly. 'Good point, Stan. How did he get back to Craignure so that he could make his way up to collect his 4 x 4?'

'An' if he did help put Coghlan under the truck, that'd mean two trips up to the garage, wouldn't it?' Stan went on. 'He must've gone back to the village after the first time, because he was walkin' up the hill only seconds before he drove his Suzuki away when he saw Lachlan McBride.'

I smiled ruefully. 'So the plot thickens.'

'Not necessarily,' Stan said. 'Could even be gettin' thinner. OK, so he did make two trips. So what? Maybe Keay did the lot. Drugged Coghlan, stuck him under the truck, then walked back into Craignure. He has a couple of drinks in the pub, walks back up the hill, jumps in his Suzuki an' pulls away the chocks. Be neat, wouldn't it? He set up the perfect crime, then reports the killin'. Who's going to suspect him?'

'Or maybe the killer was really clever,' I said. 'He set it up so that Keay pulled away the chocks, knowing that Keay would report what had happened, but be seen as too clever by half and become the number one suspect.'

'Christ almighty,' Calum said, 'can we move on from this bout of wild speculation?'

'Definitely,' I said. 'We'll bear in mind Keay's possible involvement or guilt, but leave no stone unturned. So, please, one of you, both of you, give me something, give me *anything*. Offer me theories. Ask questions that stimulate thought — '

'First one coming up, and very close to home,' Calum said, knife and fork clinking as he put them down. 'Was Sian's accident an accident?'

'If we trust Dougie's mechanical knowledge, and what I saw with my own eyes, then yes. The damage to the underside of the vehicle caused the loss of brake fluid, but looked accidental. However, circumstances leave room for doubt.'

'Those being that Sian's an excellent driver, there's a rapidly rising body count which means there's a killer out there, and Sian was at risk because she's linked to us nosy investigators — albeit very loosely at present?'

'Yes. Plus the presence of a man called Lachlan McBride, who's been sniffing around her for far too long and recently propositioned her — '

'For the umpteenth time — and was again rebuffed.' Stan Jones grinned. 'An' then she went and snitched on him, which must've got right up his nose.'

'OK, so the question's not answered to our satisfaction, and there's a big query against the name Lachlan. Calum?'

'Next question: what do we do about the elegant Peggy McBride?'

'Treat with caution,' I said. 'I've been mulling over what Andrew Keay said about going out there the night Coghlan died — and I've just remembered that Coghlan was also there.'

'Christ, he was, too,' Calum said. 'In Salen visiting a crony, she said, and he called in.'

'So the easy answer to your question is that her background, and the behaviour we've witnessed, makes her too untrustworthy to work with, or for, and we walk away and go back to Liverpool — '

'Willie Vine wouldn' like all those implied commas,' Stan said, leering.

I leered back and went on, 'Trouble is, walking away is difficult because Peggy was right first time: at least one of these deaths presents us with a mystery to die for.'

'The death of Bridie Button.'

'Yes, that one. Firstly because if it is a crime, it's impossible. Secondly because I believe that if Bridie hadn't died, the other murders wouldn't have been committed.'

'Looked at like that,' Calum said, 'if we work backwards we should go one step further: this all started *when Bridie walked out on Dougie McCafferey.*'

'Which points the finger at Dougie, the jealous husband of a two-timin' wife,' Stan said.

I nodded. 'So, now the *big* question: if Dougie did kill Bridie, how did he commit the impossible crime?'

'Well, it's obvious he made a mistake,' Calum said, 'because from what we've pieced together we know he believed *Coghlan* was driving — '

'Forget the mistake,' I said. 'He killed someone — but how did he do it?'

'I'm coming to that. Look, concentrate on the fact that Coghlan was driving. Now, Jim Gorrie told me that when the truck was recovered, one of the front tyres was blown. On the face of it, of so little interest that nobody's mentioned it, right? Just one more item to add to the accident damage, because Gorrie reckoned it blew when the truck went off the road and through the fence, and the police agreed with him.'

'Yeah, right, so why're you bringin' it up?' Stan said.

His blue eyes were alight, his thin face flushed under the white whiskers he called designer stubble. Calum was extracting a cigar from a packet and fumbling for his matches. He looked at me.

'What if the tyre was shot out with a rifle?'

'Great minds,' Stan said. 'Me an' you, Cal, what an ace team. That's exactly what I was thinkin', and if that's the way it happened it turns an impossible crime into a straightforward shootin'.'

'Into a miracle,' I said. 'Doug McCafferey was driving a Land Rover, in appalling conditions. What did he do, lean out of the window and fire a rifle one-handed? If he'd managed it at all, he'd have hit a *rear* tyre.'

'I wasn't thinking of McCafferey,' Calum said.

Smoke was rising in a blue haze. He was sitting back, deep-set eyes pensive, his hand up and stroking his beard.

'Go on,' I said, 'amaze us with your erudition.'

'Aye, well, you remember I said that working backwards from Gorrie to Coghlan to Bridie led us to a conclusion. Actually, that was misleading. For the troubles between those three it might, but we know full well that Ray Coghlan had been an all-round bastard from the day he was born. So what if we went back not a couple of weeks, but a couple of years, and looked at another of his victims?'

'So that's what you're getting around to,' I said softly. 'Stuart McBride disappeared two years ago, didn't he, shortly after Ray Coghlan had caused the death of his stepson Alec? A long time before that he'd lost money in a scam run by Coghlan — and, according to Peggy, Stuart loved hunting and was an excellent shot.'

'It also keeps it in the family,' Calum said. 'Dougie told you Bridie was an orphan.

There's no family on that side to grieve for her, so it's hard to see anyone other than the McCaffereys or the McBrides wanting Coghlan dead.'

I reached for my glass, saw that it was empty, realized I didn't want any more anyway. Stan was ahead of me.

'I'll do the coffees,' he said, and set off for the kitchen.

'You realize where this theory leads us, don't you?' I said to Calum.

'To the man's son.'

'Of course. If Stuart McBride roamed the moors shooting rabbits or deer, it's possible he took Lachlan with him. If Lachlan is also an expert shot . . . '

Calum was nodding slowly, thinking it through.

'Bridie followed the same routine every Friday after she moved in with Coghlan,' he said. 'Into town to do the shopping, then back home on the midday bus. That routine was familiar to everyone in Craignure. If a man was planning on murdering Coghlan, he would have known Coghlan's truck was in for repair, but probably missed any change in Bridie's routine because he'd have to make sure he was in position in plenty of time; he would leave town early. So he's out there, in position, high-powered rifle at his shoulder, the truck comes along and, expecting Coghlan to be driving, he squeezes off a shot — '

'Headlights make the shot easy — '

'Or night sights. Whatever. And he can't check the corpse, because Doug McCafferey is right behind the truck in his Land Rover.'

I nodded. 'So it's workable?'

'Gives us another suspect or two,' Calum said, 'even if one of them hasn't been seen for two years.'

'According to Lachlan,' I said, 'he was at the garage on the night Coghlan died.'

'Fits in nicely. He was rectifying a big mistake: he'd murdered his surviving stepson's wife.'

Stan returned with three steaming mugs, the roll-up hanging from his lips streaming smoke over his shoulder. He plonked the mugs down, slopping coffee, and slumped back into his chair.

'If this Stuart feller murdered his stepson's wife usin' a rifle, then got it right and murdered Coghlan by droppin' a truck on his head, who murdered Jim Gorrie, and why?'

'Stuart's as good a suspect as any, until we dig deeper,' I said. 'The reason? — probably because Gorrie saw something, discovered something, and was about to go to the police.'

'Yeah, right.' He yawned. 'So is that it? Cos it's gettin' late, an' I'm knackered.'

'You sure it's only ten years you can give me?'

He sneered. 'I could give you twenty, and still not get decked by some stroppy Jock.'

'Don't speak too soon. Tomorrow I want you and Cal to get the investigation moving. Circulate, converse with the locals. Talk about hunting and shooting. Drop Lachlan's name into the pot. Find out where Jim Gorrie was on the night Coghlan died. See what the feeling is about Peggy's house being burnt down, and who might have been responsible. Same goes for Sian's accident: has anyone been criticizing her; has there been animosity towards her, and if so by whom?'

'That's me an' him sorted,' Stan said wearily. 'What about you?'

'I'll talk to Vales and Hills about the damage to Sian's 4 × 4. Then I'd like to know more about Lachlan and, indirectly, his father, Stuart. I could ask Peggy, but I think I'll go across to Oban and talk to Lachlan's partner at the computer business they run. That means the ferry, which will give me a chance to check on Dougie's alibi — apparently he was in Oban the night Coghlan died, and the alibi was noisily and obviously confirmed by Lachlan when I was with Peggy

— which makes it iffy. I can also find out from Nellie McBride if her brother Lachlan was there the night he was away from Sian's course, though that won't tell me much. He wouldn't firebomb his mother's cottage — and I can't think of anything else exciting happening that night.'

18

Monday

'Doesn't it strike you as a strange coincidence?' I said. 'Within days of each other, two vehicles go out of control driving from opposite directions into Maddock's Switch, and both finish up in the same field with the drivers injured or dead.'

'I can see where you're going with this,' DI Vales said, 'but I can't actually believe what I'm hearing. Are you implying that the same person somehow contrived both those accidents? And 'accident', I hope you will note, is definitely the operative word here.'

'If it was contrived by someone,' I said, 'then accident is the wrong word.'

'If it was murder and attempted murder, which is what you're suggesting,' DS Hills said, 'perhaps you can explain how it was done.'

I'd used my mobile to phone early that morning and been told that the two officers on the Gorrie murder were already at McCafferey's garage. Leaving Calum and Stan to their breakfast, I'd piled into the

Quattro and headed for Craignure. The roads were shrouded in wet mist, the tarmac like glass, and the waters of the Sound of Mull I caught brief glimpses of were iron grey and sullen as if flattened by the immense weight of the overcast skies. When I drove on to McCafferey's forecourt, there was no sign of Dougie or Peggy McBride, though I could see her Volkswagen Golf's gleaming black bonnet poking out at the end of the building.

Hills had been leaning into a police car talking to a uniformed officer. Vales was prowling about in the workshop. She saw me arrive, and came out to meet me. Because I was working for Peggy and more or less obliged to let her know what I was doing, I asked Vales if she was at home. She told me that both Dougie and his mother had been away from the premises since the previous evening — Peggy because she was sickened by what had happened to Gorrie. She had no idea where they were.

We had been standing by her Volvo talking when Hills came over to join us.

'Did you know one of the tyres had blown on Coghlan's truck?' I said now in answer to Hills' question.

'Hardly unusual in the circumstances. It had smashed through a fence and rolled a hundred yards before ploughing into a wood.'

'What if the tyre had blown halfway down the hill — and I'm talking about the road? That would have caused Bridie Button to lose control, wouldn't it?'

He flicked a glance at Vales. 'The operative word's still *accident*.'

'Not if the tyre was blown deliberately by a marksman with a high-powered rifle.'

DI Vales chuckled. 'Do you perhaps have someone in mind for this . . . what should we call it now, a contract killing?'

'Stuart McBride was an excellent shot. When I spoke to Lachlan McBride he told me he was talking to his father, here, only the other night.'

'Aye,' Hills said, 'and Lachlan McBride is the lad who plays at special forces out there on the moors with that woman of yours. That firmly establishes the level of his maturity, and the credence you should put in what he tells you.'

Vales was shaking her head, impatient, and clearly unimpressed with my theory.

'You're wasting our time, Scott. Bridie Button died in a tragic accident. I know you were there when Dougie examined Miss Laidlaw's Shogun, so you saw the damage to the braking system and you know it was caused by the underside of the vehicle striking a hard, immovable object — almost certainly a rock. It was another accident. Jim Gorrie's death, on the other hand, was cold-blooded murder.' She smiled sweetly. 'Have you any more helpful theories?'

'I'll use your words, but applied to Gorrie's death, to make a point,' I said. 'You saw the damage to Gorrie's head. You know that could have been caused when his head struck a hard, immovable object. But it wasn't, it was the other way round: a hard object was used to strike his head.' I returned her sweet smile. 'You might apply that principle to the damage caused by a rock to Sian Laidlaw's Shogun.'

★　★　★

An hour after leaving DI Vales I had an interesting conversation with one of the employees on the Caledonian McBraine ferry to Oban. It had to do with the alibi put forward by Dougie McCafferey for the time of Ray Coghlan's murder. I'd told Calum and Stan that I'd pass time during the voyage by checking the garage man's story of being in Oban that night — which meant he had travelled out and back on the ferry. Because the alibi seemed water tight — confirmed by almost everyone who knew him, absolutely precluding him from having played any physical role in Coghlan's murder — I wasn't expecting any startling revelations.

What I got was a rude awakening, an unpleasant reminder of my fallibility.

I was out on deck, collar up, hands stuffed deep into my pockets, the wind flattening my hair, and my nostrils flaring to the scent of salt spray. A big man in boots and a seaman's heavy jersey was coiling ropes nearby. We got talking. He was in his fifties, and his name was Rory. I worked the conversation around to Dougie McCafferey. Rory admitted he knew him well, and a knowing look crossed his bearded face when I began asking questions.

'This has all been gone into before,' he said. 'Is it you or is it the polis out to pin Coghlan's murder on the man?'

'The opposite: I'm working for his mother, so I'm out to prove he couldn't have done it.'

'Aye, well, if that's what you're after then you're wasting your time here. Dougie being on this ferry proves nothing of the kind.'

If I hadn't been already narrowing my eyes against the near gale, I would have blinked.

'He travelled across on the ferry, returned the same way the next morning. He couldn't do that, and be in Craignure murdering Ray Coghlan.'

'Could he not, now?'

'Well . . . how could he?'

'Come on, man. How many hours are there between the last ferry out, first one back?'

'Depends on the day, doesn't it? Coghlan was murdered on a Saturday night. I know Dougie took the afternoon ferry out of Craignure — four o'clock — so he'd have been in Oban before five. The first one back on Sunday is nine o'clock. That's, what, a gap of almost sixteen hours?'

'Whatever. As you say, it can vary. But think about it. The ferry takes forty-five minutes. A fast boat would cut that time in half, and there's a lot of owners out there who would be more than willing to take a man out to Mull for a reasonable fee.'

'Damn, why the hell didn't I think of that?'

'Aye, exactly.' Rory straightened from his work, one weather-beaten hand brushing back a thick mop of grey hair stiffened by the salt spray. 'Bear this in mind, now: I don't believe for one minute Dougie McCafferey had anything to do with the murder of Ray Coghlan. But the timing of the ferries cannot provide any man with an alibi. Once that man gets from Mull to Oban on a late ferry, he's got a whole night to do whatever the hell he likes and *still* be there to board the first ferry back

218

the next morning. Anything — you understand me? That includes *going* wherever he likes — and, as I've already mentioned, a fast boat can reach Mull in under half an hour.'

19

There's a cosy café overlooking Oban Bay, the harbour with its moored fishing boats, and the clatter and bustle of the quayside. Clutching a mug of hot sweet coffee, I sat there amid the clink of crockery and, through a nifty porthole I created with my hand in steamed-up windows, idly watched fishermen repairing tangled nets or wrestling with flat boxes packed with the silvery glitter of fish.

What effect, I wondered, would the conversation with Rory have on the results expected from me by Peggy McBride?

A seaman's few blunt words had wiped out Dougie McCafferey's alibi, yet one of the things Peggy wanted me to prove beyond any doubt was that her son Dougie had not murdered Ray Coghlan. However, the clandestine movements suggested by Rory were feasible enough to warrant checking, and it was possible that some foot slogging along the slippery boards of the quay might lead me to another gnarled seaman who would admit to taking a passenger out to Mull that Saturday night, waiting for something less than an hour in the darkness, then taking him back to Oban.

It might also be a wearying waste of time if I was chasing rainbows, or the seaman who had pocketed Dougie's cash was out on the high seas. An easier alternative was to ask Dougie McCafferey what he had been doing in Oban on that fateful night, then check his story and, if shaky, tear it to bits.

But today that wasn't what I had set out to do. Dougie and Peggy's whereabouts were unknown; I was in Oban. I had gone there with the intention of talking to Lachlan McBride's business partner, and then to Lachlan's sister, Nellie.

Refuse to be diverted. Don't be side-tracked. Stick to the plan.

When I'd finished my coffee it took me but a few minutes to locate the successful computer games partnership with offices over-looking the harbour, even less to realize that I wasn't going to get anywhere. The single-fronted premises, with full-length plate-glass window painted a dull green that gave it the appearance of a run-down betting shop, was closed. A fancy card hanging on the inside of the glass door told callers that the proprietors of GAME ON would be BACK WHENEVER. That was too vague to convince me that hanging around would be worth the effort.

I did linger for a moment on that damp

221

pavement, looking broodingly at the window's blank green surface and wondering what Lachlan McBride had decided to do when Sian's survival course collapsed around his ears. That left him at a loose end. Lachlan himself had said that a single computer game had made him rich and he was now coasting. Perhaps he was at home.

Even as the thought crossed my mind, I realized I had no idea where he lived. Jim Gorrie had told me Lachlan was a Mull local who had spent a lot of time in England, which wasn't very helpful. He worked in Oban — *when* he worked. But where did he live? Was his permanent address on Mull, in Oban or somewhere else in Scotland? Did he reside in England, keeping tabs on my Soldier Blue by scouring newspapers and turning up like a bad penny whenever an outward bound course was advertised? Or was he even now sitting in the room above the garage, sipping coffee with his mother before taking a later ferry with the intention of starting work in the afternoon?

His distinctive sporty silver Mercedes certainly hadn't been on the early morning ferry I'd taken, or I would have spotted it. Of course, he could have crossed on the late night ferry, which meant he could be, well, just about anywhere, which left me nowhere.

And what bearing, I thought bleakly, did any of my directionless musing have on the crimes that had been committed on the Isle of Mull? It was my firm conviction that the McCaffereys and the McBrides were involved up to their eyebrows. But an icy drizzle had begun to fall, lowering yellow skies were threatening snow, it was already approaching eleven o'clock and so far I had made no progress.

Without more ado, I began the hunt for Nellie McBride. A piece of cake, for an enterprising PI. The infallible guide book is the telephone directory. I remembered something Peggy had said about her daughter having a bungalow outside town, and was prepared to look for a likely address among the columns of McBrides I was sure to find.

* * *

Lachlan's sister, the only McBride in the telephone book, lived in an impressive white bungalow set in wide landscaped gardens about three miles outside Oban on the Gallanch road, with wonderful views across the Sound of Kerrera to the island of the same name that stands between Oban and the Firth of Lorn. As I climbed the steps to the front door I couldn't help wondering where she had acquired the money to buy the property.

Nellie McBride answered the door in a velvet green caftan, and for an instant I thought I was looking at Lachlan in drag. Then realization that this tall, slender woman with thick blonde hair was his twin kicked in, and I smothered confusion and managed to blurt out the feeble story I'd concocted to worm my way into her presence.

'A *newspaper* article?'

'That's right.' I smiled disarmingly. 'Lachlan's been making a name for himself. He almost died on one of those adventure training courses, yet keeps coming back for more.'

She was not impressed. 'He's done two that I know of, one in Cape Wrath where he suffered something worse than cold feet, one here on Mull — and that's just been cut short.'

'All right, so I exaggerated slightly. But he did also try to arrange some extracurricular activity with one of the more attractive instructors . . . '

The strong wind was moulding the caftan to her slim body. She was holding the door to stop it banging against the wall, but absently: Lachlan must have let her into lots of his little secrets, because she took in what I'd said and her mouth twitched in the ghost of a smile.

'So what's the article's title going to be?' she said. '*Glutton for Punishment?*'

'We thought we might establish a link between his behaviour and his father's mysterious disappearance.'

'You *what?*' Her surprise was almost comical, and rather than push the point home I waited for her to absorb the implications and either invite me in or push me down the steps.

The reaction I did observe was odd. The look on her face moved from mild amusement to surprise, then wariness. The soft dark eyes that had looked upon me as a visiting stranger, impersonally but without malice, suddenly became hard. I began to tense, expecting the curt rejection against which journalists develop thick skins, the sudden shuddering slam of the door.

Instead, she pulled it wider.

'I'm freezing to death here,' she said, her soft Scottish accent suddenly more pronounced. 'You'd better come in.'

Bungalow's aren't renowned for impressive entrance halls, but this one was large and square with an Italian stone floor, an ornate telephone on what looked like an antique oak stand and, in a shaded corner close by, an exotic potted fern that would have held its head high amid the lofty specimens in

Liverpool's palm house. Perfumes were all a subtle musk. Somewhere, coffee was brewing.

Clip-clopping across the stone tiles in high cork mules, Nellie led me through to a front lounge with wide windows making the most of a view that by now was nothing more than an expanse of water across which a squall of fine snow was being driven to blot out Kerrera. Illuminated by several table lamps with old-gold shades, leather furniture looked soft enough to cause visitors to overstay their welcome. Scandinavian sideboards in a light wood were low enough to impress without overpowering, while vases and urns tastefully displayed on available flat surfaces suggested I was in the home of a serious collector who would probably know the name for such a person.

'Must be great in summer,' I said, wandering over to the window and looking across the sloping front garden to the road where the Quattro was parked and, beyond that, a gravel shore where salt water flattened by the wind and driving snow lapped feebly.

'That's one of those meaningless pronouncements, isn't it — like saying it'll be lovely when the war's over, or when you stop banging your head on the wall,' she said.

'But true nonetheless.' I turned quickly to face her. 'And there's a sort of a war going on

226

now, on the Isle of Mull.'

'Between good and bad, the law and the lawless?' She nodded, her lips tight. 'You're no journalist. Have you not realized I let you in out of curiosity? You're Jack Scott. You're a private investigator who makes toy soldiers, a friend of that formidable woman who has Lachlan acting like a pimply schoolboy who can't keep his hands out of his trouser pockets.'

'Damn,' I said softly, 'my cover's blown.'

'Maybe you should change your car.'

'Or park it out of sight.' I raised an eyebrow. 'I suppose Lachlan told you all about me the other night?'

'What's that, a trick question?' Her hands were on her hips, her face tight with contempt. 'If you want confirmation, yes, I was unwell and it *was* the night Peggy's house got torched, and yes, Lachlan *was* here — '

'All night?'

I'd suddenly realized that if Dougie could use a fast boat to flit between Oban and Mull and commit murder, so could Lachlan; if sufficient resentment or fear had built up within Stuart McBride for him to want his wife dead, his son Lachlan might share those sentiments.

Nellie had kicked off the mules and plonked herself down on one of the big settees, her arms folded, and was watching me as if trying to read my mind.

'He came over on the last ferry,' she said, 'took the first one back the next morning.'

'Doesn't quite answer my question.'

'I wasn't well enough to keep track of his every move. He came in the evening, looked after me, gave me hot Lemsip, stuff like that — and in the morning he left.' She shrugged.

'I spoke to him on Mull. Since then there have been important developments. I wanted to talk to him again, so I caught the ferry over this morning and called at his business. GAME ON. It's closed. Do you know where he is?'

'More or less the same answer as before: I've a rough idea, but I can't keep track of him 24/7. He was here earlier, said something about heading north to see a friend in Fort William — '

'So he came over from Mull yesterday afternoon?'

'I don't know — did he?'

'Well, he wasn't on the first ferry this morning. But if he did come over yesterday — and you didn't see him until this morning — where would he have stayed?'

'He has a flat, in town, two rooms above the business — did you not see the side door, the name plate?' She was frowning as I shook my head. 'Does any of this really *matter*?'

'Not really — it's just that he isn't in the phone book — '

'He relies on his mobile.'

I smiled ruefully. 'Of course. Sorry, go on, you were saying?'

'I was *saying* that he told me he wouldn't be in work today, so when I heard that, I didn't bother opening up.'

'You?'

'Well, yes. Didn't you know? Lachlan works for me.'

I frowned. 'He told me he's one of two people running a business designing computer games, that he's a talented programmer — '

'Ha! I took him on when he was broke and drifting. Lachlan couldn't programme a video recorder without my help. I point the way, tell him what to do.'

'Then the game that made a fortune, and paid for all this' — I waved a hand at the house the furniture, the collection.

'All my doing.'

I nodded slowly, absorbing the information I'd been given about Lachlan's character, knowing that without Nellie's help I should have reached the same conclusion from my knowledge of her brother's erratic behaviour with Sian.

For a moment I thought of telling her

about the latest road accident, and how Lachlan's rejection by Sian made him a suspect — at least in my eyes. Then I decided to move on.

'That's Lachlan put in his place — but what about your father, Stuart McBride?'

She frowned. 'What about him?'

'Lachlan told me he was talking to your father on the night Ray Coghlan was murdered.'

Her laugh was short and dismissive. 'Then he's having you on.'

'Why would he do that?'

'Because he tells lies. You've experienced that. It's the way he is.'

'But when he told me he was here, he was telling the truth?'

'Jesus Christ,' she said irritably, 'if you're going to keep on pushing me I need a hefty caffeine kick.' She was up off the arm of the settee, heading out of the room and saying, over her shoulder, 'Coffee's already made, if you want some.'

I said I did, and followed her through into a bright kitchen with a tall Welsh dresser holding photographs and willow-pattern meat plates and an ornate pot that had escaped from the collection, and lots of stainless steel and shiny black work surfaces lit by grey light filtering through wood-grain Venetian blinds. An electric coffee percolator was filling the air with a delicious aroma.

I sat down at a pine table.

'Do you know where your father is?'

'He's over there.'

She gestured without looking, and I glanced across at one of the framed photographs standing high on the dresser.

'And in life?'

She poured coffee into two china mugs and brought them over to the table. Pushed sugar basin and cream jug towards me, watched while I took generous helpings from both.

'He may have run away from Peggy,' she said as I stirred, 'but he's always been there for his children, and Lachlan and I have always known where to find him.'

'But you're not going to tell me where he is?'

She ignored the question, took a sip of coffee then asked one of her own.

'What's he supposed to have done?'

I pursed my lips. 'For a start, it's possible he had a hand in the killing of Bridie Button — '

'That was an accident.'

'I think she was murdered, but by mistake: the killer was out to get Ray Coghlan. Like

231

many people, your father had suffered at Coghlan's hands.'

'Yes, but her truck went off the road in bad weather. A *lonely* road, no other vehicles.'

'A good shot,' I said, 'could have used a rifle to blow out a front tyre.'

'Right, and my father was very handy with a rifle — and this was a couple of weeks ago?'

I nodded. 'Also, rumour has it that your father left Peggy because he feared for his life. And a couple of *nights* ago, as you know, somebody tossed a Molotov cocktail through your mother's window.'

'They did indeed. And you think the person responsible for that was my father?'

'It's a possibility, and if it was, he did a good job. My colleague and I saved Peggy's life. Alone, she'd probably have died in the fire.'

'What a bloody waste of effort.'

The sheer venom in her voice jolted me.

'What does that mean? That Peggy's life wasn't worth saving? Or that we were wasting our time, because they'll get her in the end?'

Again she ignored the question.

'They? A few seconds ago my father was the guilty party; now it's 'they'.'

I shrugged. 'All that means is he might

have had help; he was there, but someone else threw the firebomb.'

'Somebody else threw the bomb all right, because my father *wasn't* there.'

'If he wasn't there,' I said quietly, 'where was he?'

'Exactly where he's been for the past three weeks.'

'And where's that?'

'I've already told you. I pointed to him.'

I heard the sigh of the wind, the rattle of hard snow on the windows, the ticking of the clock standing on the big Welsh dresser. Then I sighed, and pulled a face.

'Maybe I should take up a new career as well as getting a different car. You've been so positive that he couldn't have been here, couldn't have been there, couldn't have done this or that . . . and a few minutes ago I should have noticed you were talking about him in the past tense when you said he *was* a good shot . . . '

'My father's ashes are in the urn under that lovely photograph,' she said, at last looking in that direction, her face collapsing. 'He died three weeks ago, and was cremated the very next day.'

Her face was ashen. Tears welled, spilled over, and she dashed them away almost angrily with the back of her hand.

I said, 'Peggy had no idea. I know he walked out on her, but he was her husband and . . . well, don't you think you should tell her?'

'It's a bit late for that now,' she said, and I was appalled by the bitterness in her voice, the naked hatred in her glittering dark eyes.

20

'She let me hold that ice-cold urn — the deathly chill of it actually gave me the shivers — and look more closely at the photograph. Then, with no sign of emotion in her voice or demeanour, she told me her father took two years to drink himself into the grave. Well, the urn.'

'Those last are your words,' Sian said reprovingly.

'I know. Sorry. Much too flippant for what's really a story of tragedy. Apparently Stuart skipped from Mull to Glasgow, which is why he was never found. Well, he was a grown man, entitled to disappear if he wanted to, so nobody was really looking. Nellie would have done, but he kept in touch with her so there was no need. She said he told her time and time again that he'd always love Peggy, but he couldn't *live* with her. Firstly because she had begun treating him with contempt after he was taken in by Ray Coghlan. Secondly, because the knowledge that she despised him reminded him of the rumours: trust had gone, and he was scared.'

'The rumours being about her first

husband, Tom McCafferey, and the coronary that wasn't. Mysterious poisons.'

'That's right. And now Stuart had hit rock bottom in Peggy's estimation and she was serving him his meals with a wicked gleam in her eyes.'

'You made that up.'

'Of course. But imagine how he must have felt, gingerly tasting each forkful — or lying in bed at night, in the dark, waiting for the carving knife between the ribs.'

She was trying not to giggle because her collar bone was strapped and painful and the split lip suffered when her mouth hit the steering wheel had just healed. A tube led from the back of her left hand to the usual drip-on-a-trolley. Her jaw was a purple mess turning to yellow. Her eyes were damp with restrained merriment.

'So if Stuart was dead when Bridie Button went off the road at Maddock's Switch, bang goes your theory of a bullet into the front tyre.'

'So to speak.'

'I know. A bad pun.'

'But spot on. Unless Lachlan fired the fatal shot, which is doubtful. Again according to our Nellie, Lachlan is even worse with firearms than he is with computers.'

'I can believe that, from his showing on

those survival courses. Mental stuff like map reading was beyond him. Anything like abseiling that requires co-ordination or manual dexterity would tie him in knots.'

'So it's think up another theory, or admit that Bridie died in an accident.'

We sat in silence for a while, Sian propped up in the only occupied bed in a four-bed ward, me in a chair but leaning close enough to bask in the warmth from her body. Her hand was in mine, the tips of my fingers were on the soft skin inside her wrist and I could feel the throb of her pulse, strong, slow and reassuring.

'What about Siobhan? Any more from her, any progress in the police search for the stalker?'

'Did I tell you she gave Mike the man's name?'

'Mm. Alan Spencer.'

'Spence. Anyway, I spoke to Mike this morning, and Merseyside Police can't find him. No record anywhere. They think he made up that name on the spur of the moment and only used it with Siobhan.'

'CCTV?'

'A light-coloured car turned out of Long Lane at about the right time — a few minutes after the attack on Siobhan. But you know what those CCTV images are like. Mike said that, even with computer enhancement, they can't determine the make of the car.'

'That's hard to believe. The registration number's another matter, but make is mostly down to shape, isn't it?'

'So what d'you think? Mike's not giving me the full story?'

'It's possible. If the stalker believes he hasn't been spotted, he might strike again. Perhaps that's what Mike wants. It's one way of catching him.'

'Too risky, for my liking. Besides, wouldn't he have to get Siobhan's permission? After all, she'd be the one in danger.'

'Maybe he has, and she's not telling you.'

'You think?'

She was frowning, tiring quickly, and I could see her mind racing in six different directions at once and not liking anything it saw. Then her thinking seemed to settle, to focus on something much more pleasant, and her blue eyes crinkled as her hand squeezed mine.

'Mention of risk has reminded me, Jack. I was lying awake most of the night, thinking beautiful thoughts. About you and me with different careers, or *no* careers. All the danger put behind us, no more Shogun crashes in remote highland glens, no more assailants attacking you with sundry blunt instruments.'

Her eyes were alight with excitement.

'Remember during the Gerry Gault case,' she went on, 'I turned down a trip to Gibraltar. And, at the time, that reminded us of Charlie Garcia and the security firm his brother was keen to sell?'

'That's right. Ideally located on Main Street, in Gibraltar. Charlie's brother wanted to take early retirement and spend his days fishing out on the sunlit waters of the bay.'

'What if it's still for sale?'

'Doesn't running a security firm mean there would still be some danger?'

'Come on, Jack; danger, in Gibraltar?' She chuckled. 'Change the firm's name to Scott Laidlaw Security and we'd be using screwdrivers to fit infra-red security lights, minor stuff like that.'

'Or working on our tans while keeping a watchful eye on millionaires' floating gin-palaces down at the marinas.'

'Right. And we've already got a powerful contact in Eleanor's elderly heart-throb.'

I grinned. 'Ex-diplomat Reg, in his house near the governor's residence on Europa Road.'

Eleanor's my mother. She'd been staying with Reg in his Gibraltar home when Sian and I travelled to the Rock during the Sam Bone case. When I was unravelling the Joe

Creeney mystery, Eleanor had returned the compliment by inviting Reg to her flat overlooking Liverpool's Calderstones Park.

'Makes you think, doesn't it?' Sian said, watching me while doing her best to suppress a yawn.

'We've been thinking of it off and on for some time.'

She rolled her eyes. 'And you know what they say: you regret the things you don't do, not the things you do.'

'This,' I said, 'is a hospital bed.'

'And I,' Sian said, 'am talking about security and Gibraltar.'

I grinned. 'Right now,' I said, forcing myself to take a mighty mental leap back to reality, 'I have no regrets, but a lot of uncertainty. Like, are we tackling this case — ?'

'These cases.'

'Are we tackling these cases in the right way and, if we are — or even if we're not — what do we do next?'

'That's easy. Bridie Button's death could have been an accident, Ray Coghlan's was murder, but totally bizarre — '

'Yes,' I cut in, 'and I've got my suspicions about Andrew Keay, the GP who — as Stan put it — pulled away the chocks.'

'Suspicions in what way?'

'I think he was involved, actually played a hands-on role with Coghlan before his death. I called in and spoke to him about these bruises — '

'Which I tactfully haven't mentioned — '

'And his manner rang warning bells. I really do believe he was set up and drove away from the workshop unaware of what was about to happen. But, earlier, well, I'm not so sure.' I shrugged. 'I know he spent some time with Peggy McBride earlier that evening. Apparently she wasn't feeling well, and he made a home visit. Coghlan was there. Whether that has important implications, leads to indiscreet or even criminal behaviour by Keay, or Peggy . . . ' I shrugged. 'Sorry, you were saying?'

'Well, I mentioned the Bridie accident and Coghlan's murder, and I was *going* to say that the one *straightforward* murder happened yesterday: Jim Gorrie. Start looking into that, and see where it leads.'

'Good thinking. It's surely got to be connected to Coghlan's murder, so working on one is as good as working on both. That means my first stop's McCafferey's garage, and a talk with Doug and Peggy — if they're there.'

'Making sure to keep out of the way of the deadly Strathclyde duo.'

'Actually, DI Vales has turned quite friendly,' I said.

Then I realized my mobile was ringing.

Sian was rolling her eyes in disbelief, knowing mobile phones are banned in hospitals and wondering why on earth I hadn't switched it off. I grimaced, glanced about me for irate nurses, saw none in or near the empty ward. I climbed to my feet, walked to the window and dug the phone out of my pocket.

It was Calum. I listened carefully, nodded without knowing why — as one does when a shocking message is not quite registering — then told him I'd be on the next available ferry.

'Trouble?' Sian said, watching my face as I put the phone away.

'Another murder.'

'If there's any kind of a pattern forming,' she said thoughtfully, 'it has to be Dougie.'

'The pattern that's taking shape,' I said, 'is making nonsense of all my pet theories. It's Peggy McBride. She's been found dead in Dougie McCafferey's accommodation above the workshops.'

PART THREE

21

After warmly embracing Sian I left her to countless hours sleeping or taking her drip for a walk and made a dash for the last ferry back to Craignure. That was followed by a short, swift drive, some fifty minutes after leaving Oban, to a run-down garage that was beginning to have the taste and smell of a war zone. Complete with collateral damage.

At just after five o'clock it was already dark, but McCafferey's forecourt and the workshop premises and living accommodation flanked by the looming windbreak of lank black pines were brightly lit by police floods. Crime scene tape was flapping in the cold breeze.

There were more police visible than warranted by the two cars, and I guessed the murder squad had arrived by helicopter from Glasgow. A Portakabin had been brought in, obviously because neither workshop nor office was suitable for use as a major incident room. Light blazed from the portable office's windows and the open door. As I drove in from the road, bounced towards the pumps and drew to a halt, I saw the unmistakable bulk of DI Vales silhouetted in the incident-room's doorway, DS Hills peering over her shoulder. They were both watching me.

When I climbed out and slammed the door, Vales was already ten yards away and closing fast.

'Get back in the car.'

'Hold on a minute — '

'Just do it.'

I hesitated, caught the angry gleam in her eyes as she bore down on me — and slid back into the car. Vales came storming round the bonnet, wrenched open the passenger door and half fell into the seat. I was enveloped in a warm waft of musky perfume. The suspension groaned. I smiled inwardly. Sian would have said I was making that up. I was. Let's just say the car settled in an unsettling manner.

'Since you arrived on the island,' Vales said tightly, obviously miffed by my amused look, 'the body count's tripled. You proud of that?'

'I hadn't realized it was down to me.'

'I feel like playing safe. Maybe it's got nothing to do with you, but I'm superstitious, and with you off the island — who knows?'

'Are you asking me to leave?'

'You and your merry men.'

'The killer will still be at large.'

'But I will be at peace.'

'Ah, but I have information,' I said, 'that will definitely rule out certain suspects.'

'No suspects are ruled out,' Vales said, 'until I say so.'

'One most definitely is.'

She had slumped as much as a large person can slump in a car seat when there's very little leg room. Her neck was pulled into the collar of the same green trouser suit she'd had on that morning. She was staring broodingly through the windscreen. Her lips were dark red in a face bleached white by the glare from the flood lights, and without looking sideways I could see the reflections in her dark eyes as they flicked in my direction. She desperately wanted to know what I'd dug up, but she'd told me she wanted me to leave and asking me for the information would be a retrograde step and it was one she couldn't take.

Her jaw muscles bunched. She was fighting a fierce internal battle. I took pity on her.

'Stuart McBride died three weeks ago.'

'Jesus Christ.' She let her breath go explosively, spent a few seconds examining her thoughts then said, 'All that's done is left Bridie's death an accident by shooting down in flames your daft rifle idea of murder.'

'You're as bad as Sian with the puns,' I said. 'All right, so nobody took a pot shot at

Coghlan's truck. But knowing Stuart's out of the way does eliminate one suspect in the Peggy McBride murder enquiry.'

'Why the hell would Stuart McBride want to murder his wife?'

'According to his daughter, Nellie, he feared for his life.'

'Common knowledge. Everyone knew that. But that was when he was living with her. He disappeared, remember? That made him safe.'

'But still jittery.' I put my back against the door so I could face her. 'OK, how about this. Lachlan McBride took yesterday afternoon's ferry to Oban, and spent today with a friend in Fort William. That's another suspect ruled out. Or is it?'

'Assuming Lachlan had reason to murder his mother,' DI Vales said, suddenly looking smug, 'the value of his alibi surely depends on when Peggy was murdered.'

'All right,' I said, 'when was that?'

'Close to midnight last night.'

'And you've already checked, and Lachlan was definitely on yesterday's four o'clock boat?'

'It's a tight-knit community. Not much gets missed.'

'Unless it happens to be a murder or three,' I said softly. Then a thought struck me and I jerked upright.

'Hang on a minute. If Peggy was murdered last night, then when we were standing by your car this morning — '

'Peggy McBride was dangling at the end of a rope under those exterior stairs.' Vales gestured vaguely, her mouth twisted. 'She'd been there all night, there was frost riming her silver hair. And whoever hanged her first gave her an almighty beating with a tyre lever.' She looked at me dispassionately. 'Given what was to come, a hanging without the blessed relief of a broken neck, there are those who might consider the beating that undoubtedly left her unconscious to be an act of mercy.'

22

'She can't really kick us off the island,' I said, in closing. 'All she can do is tell us to keep out of her way, leave the investigating to the professional investigators — and so far that's what we've been doing.'

'Which is PI speak for 'we've worked our balls off but got nowhere',' Calum said.

I grinned at Stan Jones. 'Like a Doberman, isn't he? Straight for the jugular.'

I'd walked in from another of those dark and misty November nights. The kitchen was like a sauna, the air hot and damp enough to make curly hair tight, straight hair lank and, sprawling in his now customary chair alongside the stove, Calum was trying to see me through the misted lenses of his glasses.

It had taken me ten minutes to bring them up to date with all that I had learned from, or discussed with, Nellie McBride, Sian, and DI Vales. I'd got no vocal or visible reaction, but for me the interest had been in trying to read what was going on behind their eyes. Especially when I told them about the death of Peggy McBride.

That brutal killing was a watershed. We had been on the island since Friday afternoon, and Calum was right: we'd got nowhere. There were several excuses available if I wanted to use them. For a start I'd been distracted by the attack on Sian's sister, Siobhan, and Sian's injuries suffered in the serious crash — which I guessed must have written-off her Shogun — would be worrying away at the back of my mind until she was released from hospital.

But just as I hate coincidence — as those who know me well will testify — so I am loath to fall back on excuses. When the going gets tough the tough . . . well, you know that one, I'm sure, and in a roundabout way it brings me back to Peggy McBride. Because her murder had come as a shock. It didn't seem to fit into the theories I had been developing. Suddenly everything was more difficult: her death had thrown a spanner into the works, created waves, and scattered favourite theories like autumn leaves (I could see Liverpool's literary DI Willie Vine's eyes rolling at those mixed metaphors). Even when no investigative work's being done, the mind continues to chug away, and in the murders of Bridie Button and Ray Coghlan it was possible to see a pattern: estranged wife

251

living with local entrepreneur and scam artist, wrong person killed by furious husband, a day later the mistake rectified. Even Jim Gorrie's death could be explained: he was an eye-witness who'd been murdered to ensure his silence — and the pattern was undisturbed.

But Peggy McBride?

'If your thinking matches mine,' Calum said lazily, slipping his glasses down his nose and fixing me with a beady gaze, 'you've come to the conclusion that the latest murder has left us up the creek without a paddle or a compass.'

'I hadn't put it quite so colourfully, but as usual you've read my mind. Which is a good omen. If two of us realize there's a problem, all three of us can sit down and work on solving it.'

'There's another problem that's easier fixed,' Stan Jones said.

'Go on.'

'Leave Bridie Button out of it.'

'Because it's an impossible crime, and it's muddying the waters?'

'It may be muddying your waters,' he said, grinning, 'but it's givin' me a pain in the neck. Call it an accident, and get on with those victims that've been squashed, drowned or strung up.'

'Now that *is* colourful,' I said admiringly.

Calum was stretched out, ankles crossed, Stan was leaning on the table with his stubbly chin in his hands and eyes dancing, and clearly we were in danger of sinking into a morass of small talk. Something was needed to interrupt us — and something did.

It's funny how the musical trill of a mobile phone has taken over the world and attracts instant attention. Mine rang at that moment. Stan's elbow slipped off the table. Calum's glasses slipped off the end of his nose; he caught them one-handed just before they hit the floor. Suddenly, as I climbed to my feet and slipped through the blanket into the chill, dark long room, I could feel two pairs of eyes on my back.

I also heard a clatter and rattle and liquid trickle, and guessed Calum was boiling the water for coffee.

Sian was phoning from the hospital.

'I've just left you,' I said, my tone suave enough to drip oil. 'Darling, you really must try to control yourself — '

'Jack, Siobhan's just been on the phone. The stalker got into the hospital.'

'Oh, Christ, no. Did he get through? Hurt her again?'

'No. Yes.' She broke off, and I could hear her fighting to control her breathing. 'What I mean,' she said more evenly, 'is, yes he got through, but no he didn't hurt her. Mike Haggard had put a man on the ward. A woman; sorry, I'm still not thinking straight. This . . . Spence, or whatever the bastard calls himself now, managed to slip past. The usual thing, he'd got hold of a white coat and had a stethoscope dangling around his neck. The police officer was alerted when Siobhan cried out. Screamed, actually. And Spence ran, of course.'

I'd walked away from the kitchen to the front door. I opened it, stepped outside. Cold stiffened the hairs in my nostrils. The night was so quiet it was as if the thick blanket of mist was deadening all sound.

'When was this?'

'Last night. Sometime. Anytime. I don't know, don't care — but it happened and he almost, *almost* — '

'He must be mad,' I said. 'There was a police officer there, and still he tried it on?'

'She's plain clothes. And she'd slipped away. There's a coffee machine round the corner and she was getting a cup — '

'In other words, she'd left her post?'

'She was getting coffee for *Siobhan*, Jack. Look, I've just heard the news, so obviously I'm upset, but it does seem that everything's OK.'

'Do you want me to go to Liverpool? You could come with me, you know. Bruises, cracked collar bone, intravenous drip, I'm sure they'd let you go.'

She chuckled, still sounding strained, true, but it was a chuckle.

'I thought about it. Decided no. I can't expect you to give up work just because the two ugly sisters have ended up in hospital. Besides, what good would we do?'

'Mm. If my performance up here's anything to go by, not a lot.'

'Give it time. I thought once back on Mull you were going to start with Gorrie's murder?'

'Yes, you came up with that idea, and it was a good one — but only when he was the latest to die. Since then Peggy's been murdered, as you know. Not very prettily, by the way: she was badly beaten with a tyre lever, then hanged.'

'Poor thing,' Sian said softly. 'I liked that woman, Jack.'

'Yes, well, at risk of sounding callous, her dying hasn't helped the dream team. McCafferey's garage is swarming with police, and that's going to force me, us, to come at this investigation from a different direction. I've still got this gut feeling about the McCaffereys and the McBrides being as

255

guilty as hell, but Dougie's going to be too upset to talk, and Lachlan's in Fort William. Back tomorrow, probably, but — '

'Oops, I'm getting nasty looks,' Sian said. 'Me and my mobile phone.'

'I'll let you go. And don't worry about Siobhan. Mike Haggard will be livid, so Spence will *not* get a second chance.'

Footsteps. Scottish voices. The ring of authority.

'Bye, Jack,' Sian said softly, and switched off.

I put my phone away, went back inside the bothy and through to the kitchen. It was like walking from the fridge into the airing cupboard.

Calum was watching me enquiringly over the rim of a steaming mug while pointing to another standing on the table.

'It was Sian,' I said. 'The stalker got through to Siobhan's ward, but was repelled.'

'I like it,' Stan said. 'Sian rebuffs her stalker, Siobhan decides repellin' works better — '

'It was the presence of a woman PC that did it.' I picked up the coffee mug. 'Where were we?'

'I'd got around to decidin' the hierarchy needs adjustin',' Stan said, standing up and stretching like an old monkey. 'It's bottom

256

heavy, an' the wrong man's makin' the decisions.'

'No,' I said, 'it's top heavy, as it should be, but the right man's making the wrong decisions.'

'Isn't that the same thing?'

'Subtle difference. If the right man gets it wrong, imagine what the wrong man would do in your inverted hierarchy.'

Stan sneered. 'Couldn't do much worse.'

'Aye, well, you can forget the bloody hierarchy,' Calum said, uncrossing his legs and springing to his feet fast enough to endanger his coffee. 'The way it's always worked is we pool ideas. Another name for it is brainstorming among equals; it never fails — '

And then he stopped, head cocked, listening.

The hum of an engine had been there in the background like a bee out on a night mission, but had gone unnoticed. Now a car's tyres crunched up the last fifty yards of the track from Salen. Headlights washed across the kitchen window, then were extinguished. We heard a car door slam. The tramp of feet. The creak of the front door's hinges. The scrape of boots on the long room floor.

Then the curtain was whipped aside, and

Dougie McCafferey stepped through. His dark curly hair was damp from the mist, his face pinched with cold, and all trace of his habitual truculence had been washed from his eyes leaving them as dark and vulnerable as a child's.

23

'Old men,' he said. 'Three bloody old men in a run-down bothy. How bloody impressive is that?'

He was standing just inside the room, swaying slightly, his weight mostly on his heels. And, back in my seat at the table, I wondered about his eyes, wondered if what I was seeing was the inconsolable hurt of a man whose mother has been brutally murdered, or the familiar thousand-yard stare, the blank look of a hard man tanked up on whisky and out looking for trouble.

'What do you want, Dougie?'

'Did you hear me comin' up the hill? Was the engine labouring, or what? Did you not wonder why? And if you did, did you not then begin to fear for your skins, maybe wonder how many hard men can be packed into an old Land Rover? With pick helves, yeah?' He slammed a hand against the wall to steady himself, grinning wetly. 'Enough, I can tell you. *More* than enough to handle three old men sittin' there like three bloody old *women* — '

'Shut up and pull up a chair,' I said, sick of

his rambling. 'I'd known your mother for just a few days, but I was appalled when I got the news of her death. You have my deepest sympathy. But there are no men out there, you're on your own, Dougie, and you've had too much to drink. Sit down, grab a cup of strong coffee, then tell us what you want.'

Calum, back in his seat by the stove, stuck out a long leg and unceremoniously kicked a chair towards the visitor. Stan was still up on his feet. He spooned instant coffee into a mug, poured on boiling water and placed the mug on the table. Then he sat down.

Calum closed his eyes and seemed to go to sleep. Stan bent forward and began rolling a cigarette, eyes lowered to the task. I reached for the milk standing in the middle of the table and splashed some into the coffee I hadn't yet touched. Sat back, sipped my drink, idly watched Stan sprinkling a line of tobacco on to Rizla paper.

In the silence, Dougie McCafferey's breathing was harsh.

'Bastard,' he said softly. 'Bastard.'

He lurched to the table, dropped into the chair, scooped the mug towards him. Hot coffee slopped over his hands. He looked at it, lifted his hand and licked it; looked across at me.

He said, 'If you were that fond of her after

260

just a couple of days, then find out who killed her.'

'Is that why you're here? The last time we met you punched me in the face and told me to take the next ferry out of Mull.'

'Aye, well, that was then, and tragedy's overruled common sense.' His face was bleak. 'You didnae go, anyway, so you might as well make yourselves useful.'

'We're going to. And we will find the person who murdered your mother. It was a brutal crime and her killer deserves to meet the same fate — though the best that will happen is life imprisonment.' I looked straight into his eyes. 'But I must warn you, Dougie, we're also going to prove that Bridie Button was murdered.'

'Bridie died in a road accident. Unlike that woman of yours, who was lucky to emerge alive from a deliberate attempt at murder.'

For a moment I was speechless, stunned by his words.

'I thought that was an accident,' I said, finding my voice. 'The brake pipe had been damaged in an earlier impact — isn't that what you said?'

'Aye, at first glance that's the way it looked. But someone had pulled the pipe down, cut it on the upper side, then used a rock to bash it back up against the chassis. It was made to

261

look like an accident, by someone who knows about cars.'

'Sounds like a replay of Bridie's crash. That was somehow made to look like an accident — '

'It *was* an accident.'

'No. I believe you killed her. You made a terrible mistake: you thought Ray Coghlan was driving the truck; he had taken your wife and you wanted him dead. And I believe that, the next night, you and a helper somehow got Ray Coghlan under that truck and rigged a trap that Andrew Keay unwittingly sprang for you — '

'You're talking bloody nonsense; I was in Oban that night — '

'There's a way around that. You were there, in the workshop, and I believe your helper was Andrew Keay.'

'Keay?' His bearded face was incredulous. 'You're talking utter bollocks.'

'No. He was probably tricked into it, told it was some kind of prank. Agreed to it because Coghlan was so universally hated. And I think that after he had driven his Suzuki away and brought the truck crashing down on top of Coghlan, he was too scared to own up. Or maybe convinced himself there was no point. But if he was the man who helped set up the trap, then he knows the name of the killer.'

McCafferey grinned fiercely. 'That lets me out then. I wasnae bloody there, pal — '

'Not only did you murder your estranged wife and Ray Coghlan,' I went on, 'but you also murdered Jim Gorrie when you realized he was about to spill the beans. He'd seen something, figured something out, knew you'd killed Coghlan — '

'Balls.'

'I saw him a short time before he was murdered. He looked straight at me, told me he'd talk to me later.'

'Pure, unadulterated bloody crap. In the first place, I was behind Bridie all the way from Craignure to the switch. The roads were empty, and it was Bridie who made a terrible mistake: there was black ice and poor visibility and she banged on the brakes with the inevitable result. As for Coghlan' — he shook his head, his eyes black boiling with black rage — 'I wish to God I had been the man to kill him, but everybody knows on that night I was elsewhere — '

'By fast boat,' I said, 'Oban is no more than half an hour away.'

His head shot up.

'If you think that,' he said, 'you're out of your bloody mind. D'you not think I can prove where I was?'

'We'll see.' I sipped coffee, watched

McCafferey lift his mug with shaking hands and said, 'If you didn't kill Gorrie, who did?'

'The same man who murdered Ray Coghlan.'

'You murdered Coghlan.'

'Oh for Christ's sake, I'm off out of here . . . '

The chair clattered to the floor as he stood up. He stepped back too quickly, banged his heel against it and almost fell. Then he turned and stumbled blindly towards the blanketed doorway.

'There's nowhere to run, Dougie.'

'Away tae fuck.'

'What about your mother? Who would want her dead?'

He lurched in the doorway, stopped, swaying, the blanket draped across his broad shoulders like a grubby cape.

'You'll no doubt find out soon enough, so to save time I'll tell you now that in her will she leaves everything to me.' He grinned wildly. 'Knowing that, you and the polis will then have to work out if it was me killed her for the money, or the others who killed her out of spite when they discovered they were going to be left with bugger all.'

*　　*　　*

'You handled that well,' Calum said.

'It's a knack. Comes with experience.'

'And you really believe McCafferey took a fast boat back here to murder Coghlan?'

'I don't know.'

'So you're up to your old tricks, poking a stick into a wasps' nest to see what happens?'

'It got us something, didn't it?'

'Yeah, he coughed up about the will bein' in his favour,' Stan said, 'an' the others getting' sod all. But he's got to be wrong about them killin' her out of spite. If they did that, he'd still benefit, wouldn' he?'

'Oh, he's wrong about the reason,' I said, 'but, you know, without really meaning to he could have given us the names of Peggy's killers.'

'Those two kids?' Stan said. 'Lachlan and Nellie.'

'Fit, in their twenties. And there was a lot of grief and anger in that young woman.'

Calum was nodding, mentally weighing up the possibilities.

'Dougie's motive's obvious; what about theirs?'

'Nellie said Stuart McBride, their father, drank himself to death. He loved his wife, but couldn't live with her.'

'Ah ha,' Calum said. 'She was thought to be involved in the death of her first husband.

Stuart lost money and earned her contempt. Then he remembered those rumours . . . '

'If he died a broken man,' I said, 'would Lachlan and Nellie blame Peggy?'

'Apparently they watched him go downhill for two years. You said Nellie keeps his ashes in her house in a wee urn. They'll be a constant reminder to both of them of a drawn-out tragedy. Oh, yes, they'd blame Peggy.'

'Ah, but enough to take steps to avenge their father's death?'

'I don't know about Nellie,' Calum said, 'but Lachlan is a definite weirdo.'

'Yeah, but we're facin' the same problem,' Stan said. 'Dougie was off the island when the truck fell on Coghlan's head, an' wasn't Lachlan off the island when Peggy was murdered?'

'Yes, *and* when her cottage was fire-bombed,' I said. 'But what about Nellie? If he could take the ferry one way to create an alibi, she could surely take it the other to commit murder.'

'Nah.' Stan was shaking his head. He'd finished his cigarette and was rolling another. 'If Nellie did it, she must've had help. The old girl was hangin' under those stairs. Short of makin' her walk up a ladder and jump off, there's no way Nellie could've worked it.'

Calum gathered up three mugs, took them over to the stove and lit the gas under the hot kettle.

'I think you will find when you check,' he said, 'that Nellie McBride did not take the ferry across on that particular night. I'd be very surprised if she's been across to Mull in recent times.'

'If you're right,' I said, 'we're left with Lachlan, and we know he couldn't have done it.'

'Do we?'

Stan had a fresh roll-up dangling from his lips and was watching Calum pour the coffee.

'We do,' I said. 'Don't we?'

'If Dougie could commit the perfect murder,' Stan said, 'so could they.'

'Jesus Christ,' Calum said, almost bouncing the filled mugs on the table. 'Start him off on that Bridie Button caper again and he'll be out there sniffing around Maddock's Switch like a bloodhound — '

'All right, all right,' I said, pulling a face. 'Sian as good as told me to leave Bridie's death alone when she suggested I concentrate on the one straightforward murder: Jim Gorrie's. Trouble is, I'm pretty certain Gorrie's murder's connected to Coghlan's — and Bridie's, but we won't mention that. I'm sure Gorrie saw something the night

Coghlan died; he was going to talk to me about it, and somebody leaped in double quick to keep him quiet. And therein lies the problem.'

'Because you'd still like to believe Dougie murdered Coghlan,' Calum said, 'and that death's obviously connected to Bridie — if only because her death provided Dougie with the motive that sent him after Coghlan.'

'We're goin' round in bloody circles,' Stan said, reaching for his coffee. 'It's make your mind up time. Which one're we going to concentrate on?'

'He's got a little bit more than that to ponder on,' Calum said.

I frowned. 'What does that mean?'

'If you're right, and Dougie McCafferey murdered Jim Gorrie because he was about to blow the gaff, that makes him very dangerous indeed. Now, if you're right about Keay helping move Coghlan's limp, intoxicated form — '

'There's another thing,' Stan cut in. 'About Dr Andrew Keay. He was at Peggy's that night. A friend took him out there on a professional visit, remember? An' remember how when we were talkin' about this we were wonderin' how he got back to Craignure? Like, if the friend stayed at Peggy's with him, or what? Well, Coghlan was in the same boat, wasn't he?'

'No transport.' I looked at Calum, saw the quick understanding in his grey eyes. 'Coghlan's truck was in the garage, wrecked, Keay's 4 x 4 was outside waiting to be picked up. So you're saying, Stan, that perhaps Peggy took both of them back to Craignure?'

'Why not? It'd put all three of them close to the scene of the crime, wouldn't it?'

'And that,' I said, 'throws another name into the pot.'

'Indeed it does,' Calum said softly.

'I know Peggy was under suspicion thirty years ago when Tom McCafferey died, but Coghlan's death was so cunningly planned, so horrific in its nature — '

'That we never considered her as a suspect,' Calum said. 'Fine, I agree, and even now we shouldn't jump the gun: her taking Coghlan and Keay back to Craignure could have been a gesture of thanks for Keay's ministrations, and the pleasure of both men's company. And even if she was there in the workshop when Coghlan was being dragged under the truck, that certainly doesn't rule out Dougie. Which brings me back to the point I was making: if Keay was there, and helped move Coghlan's limp, intoxicated — '

'Or drugged,' Stan said.

'Yes, or drugged form, then clearly Dr Keay knows the name of the murderer. The murderer already knew he knew, but now it seems likely he's going to find out that *we* know.'

'Not necessarily,' I said. 'What if Dougie's not the killer?'

'Doesn't matter. It's highly likely he knows the killer, and will pass on what's been said here.'

'Damn. So I've made Keay a candidate for the chop?'

'Indeed you have. Furthermore, what d'you imagine Dougie McCafferey — guilty or innocent — is going to have planned for you, now you've as good as accused him of, not one, but two murders?'

24

I spent the night in Sian's room, snuggled down inside my sleeping bag and listening to the inevitable rain rattling on the rusting tin roof, the wind moaning eerily across the high moors. And for an hour at least, with the tip of my nose as cold as a puppy's and the edge of the sleeping-bag damp with my warm condensed breath, I stared into the darkness trying to make sense of the latest confused discussion.

While heeding advice and deliberately pushing the death of Bridie Button into the background, I'd gradually reached the conviction that the McCaffereys and the McBrides were deeply involved in murder. My problem was that I could find suspects with very real motives for the murders of Ray Coghlan and Peggy McBride; I could at least hazard a guess as to why Jim Gorrie had been killed, but the people with clear motives seemed to have no opportunity to carry out the crimes.

I had for some time been fairly certain that Dougie McCafferey had murdered Ray Coghlan, yet Dougie seemed confident he could prove that he was on the Scottish mainland when his hated enemy met his death.

Nellie McBride's story had set me thinking that perhaps she and her brother Lachlan had conspired to murder their mother, but Lachlan had been in Oban when Peggy was hanged, and Calum believed Nellie would have the same alibi. I agreed with him.

But what of Andrew Keay? I had spoken to the man once, and knew nothing of his background. Could he have been another of Coghlan's victims? Was Stan Jones right when he said Keay could have carried out Coghlan's murder entirely on his own, craftily setting it up to look as if he himself had been the victim of a set up?

And what about Peggy McBride? Had she used her Volkswagen Golf to bring both Coghlan and Keay back into Craignure on that fatal night, taken both men up to her son's garage and used the doctor to assist her in cold-blooded murder? Had she conned Keay into it, telling him they were playing a cruel but harmless prank on Coghlan to pay him back for his many sins, then set the trap when Keay had departed for the village? Or was it more than a con? Did she have some hold over Keay?

Unanswerable questions. I could be close

to the truth, or a million miles away and floundering. Which brought me finally to Jim Gorrie, the one person I believed might have been able to unlock at least part of one mystery.

If I was right, Gorrie had died because he was about to blow the whistle on Coghlan's killer. Manual work of any kind allows the mind to wander freely, and he had been absorbed in preparations to weld a silencer when he'd remembered something, looked across at me and signalled a desire to talk. But what had he remembered? What had he seen on the night of Coghlan's death? Who had he seen, and what were they doing?

Again, no answer. Peggy McBride was dead. Jim Gorrie was dead. And now, by poking a blunt stick in a wasps' nest, it was possible I had put another man in danger.

I drifted into an uneasy sleep beset by troubles, and awoke to find them multiplied.

25

Tuesday

I awoke in the morning (quite late) convinced that thoughts that had followed me to my sleep had been way too pessimistic. Dougie had been half sloshed when he drove back down to Salen. If he'd made it back to his garage he would have gone straight upstairs and collapsed on his bed; if he hadn't made it that far he'd probably pulled into a lay-by and slept in the car. Either way, Keay would still be alive and well, leaving me with time to whisper a timely warning in his ear.

It was with that in mind that after, yes, a late breakfast, I walked outside into the swirling mist on the fringes of which grey sheep moved like ghosts, fired up my mobile and spent a few minutes chasing the telephone number of Keay's surgery. When it was tracked down, I asked the operator to put me through.

I was answered by a harassed female voice.

'Good morning,' I said, 'could I speak to Dr Keay?'

'I'm sorry, Dr Keay's not in yet.'

I glanced at my watch. Ten o'clock.

'What time is his morning surgery?'

'It should start at nine o'clock, but — '

'He hasn't arrived?'

'That's right. We're quite busy, so we're keeping our fingers crossed.'

'Doesn't he live there? Over the shop?'

'I'm sorry — '

'Have you tried to get in touch with him? Find out where he is? Look, I'm sorry if I sound short, but this is very important. I really do need to talk to him.'

'Yes, all right, he does live here. But it seems he . . . he didn't sleep here last night.' There was a pause, during which I closed my eyes. 'Nobody's seen him. Nobody at all. Not since Monday morning's surgery. I really do not *know* what we're going to do . . . '

When I opened my eyes the phone was dead and DI Vales's Volvo was rocking its way up the track from Salen, DS Hills glowering in the passenger seat.

★   ★   ★

The steamy, cramped kitchen was crowded and hot. Calum and Jones the Van, both grey and bearded, both wearing smeared glasses, were bent over the table eating steaming porridge off tin plates, spoons clattering, their mugs of coffee contributing to the concentric pattern of dark rings on the boards. Wan light already diffused by the mist was further filtered by cobwebs draped across the window panes like the frills of grubby petticoats. The pressure lamp and stove were hissing wearily. Chairs scraped on the floor as I dragged them through the hanging blanket like a bored waiter in a greasy spoon, and cocked an enquiring eye at the two detectives.

Hills had already found two more tin mugs and spooned instant coffee and was about to pour on boiling water. He opted for a position between stove and door. Vales indicated the table, and I placed a chair behind her knees, took out my handkerchief and ceremoniously whisked non-existent dust from the seat. She scowled, then sat down and accepted the mug of coffee proffered by her sergeant. She took a quick drink, shook her head in disgust — at the supermarket instant coffee, the bothy's unique ambience, the stamp of the company she was keeping? — then turned to glare at me.

Leaning against the wall close to the blanketed doorway, I shrugged and spread my hands.

'Honestly, we'd decorate and put down fitted carpets and really make the place cosy,'

I said, 'but as we're not planning on staying — '

'You've got that absolutely right.'

'What the hell did you say to him?' Detective Sergeant Hills said.

'Who?'

'Don't piss me about.'

'Dougie McCafferey was here last night. We accused him of a couple of murders.'

'Not McCafferey, you pillock. Andrew Keay. Sunday afternoon you walked on to McCafferey's forecourt, picked up your car and drove away. You went from there to the Spar shop where you bought a bottle of Islay single malt whisky. You then drove to Keay's surgery. You spoke to the doctor for approximately half an hour before leaving and coming here.'

'Where I enjoyed a marvellous chicken curry washed down — '

'What did you say to Keay?'

'I described a number of hypothetical situations, then homed in on one that had Andrew Keay helping a killer place Ray Coghlan under his truck.'

'Helping how?'

'Drugs were mentioned.'

DI Vales seemed to burn her hand on hot tin. Her mug banged down, and she swore softly.

'You're living in bloody fairyland,' she said.

'Oh no.' I shook my head. 'Did you know Keay was called to Peggy McBride's cottage that night?'

'Christ, don't tell me you're bringing her into it?'

'Did you?'

'Yes.'

Her eyes were fixed on mine; there was no trace of the thaw I'd noticed at our last meeting. The heel of her hand was on the table, the tip of her middle finger tracing small circles in the pool of warm coffee she'd spilt.

'We know Keay was at Peggy's cottage,' she said, 'we know he treated her for mild indigestion' — she held up a warning hand — 'and we know Ray Coghlan was there. We know the three of them sat talking with increasingly well-oiled vocal chords. We know that Peggy, her indigestion much improved, drove both men back to Craignure.'

'We'd almost got there, now you've confirmed it. But, with hindsight, doesn't that now strike you as odd?'

'Why?'

'Ray Coghlan drops in to see Peggy McBride. She has a convenient attack of indigestion, which necessitates a phone call to Dr Keay. They sit in her cosy lounge while she washes down Rennies with draughts of whisky. Indigestion cured, she transports both men to Craignure. A couple of hours later, Keay drives his Suzuki away from McCafferey's workshop door and brings the truck down on Coghlan's head. A *week* or so later, and Peggy McBride's dead. Now Andrew Keay's — '

'Gone,' Vales said. 'We know not where. But that's down to your — '

'Insensitivity? Lack of tact?' I shook my head. 'No. What we've got is another bizarre twist. Late Sunday afternoon I walk in and suggest Keay played a bigger part in Ray Coghlan's murder than unwittingly springing the trap — if the springing ever was unwitting. Monday morning he finishes surgery and, like Captain Oates, walks off into the mist.' I pulled a face. 'Come on, he's a doctor, a professional man. If I'd been talking a lot of hot air he'd have thrown me out when I made what amounted to an accusation.'

'What *did* he say? How *did* he react?'

'Said he couldn't have done it. Brought up the phone call from Peggy McBride. Suggested that when the murderer was setting his trap, he, Keay, was many miles away — meaning he was at Peggy's cottage sorting out her digestive system. Which, far from proving his innocence, actually brings up the possibility of his deep embroilment in a murderous plot. Something I've no doubt he was quick to realize when he began thinking back over what had been said.'

'Did he now?' Vales said softly.

Tin clattered as Calum carried empty plates over to the stone sink. Stan Jones used his feet to work his chair away from the table and began rolling a cigarette. DI Vales watched with distaste, tried to humiliate Stan with a withering look and failed utterly. Then she waited with growing impatience as Calum poured boiled water from the kettle over the dishes and left them to soak. He turned to face us, leaned back against the sink and fired up a Schimmelpenninck. And grinned at the fuming DI.

'Have you noticed that's the only way to get those hard ridges of dried porridge off plates of any kind?'

'Shut up,' Vales said, 'and listen. All three of you.'

She was already rising from her chair as she spoke, looming large in another of the patterned, dark-green trouser suits that seemed to be some kind of personal statement. Face grim, she walked as far away as she could in that small room, then turned so that everyone present was in her field of view.

I eased my position against the wall and braced myself for the tirade.

'Everything you've said so far has been wrong,' she said. 'You began with Dougie McCafferey — '

'Sole beneficiary in Peggy McBride's will — '

'I said shut up.'

She stopped, waited, watched my mouth close and my fingers mime closing a zip fastener while trying to avoid my eyes. *Her* eyes were telling me she'd heard what I'd said, the information was new to her, but she wouldn't admit it and wouldn't give ground. I couldn't resist a smile. Her face darkened.

'Everything you've said,' she repeated, 'has been wrong. First, Dougie McCafferey: he was in Oban when Ray Coghlan was murdered. No question.'

I raised a hand. 'Permission to speak?'

Her face went pink at the military jargon. Refusal was in her eyes, but she was a detective and I'd already offered information that would either simplify or complicate her investigation. There might be more, better or worse. Reluctantly, she nodded.

'By fast boat, Oban to Mull and return is under an hour.'

'Didn't happen. McCafferey was there, in town, and he stayed there. There's woman — '

281

She broke off, left the rest to our imaginations.

'OK, that's one murder. What about Gorrie's?'

'McCafferey and Gorrie worked together, they were the best of mates. We're still checking, but I can assure you Dougie McCafferey didn't murder Jim Gorrie.'

She looked around the room, took in Calum, now stretched out in a straight chair with ankles crossed, glasses on the end of his nose; Jones the Van, a bent roll-up in his thin lips, ash on his shirt front, eyes gleaming with intelligence.

She was back with me again, about to speak, when my mobile rang. I lifted an apologetic hand. Vales rolled her eyes and went back to her chair at the table. It creaked under her weight. I dug out the phone and looked at the display. Sian.

'Stan.' I tossed him the phone. He caught it deftly. 'Take that for me, will you. It's personal.'

He pushed his chair back. Trailing smoke, he padded across the room and ducked out through the blanket.

I nodded at Vales. 'Off you go.'

But she'd had enough. She nodded to Hills. 'You do this bit.'

'The other day you were linking Lachlan

McBride to his mother's murder,' Hills said. 'You were told by my colleague that we could confirm McBride took the four o'clock ferry to Oban, and you were also told the time of his mother's death ruled him out — '

'Time of death's always open to debate.'

'Not in this case.'

'What sets this one in stone?'

'The old girl put up a fight. Have you seen the expensive watch she wore?'

I nodded. 'It was one of the first things I noticed.'

'She broke it as she fought for her life. It had stopped at ten to midnight. The struggle took place in Dougie's room. Furniture had been overturned, a railway clock had been knocked off the wall — '

'I spoke to her in Dougie's room. I also noticed that clock — and something about it.'

'Right.' Hills looked at me warily, then at Vales, then back at me, probably wondering what I was talking about. 'It was an old clock,' he said. 'A relic. The glass had shattered, the clock had stopped.'

'If you tell me that clock stopped at ten to midnight, I won't believe you.'

'It hadn't.' There was relief in his eyes. He'd caught up, and knew what I was getting at. 'It had stopped at eleven-forty — ten minutes before Peggy's watch.' He allowed herself a thin smile. 'But you were expecting that, weren't you?'

I nodded. 'When I saw that clock, it was ten minutes slow. So everything fits.'

'Satisfied?'

I shrugged. 'Not really. If Peggy struggled, her killer could be marked. Are you looking for a man with facial scratches, bruises?'

Hills was so disgusted he turned his head away without answering.

'OK, sorry, that was stupid. But there's also this: you may have ruled out the fast boat making trips between Mull and Oban under cover of darkness for Dougie McCafferey, but it still could have worked for Lachlan — and I'm pretty sure you haven't checked his precise whereabouts between those evening and morning ferries.'

'Precise whereabouts — no,' Hills said. 'But he was spoken to by police in Oban on another matter, gave them certain information, and CCTV cameras on the outskirts of the town picked up his Mercedes leaving town at 6.45 Sunday night. It's possible, though highly unlikely, that he drove back into town some other way. Cameras would have picked him up on all routes into the town. They didn't. Unless he's got more brains than we give him credit for, Lachlan

McBride could not have murdered his mother.'

'Forensics back up everything we've said,' Vales said, climbing to her feet and making for the door with a nod to her sergeant. 'Nothing at any of the crime scenes points to any of your suspects. You've been building castles in the air, Scott. For all the good you've done on Mull, you and your friends might as well have spent your time on the beach with buckets and spades, building something much more substantial out of sand.'

26

I couldn't persuade tight-lipped coppers to
tell me what information Lachlan had given
to police in Oban, or if it had a bearing on
where he had been going when he drove out
of Oban that Sunday night. They told me that
as his destination had no bearing on the case,
it was none of my business. Nor indeed
would it have been if it had been relevant, as
Vales made absolutely clear to me before she
drove away. She had mellowed again — I was
beginning to realize her bark was worse than
her bite and didn't last long anyway — but
she did stress once again that we could
remain on the island only for as long as we
kept our noses out of police affairs.

Which of course raised the interesting
question of how they would know if we
didn't?

Although I thought about it and came close
to opening my mouth, in the end I decided
against repeating Dougie McCafferey's assertion that the braking system on Sian's
Shogun had been deliberately sabotaged.
Throwing another crime into the mix wasn't
going to help the police, and it wasn't going

to help us. Besides, if it had been attempted murder, it was a failed attempt. Lachlan McBride was to blame, almost certainly, but although he had left Mull and could be in Oban, I felt confident that Sian was safe where she was, in hospital.

When I walked in after waving off to the two detectives, Stan Jones tossed my mobile phone to me.

'She's being allowed out on bail,' he said. 'Get the ferry at one o'clock, pick her up in a fast car and get back here before they change their minds.'

'At least with her back on the job we'll get results,' Calum said.

'And that,' I said, 'is probably the first sensible thing that's been said in this room all morning.'

★ ★ ★

She was battered and bruised in multi-coloured ways and carried one wing in a white sling, but she walked out of there light of foot and without a limp and I had great difficulty stopping her from running.

Despite her joy at leaving, she did take time to bid farewell to the nurses at their busy station. Afterwards, on our way to the lift, she called my attention to a particularly attractive, dark-haired sister.

'That was Jackie Green,' she said, 'the sister who phoned you when I was admitted. I forgot to tell you, our friend Lachlan was in here on Sunday, talking to her.'

'Good God! So he does have normal relationships?'

She chuckled. 'Apparently. I was pretty groggy. He waved and said 'Hi', but didn't come over to my bed. Probably scared that even in my weakened state I'd bop him on the nose.'

'I've seen that done in the army by a man with a cast on his arm. A brilliant makeshift club.'

'A sling wouldn't have the same clout.'

I winced. 'Ouch. You wouldn't use it twice. However, I did know a man — '

She punched me hard on the arm.

We'd reached the ground floor. I said, 'I was going to suggest we pop along to GAME ON and talk to Lachlan and his sister.'

'But?'

'You're a shadow of your former self. A better idea is back to the bothy.'

'And?'

'Calum's convinced your reappearance will see the return of positive results. I've bet him a tenner — '

The second punch nearly broke my arm.

★ ★ ★

A fine hard snow had begun to fall when I drove off the ferry at Craignure and turned towards Salen. Within a couple of minutes Sian was slumped sideways fast asleep, all punched out, and I drove at speed and in comfortable silence with the miles slipping away beneath the Quattro's wheels as snow swirled like sand drifting across a windswept beach.

I had a strong feeling that something was about to break. The imp of the perverse was dancing in glee, well aware that if those in authority tried to convince me of one thing, I would immediately believe the opposite. No longer daring to name names even in my thoughts for fear of disturbing the delicate balance that I was convinced was tipping my way, I still stubbornly refused to believe that all my theories were wrong.

When I slithered to an untidy halt outside the bothy I was in buoyant mood. Calum emerged like a grey bearded mountain guerrilla to help a weary Soldier Blue across the thin snow and into the warmth without jarring the healing collar bone, and I was moved almost to tears to see the way he and Stan had prepared her room.

Lop-sided with pain, Sian nevertheless

grinned as she cast her eyes over the camp bed with its plumped up sleeping bag, the gas heater in the corner of the room, the makeshift carpets bearing faded stencilled lettering from their time as hemp grain sacks, the crate at the head of the bed with a small pressure lamp throwing low light on Stan's tiny Roberts battery radio and a carafe of water that had surely been bought only that afternoon.

'You two,' she said softly, shakily. 'What *are* you like?'

'Mercenary,' Stan said from the doorway. 'Your rent's just doubled.'

'However,' Calum said, 'a reduction can be negotiated based on the cleaning satisfactorily carried out and the number of meals cooked.'

Banter in a similar vein bounced back and forth while she emptied her overnight bag on to the shelves in the orange-box bedside table, but underlying the good-natured joshing I could sense a lot of tension in Calum and Stan. Sian noticed nothing out of the ordinary, wanting only to get her head down. For me, after convincing myself on the drive in that a breakthrough was imminent, the realization that I had almost certainly got it right was intoxicating.

Once I caught Calum's eye, and he nodded almost imperceptibly. Then, sensing that they were rapidly wearing out a very different Sian Laidlaw from the woman used to scaling the high peaks of Snowdonia, usually before breakfast, he clamped a hand over Stan's mouth and bundled him out of the room.

I remained behind. Words between Sian and me were few, interspersed with squeaks of protest or murmurs of apology as I helped her awkwardly and painfully out of sling and clothes, eased her gently into the sleeping-bag and went down on one knee to hold her close — with loving care — and kiss her goodnight.

'I was doing a lot of thinking in hospital,' she said muzzily.

'Not now,' I said. 'Sleep beckons.'

'It was important, Jack. Something I thought of — and now I can't remember what it was.'

'It'll come to you.'

'Important means urgent and means later could be too late.'

'Shh.'

I put a finger to her lips, leaned close, closed my eyes and pressed my cheek to hers. It was soft and warm. I was nuzzling a warm, purring kitten.

When I opened my eyes and drew back, she was asleep.

I went out, closed the door quietly behind me then crossed the big room and slipped through the blanket and into the kitchen. Calum plonked a mug of coffee on the table, gestured to the chair.

'I feel in the mood,' I said, 'for something a bit stronger than drab old supermarket instant.'

'Inadvisable in the light of what's occurred,' Calum said. 'I have a feeling you're going to need your wits about you, which is difficult for you even with a clear head.' He grinned. 'We've had a telephone call from Gregor Neill — remember, the old boy who lives with his wife up in the hills and watches fatal road accidents?'

'Ah ha,' I said. 'He's remembered something he saw relating to Bridie Button's crash.'

'I asked him that. He said no.'

'So what then? What did he tell you?'

'Not a bloody thing,' Stan said. 'He'll tell you when he sees you, he said. And that's tonight. Like, right now.'

★　★　★

After quickly munching through a thick ham sandwich washed down with two mugs of coffee I jumped into the Quattro with Calum leaving a contented Stan Jones babysitting in the bothy.

Gregor Neill had given Calum a rough idea of how to get to his cottage, which he said would be more than sufficient because, in his rolling words, 'You're verry unlikely to hit any Spaghetti Junction affairs in this neck of the woods'.

I already had a rough idea of the cottage's location because I knew it overlooked Maddock's Switch from the north. Neill had told Calum to take a single lane dirt track that would lead us off the A849 shortly after we drew level with Loch Squabain. I was lucky. The fine snow had ceased to fall, a pale moon veiled by thin high clouds was gleaming on the loch's waters, and the gnarled oak tree Neill had picked out as our landmark was starkly outlined against the white moors.

'Two miles,' Calum said, peering ahead. 'Try and keep at least two of the four wheels on the road, my man.'

His words were spoken only partly in jest. With the passing of the clouds the temperature had plummeted, freezing the thin film of snow. Driving the Quattro up that track was like trying to ride up the Cresta Run on a bicycle with a puncture. By the time the lights of Gregor Neill's cottage's peeked over a hillock to greet us with their warm glow, Calum's tears of laughter were trickling into his beard and I was having so much fun I was reluctant to stop.

I did, of course. Behind a battered old Land Rover, and snazzy looking BMW.

'Two cars?' I said as we climbed out of the Quattro and the hairs in our nostrils stiffened with the cold.

'The Land Rover will be Gregor's.'

'Then he has a visitor.'

'At mention of which,' Calum said, crunching towards the front door, 'all becomes clear. To me, at least, but what about you? Does the word Booby jog your memory.'

'Bloody hell,' I said, stopping in mid-stride. 'Hubert Phillips and his card game. Gregor and his wife regularly play cards with Dr Andrew Keay, don't they? If he wanted to lie low, then this has to be the ideal place.'

27

The heat that enveloped us like a fuggy blanket as we walked into the cottage was redolent of dust and stale cooking, of burning logs and paraffin. We passed one heater in the hall, saw another through the open door of the front living room from where, I knew, Gregor Neill and his wife had watched Bridie Button die.

Gregor was an old man with hair like cobwebs draped over a shiny brown stone, pale sunken eyes and a bent posture that caused sensitive onlookers to wince and thrust out a supportive hand. He gestured us towards the open door, slopped away down the hall on slippers like dead beavers and disappeared into what I guessed was the kitchen. He'd said not a word.

When we walked into the living room, Andrew Keay was sitting waiting for us.

'You were quick.'

'Mm. But was it worth the effort?'

He shrugged. 'I'm sure the police will think so.'

'If this is to do with murder, why didn't you call them?'

His smile was tired. 'When we spoke you said you were the expert — '

'I tend to exaggerate.'

'Perhaps, but you got remarkably close to the truth. I thought you deserved to hear the full story of what happened on that night.'

'That would make a welcome change; probably a first for us, on Mull.' I moved closer to the fire. 'I've brought along my learned colleague, Calum Wick. He took Gregor's phone call.'

They nodded to each other. Keay was managing to look uncomfortable and uneasy in a comfortable easy chair near a log fire settling like glowing lava in the dog grate. Calum stretched out in the chair opposite the doctor. I sat down on the big settee, facing the fire, under a central light fitting made from an old wagon wheel. The room's walls were darkly panelled and hung with ancient oils in which shaggy highland cattle stood patiently in still mountain pools. Away to my left, heavy red curtains covered the windows that would afford views over the distant road to Fionnphort and the island of Iona.

'I wouldn't be doing this, wouldn't be talking to you again,' Keay said, 'if I hadn't remembered being called in my professional capacity to treat Peggy McBride.'

'Surely we've talked about that already?'

'That was the first time. Severe indigestion. Which is what Peggy said she had, and what I believed when I got a lift out to Salen.' He took a deep breath, shook his head, clearly overcome by emotion.

'Peggy McBride called me out that night,' he said when he'd recovered, 'not because she was ill, but because she wanted help killing Ray Coghlan.'

'Christ,' Calum said. 'The woman hired us. What the hell was she playing at?'

'She wanted us to concentrate on proving Coghlan murdered Bridie Button, which I believe is a ridiculous notion,' I said. 'With all that hate burning inside her she probably forgot she could be in danger.'

Keay was nodding. 'Of course, she didn't tell me she wanted to kill him,' he said. 'When I got to the cottage, Coghlan was sitting by the fire. Peggy took me into the kitchen, supposedly for me to administer the indigestion remedy, and she told me she wanted to play an elaborate prank on the man. A *wicked* prank, but one she felt he deserved. She wanted to get back at him for stealing her son's wife.'

'A thought springs to mind,' Calum said. 'If you knew the prank was wicked — no, more than that, bloody *dangerous* — why would you, a doctor, pillar of the community and all that, be willing to play along?'

Keay sighed. 'Because a long time ago, when Lachlan McBride was in his teens, I supplied him with certain substances.'

'Which of course leads me to ask why on earth would you do that?'

'And gets us nowhere.' Keay waited for Calum to realize he was not going to get an answer and spread his hands in defeat, then said, 'Certain substances came into it again, later that night, when Peggy had driven us to the garage. Coghlan was drunk, barely able to stand. We got him into the workshop and it was quite easy to . . . tranquillize him and make him comfortable.'

I grimaced. 'Nicely put.'

'And then,' Keay said, 'I walked down to the village.'

'Your Suzuki was there, outside. Why didn't you take it then?'

'The keys weren't there, nor in the workshop office. Peggy said she'd find them, leave them in the vehicle. As it was reasonably early, and I drop into the pub most nights, I agreed.'

'And left, leaving Peggy with Coghlan, in the workshop.'

'I thought nothing of it. The idea was that Ray Coghlan would wake up and howl the place down when he realized where he was

. . . or something like that. I didn't expect Peggy to stay; she told me she was going up to Dougie's rooms to wait for the fun to start.'

'Peggy McBride was sixty, a slender woman,' I said, frowning. 'Are you asking us to believe she set the trap on her own? Connected that wire rope to the vehicle stands with iron shackles? Fed the loop of cable out beneath the doors? Hooked it over your tow ball?'

'Her first husband owned that garage until the day he died. She'd helped him for many years, probably changed car tyres on her own when it was done the hard way with two tyre levers and a rubber mallet.'

'Mm.' I nodded. 'The first time I saw her I noticed her hands. Strong. Capable.'

'Capable of murder,' Keay said, 'and it was the hands that gave her away. You see, she must have been in too much of a hurry to look for leather gloves.'

'Ah.' I nodded understanding. 'This was the other time, the second time she needed your attention — and this time it was genuine?'

'That's right. Old Bowden cable or wire rope, whatever you want to call it, can tear the skin from your hands. Peggy's were severely lacerated. She called me to her cottage the day after Coghlan died, told me she had got tangled up in brambles.'

'And you believed her?'

'I — '

'Thought nothing of it?' Calum was clearly exasperated. 'OK, so go back a bit. When Coghlan turned up dead, did you not wonder what had gone on after you walked out of the workshop and set off for the village?'

'I thought someone else had come along, found Coghlan — '

'Jesus,' Calum said. 'Don't try that one on Jack here, because my friend never, ever, believes in coincidence.'

'I was in denial,' Keay said, his voice ineffably weary. 'Then, this afternoon' — he looked at me and nodded — 'yes, this afternoon, today, finally, I allowed myself to acknowledge what I had known all along: the injuries to Peggy McBride's hands led back to that old wire rope, and proved conclusively that she had arranged a clever trap that led to the death of Ray Coghlan.'

'How convenient,' I said, 'getting to the truth when Peggy McBride is dead.'

'Inconvenient for me,' Andrew Keay said. 'I'm left all on my own, an accessory to murder.'

* * *

300

I called DI Vales on her mobile when we got back to the bothy, told her that Andrew Keay was at Gregor Neill's cottage and had confessed to his part in the murder of Ray Coghlan.

'His part's already known,' she said. 'He's the poor bloody sucker who pulled the trigger.'

'If you want to stick with that analogy,' I said, 'then he was there even before the gun was loaded. With Peggy McBride. As he will tell you.'

I rang off. Stepped out on to the crackling film of snow. Followed Calum into the bothy and walked through to the warmth and growing familiarity of the kitchen.

Sian was there with Stan Jones, sitting at the table with her arm in its white cotton sling resting on the boards in front of her. Her fair hair was drawn tightly back into its usual pony-tail, but she had only one usable arm and I knew Stan's thin fingers must have helped her with the elastic band. She was watching me watching her, as always reading my mind. A gentle smile brought a slight curve to her lips, but her face was pale, her eyes haunted.

★　★　★

'You remembered what you were thinking about in hospital?'

'No. At least not the bit I meant. That's still floating around somewhere, possibly never to return. But there's something else.'

'As important?'

She nodded. 'Maybe more so. Remember I told you Lachlan McBride was in the hospital on Sunday?'

'I do. He was talking to that pretty nursing sister. Said hello to you, but didn't come over.'

'Actually, he didn't say hello to me.'

'He didn't?' I glanced across at Stan. He was looking down at fingers working on tobacco and paper. Sian's lower lip was trembling. She held it gently with her teeth.

'Then who *did* he say hello to, Soldier Blue?'

'*Whom,*' she said, and even as she smiled, her eyes flooded. 'He said hello to Siobhan, Jack. He slipped up, saw me, but his mind was on what he was going to do and he got the name wrong.'

'Jesus,' I said, agony in my voice. 'To get the name wrong, he had to know the one he blurted by mistake. And if he knows your sister's name, if it's familiar enough to be lodged in his brain — '

'That's what I'm saying: Lachlan McBride *must* be the man who attacked Siobhan. And I'm responsible.'

'Oh, come on.'

'Jack, think what happened. Lachlan propositioned me. I rebuffed him.' She flashed a tremulous look at Stan, who smiled and winked encouragement. 'That night he asked for time off. He said he had to go to Oban to see his sick sister. Instead, he must have driven to Liverpool and . . . ' She swallowed, shook her head in numb despair.

'If that is how it happened,' I said, 'how did he get from Siobhan to you? And why?'

'All I can think of,' Sian said, swallowing, 'is that he saw my photograph at Siobhan's house, and became obsessed. Remember, she got fed up with his harassment, called him in to talk it over — and suddenly the stalking stopped.' She smiled shakily. 'Sounds big-headed, doesn't it? One glimpse of me, and not even in the flesh.'

'Could he trace you from a picture?'

'Didn't have to. If he wheedled my name out of Siobhan, he could Google me. I'm there on the internet, linked to outward bound courses. In fact, events just about prove that's the way he did it. I first knew him as Mark Deeson on that course at Cape Wrath — and that was very soon after he stopped stalking Siobhan. She knew him as Alan Spence, we know him as Lachlan McBride . . . '

It was like one of those modern TV adverts where lots of odd-shaped coloured bits and pieces miraculously float together to form something totally unexpected and mind-blowing. Snippets of information tucked away in various pockets of my brain suddenly burst forth, swirled, combined and began to arrange and rearrange themselves into a story of horror. An unfinished story.

I sat down at the table and took Sian's good hand in mine. She gripped it, ducked her head to wipe her eyes on the cloth of her sling, gave me a bright, tremulous smile.

I looked at Calum. 'Do we know where Lachlan is now?'

He shook his head, no.

I dug out my mobile phone, punched in some numbers, waited impatiently.

'Mike?'

'Ill Wind,' a thick, clogged voice answered. 'Are you operatin' in a different time zone up there?'

'Mike, have you been withholding information?'

'Wrong way round, old son. *You* withhold, but I have no reason to disclose *anything* to amateur PIs.'

'This concerns the attack on Siobhan Laidlaw. What make of car was caught on CCTV pulling out of Long Lane?'

'Picture was rubbish, not enough light, jerky, couldn't make it out — '

'Bollocks. Look, Mike, I know you're keeping that information under wraps so the press don't get hold of it and let the cat out of the bag, but I think I can give you the name of the stalker. Real name.'

There was a soft rustle as of a duvet and I pictured the Liverpool detective sitting up and swinging his legs off the bed, heard a feminine voice raised in sleepy protest, the sound of a drawer sliding open and a rattle and the snap of elastic as Haggard grabbed pen and black notebook.

'Go on, let's have it.'

'No. First I need to know — '

'Take heed, Ill Wind: you withhold information at your peril.'

'I know that. But I said I *think* I can give you his name. I need to know for sure before I make what could be accusations, and I cannot be sure until you tell me — '

'A Merc sports. Silver. An', believe me, the CCTV was definitely too dark an' grainy to read the number plate.'

'The make's enough. That's given me enough reason to push on and make more enquiries.'

'What's that mean? You stroll up an' ask this feller if he did it?'

'I'd probably do that, if I knew where he was. But I don't, so I need to think hard.'

'Don't make me laugh. Willie Vine thinks. That Gay Gordon of yours does, once in a while. But you — '

'Thanks, Mike. I'll get back to you.'

'When?'

I hesitated. 'Let's put it this way: don't go back to sleep.'

I clicked off and found myself cloaked in silence and the focus of rapt attention. Two men with grey-streaked beards and a woman sporting purple facial bruises fading to yellow and her arm in a sling were watching me with impatience belied by their stillness. Calum was by the stove, caught and frozen on the turn with his fingers poked through the handles of four tin mugs I knew were very hot. Stan Jones had a rolled cigarette in open gummed paper poised close to his lips, the tip of his tongue out ready to begin licking. Sian was watching me with lips parted, eyes imploring yet terrified at the thought of what I might say. She didn't appear to be breathing.

'The CCTV near Long Lane,' I said, as triumphant as Chamberlain returning from Munich, 'picked up a silver Mercedes sports car. Right time. Right place.'

'Gotcha,' Stan Jones said — then grinned

sheepishly as the half-formed cigarette came apart in his fingers.

I pulled a face. 'I'd like to think so, but there is one big problem. As far as we know, Lachlan McBride *was* in Oban with his sister on the night Siobhan was attacked in Liverpool.'

Calum placed the four steaming tin mugs on the table and made a great show of splashing whisky into each. He sat down, drank deeply and with relish, then looked at me through steamed-up glasses.

'Who says?'

'He did, several times. Lachlan. So did she. Nellie, his sister.'

'She would, wouldn't she?' Stan said. 'Doesn' mean he was. Not all night.'

'The day after Siobhan was attacked,' Calum said, 'you and Sian drove to Liverpool in the morning and were back here the very same night. You did that in a crap Audi Quattro. Imagine what a man could do in a Mercedes sports car. A *young* man who, unlike you, is capable of driving very fast indeed.'

'How do we prove it?'

'Go 'n' ask her,' Stan said. 'Third degree, bright light in the eyes . . . '

'If she sticks to her story, it's their word against ours.'

307

Sian was looking thoughtful. She frowned into her drink, then looked at me.

'Didn't you say when you saw Lachlan at the garage that first day on Mull — Friday, wasn't it? — that he'd had his car in earlier for MOT?'

'Yes, he had, according to Jim Gorrie.'

'And then when you saw him again on Saturday, he was in again, this time for repairs.'

'That's right. His alternator had packed up, he'd probably run his battery flat.'

'In that case his mileage will have been recorded, Jack,' Calum said, instantly realizing what Sian was getting at. 'Twice. Immediately before Oban, immediately after.'

'If he went to Oban an' stayed there he'll've done no more than ten miles,' Stan said.

'On the other hand,' Sian said.

I pushed away from the table and stood up.

'I want two volunteers,' I said. 'You, and you.' I pointed at Calum and Stan. 'Finish your coffee, don dark clothing — '

'That'll make us really invisible in the snow,' Stan said.

' — and prepare for action. We are proceeding to Craignure by fast car where we will obtain from McCafferey's garage, by the most suitable means at our disposal, documents vital to the success of our investigation.'

'We break in,' Calum said.

'If Dougie's not there — yes.'

'And if he is?'

'We, er, break in.' I grinned. 'Only much more quietly.'

28

Although we had been told by DI Vales that Lachlan McBride had left Mull, Stan Jones insisted on staying behind to guard Sian.

'The day I start believin' coppers is the day I know someone's been nickin' me marbles,' he said. 'If that bastard beat up Siobhan, he could be out there lurkin'. Christ, Sian told him where to go and since then he's already tried for her once, hasn' he?'

I rocked my head from side to side, unsure.

Stan scowled. 'Come on. Dougie told you someone fixed the Shogun's brakes so Sian went off the road, and who else had motive or opportunity? Nobody, that's who — only Lachlan McBride.'

Sian rolled her eyes, but there was renewed apprehension there and she was obviously pleased and relieved that Stan was staying with her. Even without that reaction, Stan knew his words carried weight. He looked at me for my nod of approval, got it, and when Calum and I walked out to the Quattro he was helping Sian through the chill of the long dark room and back to her bed next to the orange-box like an elderly night porter in an exclusive private nursing home.

It was a cold, clear, moonless night. The fast drive from Salen to Craignure passed without incident despite icy roads coated with a thin layer of fine snow across which the Quattro's tyres sped with a constant, crackling hiss. Twenty minutes after leaving the bothy I once again drove through the village and up the hill I had walked five days ago; once again looked across the barren forecourt with its ghostly, rusting petrol pumps and ragged pines standing tall and black against the night skies. But this time I proceeded with extreme caution. I stayed on the road, all lights switched off, until I had almost passed that exposed open space. Then I turned left and inched the car across snow and gravel. I hugged those towering pines, with stones popping alarmingly under the tyres and my eyes fixed on the staircase at the end of the building and the upstairs windows behind which light glowed.

At any moment I expected the door at the top of the stairs to bang open, light to flood out, a loud voice demand to know what the hell we were doing.

Nothing happened. No window curtains twitched. The door remained closed, and when I pushed the button to wind down the electric window next to Calum I could hear, faintly from on high, the soaring guitar solo from *Brothers in Arms*, by Dire Straits.

'Not exactly a hymn praising Dougie and Lachlan's relationship,' I said.

'At least you know he has got a CD player,' Calum said. 'And, as he's entirely on his own now, we know it must be Dougie in there.'

I pulled to a halt in deep shadows.

'Mm. Nevertheless, I think we'll pretend he isn't.'

'Why?'

'If we break in, leave evidence so that he knows what's happened, and knows who did it — he might slip up.'

Calum's teeth gleamed as he grinned in the darkness.

'Right. He'll misconstrue our reason for being here, inadvertently reveal hitherto unknown facts that may incriminate — '

'Jesus Christ,' I said softly, 'you and Willie Vine.'

'Aye, lots of syllables in there, I'll admit, but am I right?'

'You are. And in case you're wondering how we get in, there's a door set into the back wall that will allow easy ingress.'

'Ingress?'

'Opposite to exit,' I said, 'but we'll use it for both.'

I flipped the car door open and climbed

out into the cold. As I stepped sideways, a branch stroked my cheek like an icy finger; when a sound drew my eyes, I saw two unmoving amber eyes watching me from the shadows.

Calum joined me. We walked around the end of the building as silently as cat burglars. I glanced up with a surge of anger and revulsion as we passed close to the stairs from which a killer had hanged Peggy McBride. Then we were at the back of the workshop. Gingerly, keeping close to the building, touching its walls' unpainted boards for balance, we picked our way along a grassless open area of slick packed earth. A heap of oil drums stood next to a stack of worn tyres leaning like Pisa's tower. Two crumbling concrete ramps like the thick walls of a roofless bothy were home to countless misshapen, empty oil cans. Rusting engine blocks lay everywhere, and I heard Calum curse as he tripped over one of several snaking lengths of worn wire rope.

I experienced another unexpected frisson of revulsion and anger as I recalled how Peggy McBride had used just such a length of wire rope to bring several tons of metal crashing down on a drugged Ray Coghlan.

Then, ahead of me, Calum had recovered his balance and located the door in the rear wall. His long legs straightened and he stretched to his full height. He tried the handle. The door swung open. Disused hinges squealed. I winced at the harsh grate of wood on gravel.

'Not used that much,' I said.

'So if he hears it,' Calum said, 'he won't know what the hell it is.'

'You wish.'

We stepped inside the workshop.

'Leave the door open.'

'As canny burglars do.'

'All we're after is numbers that add up to a crime, and we'll carry those in our head.'

Calum switched on his Maglite. A needle-thin white beam like a laser pierced the darkness. Weak reflected light revealed the mangled bulk of the wrecked truck, the welding equipment, the gaping black hole of the inspection pit where Jim Gorrie had died in a sump of oily water.

'There,' I said, and Calum crossed the floor to the office. I followed him in, bumped into him as he was almost knocked backwards by the smell of dirty oil and stale cigarette smoke, the sight of the littered desk and floor.

'It was just like this,' he said, 'the last time we broke into a garage.'

Still behind him, I put a hand on his shoulder and chuckled. 'Ronnie Maguire's garage in Old Swan, Liverpool. The Sam Bone case.'

'Aye, but this time no dogs, no big man sitting in the chair waiting to clobber us.'

Behind us there was a short bark of laughter that spun us on our heels, heads up, eyes as wide as startled fawns.

'Just a man with a shotgun loaded and cocked,' a harsh voice said, 'standing blockin your way out and asking what the fuck you two think you're doing?'

*   *   *

'Actually,' I said, as Dougie McCafferey clicked on the lights and the naked white bulb seared my eyes, 'I was trying to work out how to get into your computer.'

'No.' Dougie shook his head fiercely. 'I know damn well what you're up to, and it's got nothing to do with technology. You two are here to look again at that truck. You're going to crawl all over the cab, look at what work was done on it before it went out, fix your bloody peepers on the new mirror and anything else that's still in one piece and you're going to make damn sure you find something, something that will back up your wild bloody assertion that I murdered my wife.'

'Unintentionally.'

'Aye, well, Bridie or Ray Coghlan, accidentally or on bloody purpose, I've told you you're wrong about the road and Maddock's Switch and you bloody well *are* wrong.'

'If you didn't do it, what can we hope to find? Why are you in such a blind panic?'

'Me?' McCafferey said. 'In a panic?' He grinned, but there was a crazed look in his eyes, and I took a step backwards, wondered what Calum was doing behind me. 'Listen,' he went on, 'it's you that's standing in front of a loaded shotgun, pal, and after what's been happening around here I reckon I'd get away with blasting the both of you — you understand that?'

'What good would that do?'

'Get you off my back. Get shut of all that talk of me somehow killing Bridie. Did you know until you came here, nobody was bothering? Accidental death is what it was, right, and it would have stayed that way. Then you two step off the bloody ferry and the crap hits the fan.'

'What about Gorrie?'

'Eh? Gorrie? What about him?'

'He was murdered. Why? Did he see something? If he did, was it to do with Bridie's death? Or Coghlan's? Was Jim Gorrie an eyewitness?'

'You could put it like that.'

'When you two have finished squabbling,' said Calum, Mr Insouciance, talking through a yawn, 'maybe we can get around to figuring out how Lachlan managed to put a couple of thousand miles on his Mercedes clock in just a few days.'

That surprised even me.

'A *couple* of thousand?'

'Siobhan was got at twice, remember?'

I nodded understanding, my lips tight. 'He was caught on CCTV again. This time in Oban. You think that's where he was going? Liverpool?'

'I not only believe that, I'm quite sure he admitted as much to Vales and Hills.'

'And they didn't tell us because . . . ?'

'Well, in addition to the point Vales made about telling you bugger all, it wasn't relevant.'

'Of course. It's what I thought at the time. They're investigating murders on Mull and know nothing of what's been going on in Liverpool. Lachlan's destination meant nothing to them.'

'Which is exactly what it means to me,' McCafferey said. 'What the hell are you on about?'

'The reason we want to get into your computer,' I said patiently, 'is because your

317

brother's car has been in here twice. It was booked in on Friday for MOT, then on Saturday he wanted Jim Gorrie to look at the car's charging system. We'd like to check the mileage, see how far he drove in . . . oh, the twelve hours or so between those visits.'

'And what was all that about Liverpool?'

'Put down the shotgun, check those figures for us, and if they tally with what we expect to find then we'll tell you what we believe your brother's been up to.'

For a moment he hesitated, but I'd been right about *Brothers in Arms* not quite symbolizing the relationship between the two men and he was looking at the possibility of Lachlan McBride being in some kind of trouble — and the idea was pleasing.

He pushed past me, slammed the shotgun down on the desk hard enough for Calum to wince and me to brace myself against the expected lethal charge of buckshot — the muzzle was pointing in my direction — and sat down at the computer. Switches clicked. The screen lit up. He set about logging on.

We left him to it, wandering back into the workshop with our footsteps echoing in the emptiness and the light from the office flooding across the greasy floor to send our shadows racing towards the yawning pit.

'If our suspicions are proved correct,'

Calum said, 'what's the next step?'

'I get back to Mike Haggard with the name and the registration number. Inform DI Vales, as the crime's on her patch.'

'And reflect, with due deference, on Sian's excellent performance so far.'

'Mm. You're right. And our dismal showing. Andrew Keay confessed. Sian spotted Lachlan's fatal slip while lying in a hospital bed. Meanwhile, the two able-bodied members of the team — '

'Does Stan the Van not count?'

I grinned. 'He's a middle-aged scally, on the puny side — '

'But brainy.'

'OK, but even if he's in, we're no closer to finding out who murdered Jim Gorrie and Peggy McBride.'

'How can we hope to get close?' Calum said. 'We've questioned no suspects, made not a single worthwhile move in any direction.'

'Backwards springs to mind.'

'But isn't exactly helpful.'

I looked over my shoulder.

'Could be. Dougie's got something.'

McCafferey was walking out of the office, holding a yellow Post it note.

'MOT was done at 72,500 miles,' he said. 'When Jim booked him in for repairs on

Saturday, the clock was reading 73,300.'

He handed me the note. I looked at Calum.

'Eight hundred miles. That's about right, isn't it?'

He shrugged. 'Roughly a hundred miles to spare either way. But it matters not. We know he didn't clock that mileage driving on and off the ferry.'

Dougie had his hands thrust into his pockets. His face had darkened. His chin was jutting belligerantly.

'He told us Nellie was sick. Said he was off to Oban for the night to see if she needed anything, then rushing back the next morning for that daft outward bound course.'

'Those figures tell a different story,' I said. 'We're pretty certain he broke the speed limit pushing that Mercedes to Liverpool. Round about midnight, in a quiet street, he used an iron bar to half kill a woman who was walking home. Then, probably believing she was dead, he drove like the clappers back to Oban and caught the morning ferry to Mull.'

'If he was here now, with his car,' Calum said, 'you'd almost certainly find he's clocked up another eight hundred miles. We believe he found out the woman was still alive, and tried for her again in Liverpool's Royal hospital.'

'Did he now, the wee bastard?' Dougie said. The light from the office was bouncing off the walls, turning the tight circle of our faces into eerily pale masks with eyes like poked holes. Dougie's dark eyes looked luminous, almost lupine. There had been anger blazing in them, but suddenly, as the seconds ticked by, they became shrewd, knowing.

'If you're right, that was a wicked thing to do, but it happened a long way from Mull and so does'nae trouble me too much. But here, very much closer to home, there's a couple of murders crying out to be solved. And if the boy Lachlan could do that to a woman in Liverpool, then he's cruel beyond imagination, and capable of the utmost brutality.'

'Unfortunately,' I said, 'the second trip to Liverpool gives him an excellent alibi for the time of your mother's murder.'

The look in the shrewd eyes was suddenly scornful.

'If you think that, he's going to run bloody rings round you. Time means nothing, pal. Christ, when it's midday in Glasgow they're having an early breakfast in Florida. Figure out how airline passengers handle that, and you and your PI friend will maybe get somewhere.'

29

'DI Vales, please.'

'Who the hell's that? D'you know what time it is?'

I was phoning her from the Quattro, on her land-line. At home. A gruff male voice had answered. Heavy with sleep.

'I do,' I said. 'It's almost midnight, and I apologize. Would you tell your wife it's Jack Scott.' Wife? Partner? I closed my eyes. 'I have information that may help solve a crime, but I need to ask her just one question.'

Silence. Then, 'A minute.'

I heard him muttering with his hand over the phone. Then Vales came on.

'I thought I told you to keep your nose out of police business.'

'That was Strathclyde, not Merseyside. The police I'm helping are more than three hundred miles away, in Liverpool. In the early hours of Saturday morning, a woman was badly beaten. The police think the man who attacked her used a tyre lever.'

I waited, let her think back to Peggy McBride and put two and two together.

'A witness saw a car drive off,' I said.

'Nearby CCTV cameras picked up a light-coloured Mercedes, moving in the right direction at about the right time.'

I smiled smugly as I heard Vales grunt. Shock? Satisfaction? Or dazzling thoughts of promotion?

'Then,' I went on smoothly, 'in the early hours of Monday morning, a man wearing a white coat and carrying a stethoscope tried to get to her in her hospital bed. The woman recognized him as her attacker.'

'And you think — '

'Before I put into words what we both surely know, let me ask that question: did you know where Lachlan McBride was going when he drove out of Oban on Sunday night?'

'We did.'

'So — where was he going?'

'He told Oban police he was going to Liverpool,' DI Vales said.

★　★　★

'Mike?'

'This had better be good.'

'What's up, running out of whisky, nothing on TV, no cigarettes?'

'All three. Plus bored waitin' and patience is in short supply.'

'All right, see if this helps.' I winked at Calum, watching from the passenger seat. 'The Mercedes belongs to a man called Lachlan McBride. He left Mull on the night Siobhan was attacked. Mileage recorded at a local garage before and after the first trip puts Liverpool within range. He also left here on Sunday night, the night — '

'Yeah, yeah, the night a phoney doctor turned up at the Royal.'

'Right. Mileage for the second trip can't be checked, because he's not been seen since, but he did tell Strathclyde police where he was going. Liverpool. You've got him.'

Haggard had been grunting as he wrote furiously. I listened, gave him the Merc's registration number when I sensed a pause.

'How'd you get on to this?'

'He slipped up. Sian was in hospital in Oban — '

'Sian? I thought she was wonder woman, terror of the Cairngorms; indestructible.'

'Maybe she is. She drove into a Scottish field and wrote off her Shogun, but survived with cracks and bruises; she'll tell you all about it when we get back. Anyway, this man Lachlan, the stalker you're looking for, was talking to one of the nurses. He saw Sian, called hello — but he used the wrong name.'

'Don't tell me: Siobhan?'

'Right.'

'Dickhead. OK. We'll get on to this now, it'll give Willie Vine something to do instead of sleepin' the night away.'

'And thanks.'

'For what?'

'No, Mike, that was you thanking me. Or was I dreaming?'

He chuckled. 'That,' he growled, 'or I'm goin' soft in my old age.'

The phone clicked off.

30

The deserted road to Salen. Dipped head-lights bouncing back off hub-high white mist. Tyres hissing. The heater a comforting background hum, circulating hot air bringing out expensive new car smells that had never left the Quattro.

Calum stretched out and yawning in the passenger seat.

'Midnight in Glasgow,' he said suddenly, 'and they're having an early breakfast in Florida.'

'Mm. Overlooking an azure pool out of Hockney. Palm fronds rattling in the warm breeze. Bit of a contrast between that and the bothy's kitchen on a November morning.'

'He's given him to us, hasn't he?'

I glanced sideways. 'Peggy's killer? I've been too busy on the phone to give it much thought. But I've *started* thinking, and I did just recall something Nellie said to me on Monday when I was leaving her bungalow. I'd said I thought she should tell Peggy that Stuart had died. There was a lot of . . . I don't know, bitterness and *hatred* in her eyes when she said, 'It's a bit late for that, now'.'

'And you thought, what?'

'Well, not very much. I suppose I was thinking, well, yes it is: he's dead, and nothing can be changed. But now, thinking back, I'm sure she meant something else.'

'Aye, and I can see where this is going,' Calum said. 'It's rarely too late to announce a death, but it would be too damn late by far if the person you want to tell has herself been murdered.'

'Right. I think she knew Peggy was dead. If she did — there was only one way she could have found out.'

'From her killer: Lachlan.'

I nodded absently as I negotiated a sweeping curve and flicked the main beam on and off in an attempt to penetrate the thickening mist.

'What did Dougie say next?' I frowned. '*Figure out how airline passengers handle that, and you'll maybe get somewhere.* So, how do they handle it?'

'Flying out, they put their watches . . . back, is it? I can never work it out.'

'America's to the west. The sun gets there later so, yes, it's back.'

'But Lachlan McBride up there in Dougie's room with a dead woman,' Calum said, 'must have put those timepieces forward.'

I drove in thoughtful silence for several minutes, balancing what Calum had said with what it implied, and what I knew happened to a body after death.

It's become a sort of convention in mystery novels that, when a victim's wrist-watch has been broken in a struggle, the amateur sleuth looks at that frozen moment of time and seizes on it as the time of death. Peggy's watch had been smashed at ten to twelve, so that was when she died. DI Vales and the Strathclyde police seemed to be using that as a reasonably reliable guide, though they'd certainly be making other checks. Some of those would involve body temperature, and the degree of rigor mortis.

A dead body cools at an average rate of 1½° an hour. However, loss of warmth will always depend on environmental conditions. Peggy McBride had been hanging beneath an external staircase at the side of McCafferey's garage, overnight, in winter.

Rigor mortis begins in the neck and jaw after about four hours, is usually well established after twelve hours, and gone in thirty. The stiffening is caused by the loss of adenosine triphosphate (ATP), which is the source of energy required for muscle contraction. However, rigor mortis is one of the poorest guides to time of death because it

328

can depend on the victim's weight, the temperature of the environment and, crucially, activity at the time of death.

A skinny person develops rigor mortis rapidly, and a struggle will hasten its onset because ATP will already be depleted when death occurs. Peggy McBride, a slender woman with little flesh on her bones, had struggled valiantly against her attacker.

'It's not hard to work out,' Calum said, after a while spent drumming his fingers on the arm rest and several glances in my direction. 'Lachlan boarded the ferry at four o'clock. Peggy was already strung up under the staircase. He wanted it to appear that she'd been murdered much later, giving him an alibi. So he put watch and clock forward, cleverly leaving the clock its usual ten minutes slow.'

We were approaching Salen. I slowed, pulled into the village, turned left opposite the blackened ruins of Peggy's cottage and kept the car in third to roar up the track.

'Vales and Hills were guided by those broken timepieces,' I said, 'which we now believe were altered by McBride. But other, more reliable checks would be made. I've been trying to work out if, from the body, the pathologist could get close to determining the actual time of death.' I flicked a glance at the sprawled figure in the passenger seat. 'We're looking at something over four hours' time difference, Cal, but not very *much* over if Lachlan raced for the ferry as soon as he'd killed her. Given the circumstances, I don't think it would be possible. I think they'd settle for round about midnight.'

'So unless Lachlan left his fingerprints on those watches, or forensic evidence elsewhere, he could still get away with murder?'

'Only for a time,' I said, pulling up in front of the bothy, 'and time's against him. Which is ironic, isn't it? He fiddled with time to create an alibi. Now, because he slipped up with a name, he'll be locked in a cell for a different crime and the police will have all the time in the world to question him about murder.'

Calum stretched, clicked open his door to let in the cold.

'Do we tell yon Strathclyde 'tecs what we've worked out?'

'Dougie McCafferey half worked it out for us, didn't he? Since we landed on Mull, other people have been doing our job.'

Calum grinned. 'Aye, and long may it continue.'

31

My Soldier Blue wouldn't stay in bed. She had dark rings under her eyes and her cheeks were hot but she was in the kitchen with a bleary-eyed, harassed-looking Jones the Van and, as we pushed our way through the blanket, there was the splash of water being poured into tin mugs and the instant smell of coffee. Or should that be the smell of instant coffee? Damn it, who cares? It was hot and wet and welcome. Mull in November had turned out to be an island where coffee kept us alive. We sat down with sighs that were almost contented.

'Mike Haggard's looking for Lachlan McBride,' I said. 'When he's in clink for attacking Siobhan, he'll break and confess to the murder of Peggy McBride.'

Finished dishing up the coffee, Sian had turned to a cracked mirror hanging on a nail and was fixing her pony-tail. One-handed. With Stan's help.

'Then that's over, thank God.' Her reflected eyes met mine. 'So what does that make it, two down, one to go? Jim Gorrie?'

'Two down *two* to go,' I said, 'if you count Bridie Button.'

'Thought we were ditchin' that one?' Stan said, giving Sian's blonde head a pat as he finished.

'Getting back to Dougie McCafferey,' Calum said, watching Sian, 'he didn't just give us Peggy's killer. I think when he talked about us crawling all over the cab, he was directing us to where we should look for Bridie's killer; more than that, he was all but writing out a confession.'

He looked at me, waiting for his cue.

'What did he say?'

'We'd fix our peepers on the new mirror, or words to that effect — '

'Mirrors are out, they were dumped long ago,' Stan said scathingly.

'Actually, no,' Sian said sweetly. She smiled at me triumphantly. 'Guess what? I remembered what I worked out in hospital. I'm pretty sure I know how Bridie Button was murdered. And who did it.'

'The who is reasonably easy,' Calum said. 'It has to be Dougie.'

'The how,' I said, 'is a little more difficult.'

'Also quite easy, as most tricks are when they're explained,' Sian said. She beamed in my direction. 'You see, I remembered, in great detail, what happened to me when the Shogun went off the road. Then I turned everything around, like they do in those

332

rugby replays on TV where they look at an incident from the reverse angle; I looked at the mirror image of my experience, and came up with what could be the answer.'

'If you're thinkin' of mirrors as the answer,' Stan Jones said, head down as he rolled a cigarette, 'you're off your trolley. I've told you, we've been into that, an' it won't work.'

'Why not?'

He looked up, misshapen ciggy poised between two nicotine-stained fingers.

'Because Dougie was behind the truck all the way from the garage, wasn' he? So she had to know he was there, an' there's nothing he could've done usin' her mirrors.'

'No she didn't, and yes there was.'

I was grinning at Stan's gobsmacked scepticism, intrigued by what Sian was saying.

'Enlighten us, Soldier Blue.'

'What did those two witnesses say, Jack?'

'The ones up in the hills, Gregor Neill and his wife?' She nodded. 'Something about seeing the truck's lights, with another vehicle some way behind. Right?'

'Roughly — but roughly's not good enough. What Gregor Neill *actually* said was they saw the truck's lights, and then he went on to say, 'And shortly afterwards I saw the lights of another vehicle, about fifty yards behind it'.'

'Right, I remember. But what of it?'

'Well, why shortly afterwards? — which suggests at first he didn't see them, then he did. The two vehicles were close together. Why didn't he see both sets of lights at the same time?'

'Because . . . ' I frowned. 'I don't know. Vales pointed out that Dougie had to catch up. The land undulates. Perhaps the Land Rover was obscured by a ridge, by trees, then it came out into the open.'

'You were up there talking to Andrew Keay when it was dark. I was doing adventure training in that area, Jack, and in the course of my work I've been very close to the cottage where those old dears live, in daylight. Their view of that section of road is unobstructed.' She let that sink in, then said, 'What if Dougie had his lights switched off? Then, suddenly, he switched them on.'

Calum was playing with his John Lennon glasses as he listened, sliding them up and down his nose by holding them with the fingers of both hands as he slowly nodded his head. Now he held them still and squinted at her owlishly through the smeared lenses.

'What, no lights, in the dark, all the way from the garage?'

'Yep. All the way. Driving blind.'

'Aye, he could have managed that, I

suppose,' he said, 'if he'd kept the truck's tail lights in view. But what would be the point? From the truck's cab it looks like there's nothing behind, then he switches his lights on and suddenly there is. But so what? That's not going to send Bridie into a panic, send her careering off the road into the trees.'

'OK, so now it's back to me,' Sian said, 'and my exciting brush with death at Maddock's Switch.'

'But looked at from the reverse angle.'

'Well, let's first do it the right way round. So, my little party is heading back towards Craignure from a map reading exercise near Ben More, a bright morning has turned very dull, light is bad. I'm leading in the Shogun. It's getting darker by the minute, and starting to drizzle. I drive over the brow of a hill, and find myself looking down on Maddock's Switch. As I drive down the hill, I apply my brakes — and, as you know, nothing happened. The vehicle behind me sees the Shogun gathering speed, but thinks I'm driving recklessly, much too fast. The driver, an ex-para, already has his lights on. Now he flashes them — repeatedly. I see them in the mirror, they register — but then, of course, everything goes haywire and I finish up in a field.' She grimaced. 'And it wasn't until earlier today that I replayed those images, and realized *what they would have led me to believe if I had been in Ray Coghlan's truck, driving in the other direction.'*

Calum was grinning at me. 'Didn't someone dub those mind games lateral thinking?'

I nodded. 'That was a clever Maltese feller called de Bono.'

'Right,' Calum said. 'Being a woman, Sian probably puts all the clever stuff down to intuitive thinking — but no matter what you call it, I'm pretty sure she's got there.'

I stared at him. 'You can see what she's driving at?'

'An odd choice of words considering the subject under discussion, but, yes, I think so. Although I'm sure there'll be more explaining to do before it's wrapped up in its entirety — right, Sian?'

'Mm. I certainly haven't got *all* the answers — although I'll be surprised if you and Jack can't fill in most of the missing bits. I've been doing the brainwork,' she said, somehow managing to put tongue in cheek, 'while you two foot soldiers have been going over the crash site, examining truck and garage. You must have found something.'

'Yes, but I can only provide answers when I know the questions,' I said, 'so, go on, get on with it, Cal, explain the explanation.'

'All right, but listen closely, and no conferring with Stan if you don't understand.' He winked at Sian, clearly enjoying himself. 'Looking at it first from Sian's angle, think about the road. The way Sian was travelling into Maddock's Switch, the road goes steeply downhill, and at the bottom swings *sharp right and up.* Now visualize any car's interior mirror. It's located high up, and to the driver's left.'

He stopped, looked at Sian. 'Am I getting close.'

'Absolutely spot on,' she said softly and approvingly.

'OK, so, there's a car behind Sian, flashing his lights. They're both going downhill. She sees those lights in the interior mirror which, we've established, is high up to her left.' He paused, letting that sink in, then said, 'Now, Jack, put yourself in the Shogun, coming downhill, you're sitting there looking at the following lights flashing in that interior mirror — and imagine what you would be looking at *if the mirror wasn't there.*'

'Fields,' I said, after a moment's thought. 'Ahead of her — of me — the road's swinging right, and up, so if the Shogun's pointing downhill and I'm looking *left* and slightly up and the mirror's taken away I wouldn't see the road . . . ' I stopped. 'Bloody hell.'

'By George,' Calum said joyfully, 'I think he's got it.'

'I think I have,' I said. 'And if I'm right — I must be right — then it's fiendishly clever.'

'Care to take over?'

'Lord, no. I'm coming in a poor third, you go on and finish it.'

'Not much point. It's just about done, as I think you now realize,' Calum said. 'All you do now is go through the same process, but this time it's you or Bridie, in Coghlan's truck, coming fast in the opposite direction. And . . . ?'

'All right. So, she's coming down the hill from the direction of Craignure, with the road at the bottom curving *left*, then up,' I said, nodding quickly. 'If she now looks beyond the mirror — high up, to her left — she won't be looking at fields, she'll be looking at the road as it climbs to the next brow.'

'Or, looked at slightly differently,' Calum said, 'as it swoops down towards her.'

'That's what I worked out,' Sian said. 'It was a terrible night, roaring wind, driving rain and sleet. So I thought, if Dougie had his lights switched off, Bridie wouldn't hear or see him and she'd have no idea there was a vehicle behind her. If Dougie waited, and waited — then, halfway down that terrible hill, switched his headlights on, full beam — she'd suddenly look up and left to see those lights blazing at her in that mirror and for that crucial, critical moment would be convinced a vehicle was tearing towards her down the opposite hill — and she'd slam her brakes on.'

'Hold on, hold on,' Stan said. 'Why would she think that? She knows there's a mirror there in the cab, she's *used* to it; she's a good driver, a young kid with fast reactions and the first thing she'd think is there was something *behind* her.'

Sian looked at me. 'Jack?'

'There was a mirror in the cab. But think what Dougie said to us: we'd be looking at the new mirror. It *was* a new one, wasn't it? I noticed that the first time I saw the truck. I think that's what Dougie was doing. I don't think there ever had been a mirror in that cab, so he put one there. Telling nobody. Knowing, *hoping*, that on that dark night the driver wouldn't notice the new mirror until Dougie flicked on his lights going down that hill.'

'Still won't work,' Stan said. 'If there'd never been an inside mirror, there'd have to be a wing mirror. By law.'

'There was.'

'So even if Dougie had stuck a mirror in

the cab, she'd still see the lights in the wing mirror — out of habit because she didn't know there was an inside mirror — and that'd tell her the lights were behind her.'

'That was the beauty of the scheme,' I said. 'Drivers of those battered trucks, often overloaded, *do* get into the habit of looking into wing mirrors, even if there is an interior mirror. And, as you say, that's the mirror Bridie would be used to. If there was a truck behind her, that's where she'd see the lights.'

'Then what did Dougie do, take the wing mirror off?' Sian said.

'No, he didn't,' I said.

'Damn,' Sian said. 'So, what then? How did he work it — or has my marvellous theory just been shot down in flames?'

I looked at Calum. 'Have you worked that bit out?'

'We both have, haven't we? Sian said we must have found something at the crash site. We did. We picked up broken glass, thin enough to have come from a smashed wing mirror.'

'Yes,' I said, 'and I remember watching Jim Gorrie light his oxy-acetylene equipment. A welder's routine is to light the acetylene first, then introduce the oxygen — but before you turn that second knob, the acetylene burns with a yellow flame that sends black flecks floating in the air and coats anything it touches with a film of soot. I saw the silencer Gorrie had been welding.'

'Yes, and we both saw those fragments of glass, picked them up, looked at them closely,' Calum said. 'Tiny as they were, we could see they were coated with soot.'

'So spell it all out,' Stan said, 'just so we've got the story right when we swagger into the cop shop.'

'Dougie bolted a new interior mirror in the truck's cab, and coated the right-hand wing mirror with soot,' I said. 'When he followed the truck, he drove with his lights off. He switched them on, full beam, when the truck ahead of him was swooping down towards Maddock's Switch. Unaware of the new mirror, and accustomed to watching following vehicles in the *wing* mirror, Bridie was suddenly faced with lights blazing at her from what seemed to be the direction of the road ahead. She was probably going too fast. The brain slipped smoothly into survival mode: narrow road, icy conditions, vehicle approaching fast, take evasive action — stamp on brake, pull over. And, as Dougie McCafferey had planned, that instinctive reaction on an icy road sent the truck smashing through the fence and into the trees.'

'Dougie McCafferey had killed Ray Coghlan,'

Sian said softly. 'Only he hadn't, of course — as he would quickly find out.'

'Yes,' I said, 'and that's why Jim Gorrie died. When he was about to weld that silencer he suddenly looked up, and seemed to freeze. Then he called to me, said he'd talk to me later.'

'He'd worked it out,' Calum said. 'And probably confronted Dougie.'

'And when I put it to Dougie that Gorrie had died because he was an eyewitness, he said, 'you could put it like that'. You cut him off, Cal, or I could have challenged that remark. Because I think what he meant was that Gorrie was an eyewitness, not to the killing of Coghlan, but to the clever work that led to the death of Bridie Button. Gorrie had watched Dougie at work, but not realized what he was doing until it was much too late.'

'I,' Sian said, 'am bloody exhausted just listening to this.'

'You started it by working out a compli- cated mystery' — I winked at Stan — 'while lying on your back looking up at a hospital ceiling.'

'Makes you wonder why we've been workin' so hard,' Stan said.

'On past cases. This time we've done little, achieved less, and by way of a fee we're going to get what we deserve: a big fat zero.'

'No change there,' Calum said, 'to coin a phrase.'

'So why don't we go home?' Stan said, looking hopeful.

'Because the fat lady — '

'Isn't singing.' Sian groaned. 'I know. But what exactly do we have to do to get her up on stage?'

'We'll sit here drinkin' and natterin' while you go an' lie down again,' Stan said, grinning. 'If it worked once . . . '

'Be nice,' I said, grimacing. 'Instead we'll finish our coffee, then I'll talk to DI Vales — again. I'll try to reach her on her mobile to avoid the grumpy male; she'll probably go ballistic.' I looked at Calum. 'That done, in a valiant attempt to get just one thing right without any help from friends or enemies, you and I go after McCafferey.'

Sian pouted. 'What about me?'

'You were our lifeline in the Danson case, and here on Mull you've been our brains. Without you, we'd still be floundering. But now it's back to Stan again, and I think you just heard him outline your plans for the next few hours.'

'What, sit here nattering and drinking?' She smiled shakily. 'I'll be worried sick. If I'm back here, then I want you to keep in touch, tell me what's going on, who's winning.'

'Don't I always?'

'Win? Well, yes, but you don't always keep in touch because most times I'm there with you. Sometimes ahead of you, trailing suspects . . . or . . . or turning up in the nick of time with brightly coloured canoes.'

'But not this time. This time, I want you safe.'

'With Stan.' She nodded, grinned at the little man with the white beard and the smouldering roll-up. 'I'll enjoy that. At what we do — '

'Natter, and drink coffee,' Stan said.

'We make an excellent team — right, Stan?'

'Oh yeah,' Stan said, rolling his eyes, 'smoky, an' the one-armed bandit.'

32

I phoned DI Vales from the car before we set off.

'Are you at home?'

'No. We've been called out to an incident. At Fionnphort. I've got no time for small talk, so what the hell do you want now?'

'Small talk's a long way from my mind. I called your mobile,' I said, 'to let your husband catch up on his sleep.' I waited for her to tell me he was actually her partner and point out that if that wasn't small talk then what the hell was, but she had moved the phone away and was talking to someone and I could hear male voices shouting, the crackle of a radio.

'Get on with it, Scott,' she said, coming back, 'or I'll cut you off.'

'I can prove that Dougie McCafferey murdered Bridie Button. By mistake, but it was definitely a deliberate killing.'

'Either you're dreaming, or you're on something illegal. That was a tragic accident.'

'Dougie tampered with the truck's mirrors, inside and out. When we spoke to him a short while ago he practically told us where to look, as good as confessed to what he'd done.'

'Empty road, crap weather, two vehicles, the one behind watching a drama unfold. Accident, Scott. Back off.'

'Murder. He also murdered Jim Gorrie, because Gorrie tumbled to what he'd done — '

'Proof?'

'I saw Gorrie before he died. He was about to tell me something, said he'd talk to me later — '

'You're going over old ground, Scott. We've already talked about this. You pointed out that the next time you saw Gorrie, it was too late. So have you got anything new?'

'One of the tricks McCafferey used in his plan to murder Ray Coghlan — because that's who he was after — involved welding kit, oxy-acetylene. I saw Gorrie with that kit, saw him look at the yellow flame and the soot before he turned on the oxygen, saw realization hit him.'

'But you've got nothing new?'

'It's not needed — and you're wasting your own time with these questions. You've got a job to do there, I'm in my car and we're going to the garage to confront Dougie McCafferey.'

'Oh, no!'

'This time,' I said, 'he'll realize the game's up — '

'Scott, I'm ordering you to stay away.'

'Can't hear you, the signal's breaking up. If you can hear me, then make sure you pull into the garage on your way back from Fionnphort and we'll give you the man who murdered Bridie Button and Jim Gorrie — '

'Jesus Christ.'

I switched off. Looked across at Calum in the Quattro's passenger seat, the glow from the dash lighting his bearded face.

'She congratulated me on my perspicacity. Wished us both luck and thanked me for my help.'

'Aye, I think I heard her referring to you as the Saviour,' Calum said drily.

★   ★   ★

The cold clear night had rapidly deteriorated. Heavy cloud had swept in from the north-east. As I drove down the long hill, pulled off the track in the centre of Salen and pointed the Quattro towards Craignure, the car was buffeted by strong winds whistling across the Sound of Mull and threatening to push it sideways into the fields. Fine snow carried by the wind quickly coated the car's near side. The wipers slapped, building up solid white banks at the extremity of each stroke. Warm, cocooned, I gazed through a

347

decreasing arc feeling like a U-Boat commander squinting through a periscope coated with the flying foam of an angry sea.

We said little on the twelve-mile journey. Both of us were expecting an angry confrontation with Dougie McCafferey in his upstairs living accommodation; neither of us was anticipating any major problems. We had all the answers, two of us against one of him seemed to rule out violence, and, well, if not exactly plain sailing we were certainly looking forward to handing Bridie's killer over to a disbelieving DI Vales; doing a bit of preening and gloating at the end of yet another successful investigation.

Perhaps I should have tried what Stan suggested and gone to lie down and gaze pensively at a convenient ceiling. Because the thought that Dougie might have slipped up when he blurted out the bit about mirrors, that he was a big strong man who had killed twice and, if backed into a corner, would almost certainly use the shotgun whose twin gaping muzzles we had already gazed into — well, it didn't cross my mind.

33

The building was in darkness.

Past one in the morning, now, on a bleak winter's night, so hardly surprising that there were no lights glowing in the upstairs windows. Did that make our task easier? I could see Dougie's Land Rover parked near the outside staircase, the big breakdown truck tucked away at the other end of the building. Knowing that no signs of life didn't rule out the possibility of his being somewhere, watching, I switched off all the Quattro's lights and in the sudden blackness again cruised almost all the way past the forecourt and turned in at the last moment to park up against the pines. Switched off the engine. Leaned back.

The wind was strong enough to bend the tall trees. Snow was blowing horizontally against the rusting petrol pumps standing out against the dark timber of the building like indistinct ghosts. I could hear its icy rattle on metal and boards, the whine of the wind through the high wires, the fierce rustling of the black pines.

'Reckon we can creep up those stairs, kick

the door down and charge in, subdue him with little-known wrestling holds and render him incapable of resistance?'

'No.'

I grinned. 'Sorry. That was me being nervous. Makes me talkative, you laconic.'

'Got to do something,' Calum said, 'or we'll still be sitting here when Vales arrives.'

I glanced sideways. 'You could pass for a Mormon.'

'At this time of night,' he said, 'I could pass for John the Baptist.' He looked at me with raised eyebrows. 'What's your point?'

'Mormons knock on doors. Won't go away. You could keep him occupied at the front door — '

'There is no back door.'

'Ah. Then we're stuck with plan A.'

'Which is?'

'We both go up and knock on the door.'

'If we're going to do that, without stealth,' Calum said, 'you might as well drive over there and save us an unnecessary walk.'

I switched on engine and side lights. Pulled away from the trees. Drove at an angle across the forecourt towards the exterior staircase. Halfway there, lights suddenly blazed. White halogen beams shot out from the other end of the building. A powerful engine roared. Then the breakdown truck burst into the open. The big rear tyres spun on the thin snow, spraying gravel and ice. Then they caught, bit, and the long bonnet lifted as the truck surged forwards.

'Christ, that must be Dougie,' Calum said. 'Cut the bugger off.'

'What, block the way out with this expensive toy,' I squeaked.

But before Calum spoke, before those big tyres bit through the snow, I was already spinning the Quattro's wheel and ramming the accelerator to the floor. The breakdown truck had more power, but more mass to move. The Quattro was lighter, already moving, and had the start.

Light from the truck's halogen headlights was bouncing back from trees and the wall on the other side of the road. The forecourt was turned into a floodlit arena. In that bright reflected light I could see Dougie McCafferey's pale, bearded face high up in the cab. His head was turning desperately as he looked first at the road, then at the Quattro. He was gauging the converging angle of both vehicles. The computer in his head was calculating who was going to come out in front.

He was pushing the breakdown truck in an arrow-straight line. I was pulling the Quattro in a tight anti-clockwise circle. At the speed I was travelling it was obvious I was going to cut across his path. He was three-quarters of the way across the forecourt. The vehicles were on a collision course.

He couldn't make it. He was going to lose, and he knew it.

Suddenly he veered away. Baffled, I kept going. Instead of closing, the vehicles were now on parallel courses. I looked up. The truck's electric passenger window slid down. And, belatedly, I remembered that Dougie McCafferey had a shotgun.

'Cal, get down, cover your head,' I yelled.

I was now too close to the truck. Dougie must have been hanging on to the steering wheel, leaning as far as he could across the big cab. Above my head, the shotgun's twin barrels poked out of the passenger window. As they tilted downwards, I slammed on the Quattro's brakes. Then Dougie pulled both triggers.

There was a deafening bang. A dazzling flash of yellow flame. I shut my eyes. Ducked down. Flung my bent arm up across my head and face. Then my window disintegrated in a million fragments of sharp, glittering glass. A swarm of angry bees stung my scalp, my forehead, my neck. The back of my right hand felt seared by the shotgun's muzzle blast. Suddenly all my exposed skin was hot and wet.

Calum had been thrown forward. His grey hair glittered as if sewn with sequins. He was looking my way, grey eyes yellow in the reflected light.

'OK,' I said thickly, 'I think I'm OK.'

Grimacing, I straightened my arm and shook it. Glass flew like buckshot. The inside of the door was spattered with blood. I ran my fingers through my hair. Glass rained on my shoulders. When I dragged a sleeve across my face and head, it pulled across tiny open wounds, and more blood. I eased my foot on to the brake and drew to a halt. The truck was already accelerating. It cut across the front of the stationary Quattro, and rocked on to the A849. Numbly, I watched the receding tail lights. Then they were gone. All that was left was a muted, fading roar. To me it sounded like the echoes of McCafferey's coarse, mocking laughter.

'If you're OK,' Calum said, 'why sit there twiddling your thumbs while our man escapes?'

'I'm shedding silent tears for my ruined car,' I said, and Calum chuckled.

'Aye, well, it was going to end up bent, so maybe this way was best. And as it's still drivable, and powerful to boot, it's back to my question.'

'I'm also wondering where he's going.'

'My guess is Ray Coghlan's place. Memories of the woman he killed. In the foothills, according to Jim Gorrie. A fine place to make a last stand.'

'You think?'

'Well, it's all over for him, so he might as well tough it out.'

I pulled out a handkerchief and mopped my bleeding face and head. More glass pattered on the carpet. I screwed up what was now a damp red rag, shoved it in the door pocket. Then I put the car in gear and pulled out on to the road.

★ ★ ★

I was pushing the Quattro hard, leaning sideways in my contoured seat to keep my torn and blood-streaked countenance out of the icy draught blasting through the shattered window and spinning inside the car like a trapped cyclone. Despite the darkness, strong wind and thin, driving snow, I was hitting sixty on the straights and taking the bends at the limit of the tyres' cohesion. Which wasn't high, given the conditions. The car was rocking crazily. Glass littering the floor was slithering from side to side like gravel on a river bottom. Several times I was forced to steer into a rear-end slide as the tyres lost

354

their grip. After the third nerve-racking recovery, Calum, clinging to the grab handle, put a voice to my thoughts.

'You realize this is an action replay of Bridie Button's last drive?'

'Mm. That's what's worrying me.'

'Aye, it was a truck she died in, wasn't it?' He flicked me a glance. 'You think that's it, that's what's on his mind? Down the Switch, slam on the brakes and end it all in those woods?'

I shrugged, only half listening. The wind was roaring through my glassless window. My collar was up. The stinging from countless flesh wounds had stopped, probably because my face was frozen. My skin was stiff with dried blood and possible incipient frostbite.

'If he's crazy enough, he'll see it as a way out,' I said at last. 'If he's not, he'll realize firefighters and paramedics could pull him from the wreck alive, but qualifying for the Paralympic Games.'

'We'll know soon enough,' Calum said. 'You've caught him.'

Ahead of us, big tail lights winked like a monster's red eyes as flurries of snow swept in off the moors.

'A mile or so to Maddock's Switch.'

'He's taking it steady,' Calum said. 'I think our first guess was right. He's heading for

Coghlan's place. He wants to see his story in the national dailies: *Double killer holes up in highland retreat. Police fear long stand-off as siege enters third day.'*

'If Gregor Neill and his wife are at their window watching this,' I said, 'they'll start believing in ghosts.'

'Switch your lights on and off a couple of times,' Calum said, 'and they'll be stumbling to the drinks cupboard.'

Then, ahead of us, the glowing tail lights disappeared as Dougie McCafferey drove over the crest and began the steep descent to Maddock's Switch.

He was a third of the way down when I took the Quattro over the crest after him and the truck's tail lights were once again in view. A third of the way down, and driving fast but with care down the very centre of what was for most of the way a single lane road. Not possible in built-up areas, but here, well, there was no likelihood of traffic, he was getting away with it, and by halfway down it was clear he had no intention of turning his expensive breakdown truck into a crumpled wreck.

'Getting over confident,' Calum said suddenly.

He was. Ahead of him at the bottom of the dip was the stretch of adverse camber and the sharp left turn into the short steep climb to the next crest. But the truck was gathering speed. Watching him, I realized what he was doing. The man knew the road. He'd drifted away from the centre of the narrow road and was going down the hill with his right hand tyres brushing the frozen grass at the road's edge. That put him on the wrong side of the road, but when he reached the bend he would be in the ideal position to take the curve. He would cut across, clipping the apex, Lewis Hamilton on ice. Despite the gravity of the situation, I found myself grinning at his audacity.

Then it all went pear-shaped.

The night landscape was lit up as if by phosphorous flares as headlights appeared high up, ahead of us, beyond the dip that was Maddock's Switch and on the other side of the hill. They swept across the sky, brilliant searchlights illuminating swollen clouds and vast swathes of wind-driven snow, then dipped to the tumbling white moorland, dark stands of trees and ancient drystone walls as a fast car leaped over the crest at the top of that short climb and raced down the slope towards the bend — and Dougie McCafferey.

Just like Bridie Button must have done, with the same feeling of blind panic, he saw the danger. But for Dougie, the dazzling

357

lights bearing down on him were not the result of trickery, not created by an evil reflection, but grim reality. I saw the truck's stop lights flicker: he'd touched the brake, hesitated, realized the danger and hesitated before lifting his foot.

Then, on the speeding car's roof, a blue light began to flash. At the same time the howl of a siren split the night air.

'DI Vales,' I said and, skin pricking with apprehension, I pulled over to the side and eased the Quattro to a halt on that treacherous slope.

Ringside seat.

Dougie McCafferey and the police car were closing fast, already too close for the luxury of a leisurely stop. The two vehicles, rapidly descending steep hills, were racing recklessly from opposite directions towards the deadly bend known as Maddock's Switch. No slowing. No sign of giving way. Their drivers were trapped in an impossible dilemma: brake on those icy roads, and they'd die now; keep going, and they'd extend life by a few seconds then die in a head-on collision.

Like a scream of protest at the injustice of their position the police siren howled its manic warning. And suddenly another blaring klaxon added to the clamour. Dougie, torn by indecision, had banged the heel of his hand on the truck's horn and kept it there.

Then, at last, I saw bright red lights blaze on the wet, pitted tarmac as Dougie stood on the brakes. Heard the shriek of heavy cleated tyres, another shriller squeal from the other side of the dip. In the brilliant illumination provided by Dougie's halogen lights as he approached the bend and entered the turn I could see the police car's rear end begin to shimmy as the driver braked.

With a howl of tortured tyres that sent black smoke swirling, the police car entered the bend and came through in a broadside slide. I could see the passenger. DS Hills. He was grim-faced, arm raised, waiting in stoic resignation for the impact with the huge truck.

But the truck wasn't there. Dougie had driven with the skill that came from long experience on those roads, positioned his breakdown truck perfectly to negotiate the Switch. But there had been no margin for error; no allowance for the one-in-a-million chance of an encounter with another vehicle. The camber in the dip had been wrong for Bridie Button, it was wrong for Dougie. When the police car howled towards him and plunged into the bend just seconds after flying over the crest, he braked too hard. The truck's rear tyres lost their adhesion. Its massive rear end slid towards the side of the road. Pushed by momentum, tipped the wrong way by the road's vicious camber, the body heavily weighted with crane, winch and tools leaned too far. As it tilted beyond the centre of gravity, the truck began to go over. Weight came off the nearside suspension. The nearside tyres lifted, came clear of the road.

Then the off-side tyres slammed into the bank beyond the rough verge.

Caught in the Quattro's lights, the truck toppled sideways as it went through the fence flattened by Bridie Button. The few remaining posts sheared with the dull cracking of wet timber. Loose loops of rusted wire snagged, then snapped. The doomed truck crashed into the field, immediately rolled on to its back, went over again as momentum and slope conspired to keep it rolling. Metal crunched. Glass tinkled musically. Headlights went out. And, just before the truck came to rest on its back with all four massive wheels spinning, I again thought I heard a disembodied voice laughing crazily.

That was almost certainly my imagination.

For what seemed like several minutes but was certainly no more than a few seconds, nothing happened. The police car's blue light flashed regularly, a discoloured heart pumping. The siren died away to a muted gurgle, then choked off into complete silence. I was aware of fine snow blowing into my ear, the moan of the wind, the slow spinning of those heavy black tyres.

Then, as if at a signal, doors snapped open, four people flung themselves into the cold and we were all running, running, running. Yet even as I stepped over the wrecked fence and dropped heavily into the field to race desperately over the crackling, frozen grass, I knew in my heart we were much too late.

34

Wednesday

'So what happened?' Stan said. 'Did we win or lose?'

'Let's put it this way,' I said. 'We didn't get arrested, and that must make it at least an honourable draw.'

'Didn't get paid either,' Calum said.

'What d'you expect,' I said, 'when the client turns out to be one of the killers and ends up dead?'

Sian, slung arm cradled in her right hand and pony-tailed hair blowing in the icy morning wind, shook her head ruefully.

'You went on a bit too long, there, Jack. There was no need to explain why we didn't get paid. We *never* get paid.'

It was 9.15 and we were on board the ferry to Oban, leaning on the rail on the open deck, bidding farewell to a remarkable island. Duart Castle was lost in mist, Mull a series of indistinct soaring mountains rising darkly from the blanket of white that reached the horizon.

The Quattro, pockmarked on the driver's

side of the roof by the shower of buckshot that had been fired blind by Dougie McCafferey, was below on the car deck alongside a rusty white van. I was scarred, and stained. The injuries I'd sustained were all caused by flying glass. The paramedics who came out to Dougie took one look at them, pronounced them minor and daubed me with what looked like antiseptic war paint.

At two in the morning when Calum and I rolled wearily into the bothy, Sian and Jones the Van were asleep. We didn't wake them then, and over a breakfast of steaming porridge — cooked by Stan — we gave them only the bare bones of what had happened at Maddock's Switch. They knew Dougie McCafferey was dead, knew he had died in the field that had taken Bridie Button and almost taken my Soldier Blue. I think it was that last, terrifying thought that had put a curb on my tongue.

'He was alive when we got to him,' I said now, gazing out moodily at the flat grey seas. 'Upside down in the crushed cab, hanging in his seat belt. Blood was dripping. A case of ugly *déjà vu*. On our first day here I'd looked into the cab of the other truck and seen the stains, and last night I couldn't help thinking of Bridie. Anyway, we got Dougie down. Vales asked questions, and he admitted everything.'

I gestured helplessly. 'And then he died.'

'But didn't tell them how he'd done it?' Sian said. 'The mirrors, and the way they worked to create an illusion?'

'We did that, later,' I said, 'and Vales grudgingly accepted our version. Not much else she could do. We'd staged a rerun, hadn't we — or Dougie had. All it needed was for Vales to put a reflection — an evil reflection — in place of the police car hurtling down that slope, and Dougie's cunning scheme was explained.'

'Another one bites the dust,' Stan said.

'Several of them,' Calum said, 'but on Mull it would have been mud.'

'But not just on Mull,' I said. 'I got a call from Haggard, late last night. Lachlan's been picked up, and he's confessed.'

Sian drew in a small, soft breath, and for just a moment she closed her eyes. When she opened them again, she had regained her composure.

'To everything?'

'Everything we've suspected. He paid to have his mother's cottage firebombed. Attacked Siobhan. Fixed your Shogun. Murdered his mother.'

'What about Nellie?'

'She was involved. I don't know what the charge will be, accessory to all sorts of things

I suppose, something like that.'

'So that's it,' Stan said. 'Cue telephone call, end of one case, beginnin' of another.'

'Ah yes,' Calum said, 'but we're in a strange country.'

'You can say that again,' Stan said, grinning.

They began to trade good-natured insults, but I'd switched off. I was recalling a hospital bed, two people holding hands, and talk of a security firm in Gibraltar owned by a man who wanted out. Calum had now added to the lure of a warmer climate by pointing out that the further I was away from home the less likelihood there was of my being pestered. If that was the right word. Amateur sleuthing was something I enjoyed, though all good things eventually come to an end. Or are deliberately ended.

How had Sian put it? *All the danger put behind us, no more Shogun crashes in remote highland glens, no more assailants attacking you with sundry blunt instruments.* Had the time come?

We were all leaning on the rail, Sian and I separated by Calum and Stan. I looked along the line. She was watching me; in that uncanny way that seems to come naturally to her, she was reading my mind.

Calum sensed the look I had given her, and

stopped talking. Stan looked from left to right along the rail, clearly puzzled.

I said, 'Does it concern them? Should I tell them?'

Sian's blue eyes were dancing. 'You haven't told me yet,' she said, 'but I can guess.'

'So? Should I?'

'Well, of course it concerns them, and I'd like to think it *includes* them — though I'm not too sure about the rusty white van, all that salt air.'

Then, as Calum and Stan exchanged baffled looks, the dancing blue eyes crinkled, a smile tugged at her lips and she said, 'No, damn it, Jack, absolutely not. Christmas is when children get pressies, it's just a few weeks away, and for this one they'll just have to wait.'

THE END

We do hope that you have enjoyed reading this large print book.

Did you know that all of our titles are available for purchase?

We publish a wide range of high quality large print books including:

**Romances, Mysteries, Classics
General Fiction
Non Fiction and Westerns**

Special interest titles available in large print are:

**The Little Oxford Dictionary
Music Book
Song Book
Hymn Book
Service Book**

Also available from us courtesy of Oxford University Press:

**Young Readers' Dictionary
(large print edition)
Young Readers' Thesaurus
(large print edition)**

For further information or a free brochure, please contact us at:

**Ulverscroft Large Print Books Ltd.,
The Green, Bradgate Road, Anstey,
Leicester, LE7 7FU, England.
Tel: (00 44) 0116 236 4325
Fax: (00 44) 0116 234 0205**

DYING TO KNOW YOU

John Paxton Sheriff

When freelance photographer Penny Lane discovers a dead body on Hoylake beach she makes a terrible error of judgement. Now she must put matters right. Her overnight transformation from photographer to amateur private eye is easy, but the body count increases frighteningly, and tracking down the killer is difficult. Encouraged by her crime writer husband Josh, she finds herself at odds with the police, and rubs shoulders with villains in seedy Liverpool nightclubs. As Penny follows a trail that rakes up the past and shows her a menacing future, she's led to an unexpected and shockingly brutal success.

DEATHLY SUSPENSE

John Paxton Sheriff

When the police break into Joe Creeney's Liverpool home, his dead wife is hanging by a rope from the banisters, Joe is walking away holding the ladder and there is nobody else in the house. Yet Joe's sister, Caroline Spackman, is convinced her brother is innocent, so amateur PI Jack Scott is called in by solicitor Stephanie Grey. Now Scott, following a trail of violence and lies from a murder for which Creeney had been previously convicted, must also examine links to a woman's death in North Wales . . . and watch as more bloody killings lead him to a shocking denouement.

THE CLUTCHES OF DEATH

John Paxton Sheriff

When photographer Frank Danson took his wife Jenny to the theatre, they had two beautiful baby boys at home. But when they returned the boys had gone — presumably kidnapped. The loss was too great for Jenny to bear and Frank was left alone to grieve for his family. Then, twenty years later, the memories come screaming back. Who is sending him photographs hinting at unimaginable horrors, and taunting notes in blood? As the killings begin, amateur private eye Jack Scott must solve a mystery once buried in the past but now disinterred to make Frank's life a waking nightmare.

A CONFUSION OF MURDERS

John Paxton Sheriff

A possible murder and a man's sinister disappearance fascinate amateur private eye Jack Scott. In North Wales, Gwynfryn Pritchard's wife died face down in a stream. One year earlier, Gerry Gault had killed a girl during his knife-throwing act and disappeared that same night . . . Scott's investigation uncovers a paternity feud and a cryptic note. He is led to a retirement home where a gangster resides and it takes a brush with death, more corpses and a horrifying discovery before Scott can unravel a confusion of murders.

THE PARDONER'S CRIME

Keith Souter

1322. Sir Richard Lee, Sergeant-at-Law, is sent by King Edward II to Sandal Castle to preside over the court of the Manor of Wakefield. Sir Richard and his assistant Hubert of Loxley are forced to investigate a vicious rape and a cold-blooded murder. As the township prepares for the Wakefield mystery plays, the strangest case is brought before him. The Pardoner, Albin of Rouncivale, confesses to a crime, believed to have been committed by the outlaw Robin Hood. Sir Richard must quickly discover the truth — the stability of the realm and the crown itself may depend on upon it.